NEW EROTICA 2

NEW EROTICA
2

An anthology of sensuous writing

Edited by
Esme Ombreux

Nexus

First published in 1994 by
Nexus
332 Ladbroke Grove
London W10 5AH

Reprinted 1994

Typeset by Phoenix Photosetting, Chatham, Kent
Printed and bound in Great Britain by
Cox & Wyman Ltd, Reading, Berks

ISBN 0 352 32903 3

CONTENTS

INTRODUCTION

I t's been a real treat to edit this, the second volume
of the best of erotic writing from Nexus. I was new
to the job when I was editing *New Erotica 1*, and I
think the publisher was concerned I'd get distracted by
all the other rude material he keeps in his archives.
That's why he kept having to check on me hidden away
down there, out of sight of all the other editors who use
the building. He knows how inquisitive I am. I'm
always getting myself into sticky situations.

This time, he's let me have free run of the place
which has given me so much choice, I found myself in a
complete quandary wondering which books to select
extracts from. It's situations like that when a little
restriction comes in handy. Not to mention self-
discipline, which can be quite difficult when you're
faced with so many goodies.

I think I've finally managed to exercise enough control to select what I feel is a really good cross section of
extracts from over 150 Nexus books. 'It's growing all
the time', the publisher told me the other day. And
from looking at the list of titles currently available, I
just had to agree with him. At least, I think that's what
he was referring to. You can see for yourselves the

1

diversity of themes covered by the Nexus range. Whether the harsh regime of a correctional institution or the unbridled luxury of an Italian lakeside mansion, the backdrops to the sexual activity provide an eclectic selection of fantasy locations. From 17th-century Japan to life in the futurezone, one factor links these stories – they're all outrageously sexy.

You'll notice Nexus books have a new look as from this month. I hope you like it as much as I do. There's just time for me to wish you happy reading, and hope that you'll continue to find Nexus stories as interesting and arousing as I do.

Esme Ombreux
October 1993

THE INSTITUTE

Maria del Rey

Maria del Rey is something of a specialist in stories of dominance and submission. She has written four books for Nexus, each one striking in its originality, with settings to suit all tastes. Whether the stark, foreboding atmosphere of a corrective institution or the sensuous luxury of a secluded Greek island, Maria flavours her stories with a subtle but very effective taste of the forbidden.

Sexual intimidation can be a powerful aphrodisiac, as is proven by Maria's first novel for Nexus – *The Institute*. Rebellious young Lucy has never known the rewards of a disciplined life, and is she in for a surprise! For there is nothing quite as fearsome as the stern, uniformed mistresses of the correctional establishment to which she is sent.

Here, the regimented order of everyday life extends to exacting perverse punishment on the wayward girls in their charge. In this extract, Lucy experiences for the first time how surrender to humiliation can bring about a powerful transformation of personality.

Due to the popularity of *The Institute*, *The Institute II* is currently being written, and will be Maria's fifth novel of sexual power games.

Lucy got up and began to change. She dropped her green bomber jacket onto the bed and pulled off her trainers and socks. Looking up she saw Julie eyeing her closely. She stood to unzip her jeans and seeing that Julie was still studying her closely, turned around. She unzipped her jeans but did not pull them down immediately; she felt very conscious of the eyes burning into her back. Instead she pulled her sweatshirt up and over her head. For a second she enjoyed the feeling of the sun beating down on her large firm breasts, then she reached for the white uniform shirt.

Julie came up behind her and reached around under the arms and took hold of the naked, well-shaped breasts. Lucy froze as Julie squeezed the two globes of soft milky white flesh. Expertly she weighed them in her hands, brushing her thumbs playfully over the nipples.

Julie was delighted when Lucy began to redden with embarrassment. She let go of the breasts and took hold of the top of Lucy's jeans and slowly began to pull them down, tugging gently so that they began to drop, revealing a pair of white cotton panties. Lucy just stood stock still, her mind completely blank, overcome with horror. Julie left the denim trousers at knee level.

'You'll look so much better in your uniform,' she leered, sliding her hand up the inside of Lucy's thigh. She thrilled to the softness of the skin, the way it resisted the firmness of her touch. Eagerly she pressed her fingers up towards the soft folds of skin that the tight-fitting panties barely covered.

Finally all the anger and frustration boiled over. Sick to her stomach with revulsion, Lucy swung around and struck Julie as hard as she could.

The blow was unexpected and Julie was flung back into the centre of the room. She was dumbfounded, her look of shock was absolute. She had never been rejected by any of the girls under her charge, and this eventuality now caught her off guard. 'I'll have you later, you little bitch,' she hissed venomously. 'You've broken every fucking rule in the book. If I took you to one of the staff you'd be flogged till you fainted.'

Lucy pulled her jeans up, let her breasts remain bare and faced Julie. 'Well, if them tests were any good they would've known that I don't deal in that shit.'

'I'm going to enjoy you.' Julie glared back. 'I'm going to punish you day in day out for what you've done.'

'Just try me,' Lucy urged, her old self-confidence returning. Defiance had always been at the core of her being, and now it gave her a centre of gravity, something to grip on to in an effort to stay afloat. She looked at the whole business of Mistresses and punishments with nothing but scorn and contempt.

'Get changed,' Mistress Julie told her. She felt a little afraid of the new girl's aggressive determination. She had been a prefect for only a matter of weeks and had yet to acquire the bearing and the confidence of the others. She knew that it was her task to inform the prefect leader and the head girl of what had happened, but she was afraid to lose face. For a moment she longed to return to the simplicities of being one of the girls, to live without the responsibilities or the burden of command.

Lucy changed quickly, keeping her eyes on Julie, who stared back. Both were still testing each other, unsure who had the strongest will. Lucy had been a little intimidated earlier, but now she sensed that it was the Mistress who felt threatened.

'Follow me,' Julie ordered when Lucy had dressed. She tried, and almost succeeded, in investing her voice with the same tone of authority that had come naturally to Mistress Christine.

'Where are we going?' Lucy asked suspiciously, hands on hips, unwilling to yield an inch.

'Address me properly!' Julie demanded stridently. The two girls faced each other squarely. 'Don't forget that you're alone here,' she reminded Lucy. 'I'm the only person you know. You do as you're told or you'll be in deep shit.'

Lucy realised, with a profound sense of relief, that she and Julie were finally talking the same language. 'Yes, Mistress,' Lucy replied, though the words were rendered meaningless by the mocking tone of her voice.

'You'll be begging to get a lick of my pussy by the end of the month,' Julie warned, regaining her composure slightly.

'Yes, Mistress,' Lucy sneered.

'You've got to go to class,' Julie reminded her. 'Just try some of that crap in there and see what you get.'

'Yes, Mistress.'

'Open the door,' Julie demanded.

'Fuck you!'

Trying to ignore Lucy's triumphant laugh, Julie

finally opened the door. She held the door open and waited for her to move. She waited until Lucy was passing through the door and then slammed into her, pressing her painfully against the door frame. Lucy struggled but Julie held her tightly, using the frame to trap Lucy's right arm and holding the other with her own.

'You'll regret this,' Lucy said threateningly, giving up the pointless struggle to get free. She was held firmly between the door frame and Julie, who was taller and stronger than she was.

'That's no way to talk to your Mistress,' Julie teased. She slipped her free hand under the short skirt and stroked Lucy's soft thighs.

'What's wrong, couldn't find a bloke to give it to you?' Lucy continued to mock.

Julie ignored her, slipping her fingers into the thin white uniform briefs. She grazed her hand through the tight curly bush of pubic hair, trying to press down to the soft folds of the pussy lips that she had tried to touch earlier. She switched target and began to rub Lucy's dark nipples over the white nylon shirt; she took each nipple in turn and squeezed it between thumb and forefinger, tugging at them lightly.

Lucy shut her eyes, realising with dawning horror that the play on her breasts was beginning to excite her.

'Nice responsive nipples,' Julie observed, her eyes shining with a frisson of sexual excitement. Lucy's nipples were erect and visibly poking against the uniform shirt. 'Just as I like them, nice hard nipples to bite and suck,' she continued, managing to unbutton part of the shirt and playing with the bare breasts, exploring the feel and shape of them, always returning to the hardened puckered nipples. She realised that Lucy's breasts were sensitive to the lightest of caresses.

10

Lucy kept her eyes clamped tightly shut. The constant playing with her nipples had aroused her, her pretty white panties were becoming damp. She tried not to think of Julie; instead she remembered the last night she had spent with the two guards in the cell below the court. Desperately she tried to imagine that it was one of the men that teased her. She remembered how Dave had also used her breasts to excite her. But even the memory of two hard pricks pumping inside her could not entirely blot out the image of Julie artfully massaging the large round breasts so deliciously.

Suddenly Julie stopped, releasing Lucy, and took a step back into the room.

Lucy opened her eyes slowly. Her heart was pounding wildly and a fire was burning in the pit of her belly, inflamed by the spasms of blissful sensation that had issued from her tight hard teats. Her shirt was half open and her firm young breasts were exposed, the nipples pointing away from each other.

'Dress yourself, girl,' Julie ordered, a satisfied grin on her long thin face.

Lucy began to button up, her face burning with an angry bitter shame. She was obeying an order without wanting to, aware that Julie had again reversed the positions. It was Julie who was now confident and brash, while she was the one who was confused again and on the defensive.

Julie brushed arrogantly past Lucy in the doorway, her fingers lightly touching Lucy's thighs. Lucy looked away, unable to make any response. She followed Julie through the maze of corridors and steps. Again her instinct for survival helped her identify landmarks to enable her to navigate back to room 4C. She forced herself to take note of numbers on doors and coloured arrows painted discreetly on some of the walls.

Without wanting to she also caught herself looking closely at Julie. She wondered what would have happened if Julie hadn't stopped. She knew that if Julie had pressed their mouths together she would have accepted the kiss urgently. As she walked the wetness between her legs was a reminder of just how easily she had been aroused by the touch of another girl. The experience undermined her completely.

Julie stopped outside the first door in a corridor on the ground floor, near to the stairs that led to Mistress Schafer's office. She knocked and waited before entering, with Lucy following meekly.

The classroom was small and bright, the windows on the wall opposite looking out on to a small square courtyard. When Lucy saw the courtyard she understood the strange geography of the building. She had assumed that the building was a single massive monolith, whereas it was in fact shaped around the courtyard. The insight cheered her up slightly. Any gain in knowledge of her environment, no matter how trivial, was important to her survival.

The classroom consisted of four rows of single desks. Each row was divided into two pairs of desks close to each other, separated by a larger space, in effect leaving a long central aisle between the rows. There were a number of empty seats in the class, and Lucy quickly counted twelve young women present. Another solitary desk was placed in front of, and set at a diagonal to, the others.

The teacher, a black woman in her thirties, stood behind a large oak desk at the front of the class, on a raised platform several inches from the floor. She had soft chocolate-coloured skin; her thick glossy hair was swept back over her head and tied in a tight bun. She was dressed in a smart black jacket and short matching skirt, her long shapely thighs were clad in sheer black stockings that made her dark skin appear lighter than it was. Her face was round with full heavy lips painted a deep red and parted in an inviting pout.

'Why is the new girl late?' she demanded of Julie, in a clear stern voice that immediately brought silence to the class.

'She was disobedient and insolent, Mistress Shirer,' Julie replied dutifully.

Mistress Shirer dismissed Julie disdainfully and turned her large bright eyes on Lucy, standing nervously by the door.

'Come forward, girl,' Mistress Shirer told her.

'Yes Mistress Shirer,' Lucy replied obediently, avoiding the Mistress's penetrating gaze.

'Stand properly, girl,' she instructed, and Lucy straightened up and put her chest forward. Mistress Shirer noted the erect nipples pressing visibly against the uniform shirt. 'Tell the rest of the class your name.'

Lucy remembered to respond to the Mistress first, and then turned to face the rest of the young women. Her heart was pounding and she felt nervous. She looked at the girls, who stared back at her with undisguised interest. They were all dressed in the same minimal uniform of blue skirt and white shirt. Lucy told them her name and was told to sit at an empty seat in the third row.

She walked down the centre of the class and took her seat nearest the aisle. The desk to her left was empty. On the other side of the aisle both desks were occupied, the one nearest to her by a petite Indian girl, who looked much younger than the minimum age of eighteen, and next to her a plump plain girl who wore wire-framed spectacles, and stared back blankly.

'The new girl,' Mistress Shirer began, leaning forward against the desk so that the tops of her breasts were visible, 'has arrived at a most opportune moment. The formal part of the class is ended for today.' She stood up and then walked around to the front of the desk and sat on the edge, crossing her legs.

Lucy felt drawn to the expanse of stockinged thigh that the Mistress displayed nonchalantly. She looked round at the other girls, and felt a little relieved to find them also staring at Mistress Shirer with varying degrees of admiration, an admiration tinged with a heavy dose of apprehension. She looked up and was startled to find the Mistress staring directly at her. She took the gaze for a second, staring back with darting eyes. But then, heart pounding, she turned away, intimidated by the forbidding expression on Mistress Shirer's face. She avoided the cold searching stare, and gazed down instead at Mistress Shirer's glossy black ankle boots, the sharp heel like an upturned pyramid, the steel tips aimed directly at the floor.

'This morning I instructed the prefects to conduct a search of your rooms,' Mistress Shirer announced. She silenced the eager buzz of expectation by jumping down from the desk, the crack of her heels sending a sharp report around the room. She stood, arms folded across her chest and long lithe legs placed apart, and stared at the girls. 'The thief among you will step forward now to receive her due punishment.'

Lucy looked around the room. She felt relief that stealing still took place, it was the first sign of outward normality that she had encountered in the Institute. She recognised the girl immediately. Lucy had been in the same situation herself on a number of occasions and was not fooled by the girl, who was looking around earnestly, searching with her quick blue eyes for the culprit. Lucy caught her eye and smiled to her, letting her know that she knew and didn't care if the girl was the thief. But the girl ignored Lucy, instead sneaking glances in the direction of Mistress Shirer.

'You will be punished whether you own up or not,' Mistress Shirer told the girls. 'But if you don't own up you will regret angering me.' She waited, deliberately letting the tension build up. Receiving no response she walked down the central aisle with a slow elegant stride, a hint of menace flowing around her. The girls eyed her with a mixture of fear and fascination.

'You girls are destined for punishment,' she continued slowly, prolonging the tension.

Lucy was gripped by a sudden and irrational fear that Mistress Shirer was talking about her, she felt a dense wave of panic rising within. Part of her rebelled against the fear, refusing to be intimidated by the severe presence of the lithe black Mistress. Still another part of her felt a fearful attraction, dazzled by the menacing sexual aura that emanated from the Mistress.

'No matter how hard you try,' she paused by Lucy, 'you return again and again to your old modes of behaviour. You find that doing wrong gives you pleasure, and that the fear of capture, and consequent punishment, is the spice that draws you.'

Lucy held her breath, but relaxed when Mistress Shirer took another couple of steps and stopped at the last row of desks. All the girls at the front were craning round excitedly, relieved that they had escaped. Lucy shared the feeling of relief, feeling almost light-headed. Again she caught herself being attracted to the Mistress sexually; her eyes followed the contours of the gently curving body. Mistress Shirer wore a skintight skirt and her firm round bottom was firmly impressed on the black material. Lucy noted that no panty-line was visible and that the tightness of the skirt had gently parted the arse-cheeks, emphasising the deep rear valley between the firm globes of the buttocks.

Shocked by her thoughts, Lucy looked at some of the other girls. She saw them looking at the Mistress in the same way, the feeling of desire mixed with the same feeling of fear.

'Stand up girl!' Mistress Shirer ordered the girl sitting in front of her.

'Please Mistress . . .' the girl began to explain, her small round face collapsing. Tears welled in her bright blue eyes and her pretty little mouth was trembling.

Mistress Shirer slapped the girl's face, and the retort echoed through the silent room. The girl clutched her reddened cheek, eyes wide with dreadful anticipation of what was to follow. She looked at Mistress Shirer imploringly, but the Mistress took her by the hair and pulled her out of her seat.

'I'm sorry, I'm sorry,' the girl whined. She managed to free herself of the Mistress's grip and fell to the floor. The rest of the girls watched her grovelling on hands and knees, kissing and licking the glossy ankle boots, pressing her mouth eagerly on the shiny black leather.

Lucy was horrified. She turned and looked at the other girls, but they were watching excitedly. Many were smiling gleefully, enjoying the sight of the girl degrading herself. She turned back to the girl, sickened by the lack of sympathy shown to her by the others.

Mistress Shirer pulled the girl up by the hair, clutching a tight handful of the long brown locks. She strode purposefully back to the head of the class, her backside wiggling slightly as she walked, pulling the sobbing girl behind her.

'This filthy little bitch is a thief,' she explained,

standing the girl up to face her classmates. 'Like all bad girls she has to be punished again and again.'

'Please, I'm sorry . . .' the girl whimpered, squirming nervously.

'Unbutton your shirt,' Mistress Shirer commanded brutally.

The girl started to undo the buttons, but her hands were shaking and unable to grip the buttons properly. Mistress Shirer pulled the shirt open impatiently, ripping the buttons away. The girl seemed to shrink back, trying to pull her naked breasts away. Mistress Shirer tugged the girl's hair to make her stand properly. The girl winced and pressed her chest out, displaying the fullness of her firm breasts to the other girls.

Lucy eyed the creamy white globes with a mixture of self-disgust and unconcealed interest. Her mind was filled with the memory of Julie caressing her own breasts so expertly and, now that Julie was gone, she felt excited by the image. She had never felt this way before. It was an unexpected and peculiar emotion, it had an eroticism about it that she had never experienced before.

'Cup your breasts,' Mistress Shirer commanded the girl, and the girl obeyed, cupping her large breasts and raising them up, accentuating the swell of her flesh. The girl's face was flushing deep red with shame, her eyes were fixed firmly on the ground.

The first blow startled Lucy, who had become lost in the contemplation of the beautifully raised breasts bathed in the bright sunlight that streamed through the windows. Mistress Shirer began to lay hard sharp slaps on the naked ripe fruit held up to her, the loud slap of flesh on flesh beat out a rhythm of painful punishment. The soft white breast skin was flawed with a deep crimson tan, the impression of Mistress Shirer's fingers clearly marked for all to see. The girl closed her eyes and bit deep into her lip. Her chest was burning and stinging, the regular strokes on her breasts were painfully sharp.

Mistress Shirer varied her stroke, ensuring that each breast was spanked in turn, and also spreading the strokes over each breast, so that the girl's flesh was an even colour throughout. She paid attention to the nipples, landing several blows directly on each, so that the nipples stood out sharply and glowed a deeper colour than the surrounding flesh.

'Thank you, Mistress,' the girl whispered when the breast spanking was finished. Her chest was patterned with deep red fingermarks on a carpet of a smooth pink tan. Her chest seemed to be aflame, the smarting concentrated in the tight sensitive buds of the nipples, sending confused messages to the rest of her body. The stinging aching pain had turned into a deep red heat, warming first her chest and then suffusing slowly down to her belly.

'Let the others see how you are marked,' Mistress Shirer ordered.

The girl uncupped the two punished fruit and put her hands on her head, elbows parallel to her shoulders which she pressed back, so that the breasts were fully displayed to their best advantage. The flesh on the underside was still milky white, but it merged gradually with the scarlet fingermarked flesh where Mistress Shirer's expert hand had chastised her. The dark red-brown nipples were hard little buttons that were provocatively erect, aching for relief from the smarting ache that covered them.

Lucy was excited now by the girl's vulnerable stance, the blue skirt and torn shirt adding to the exposed look. She felt uncomfortable with the new feelings that had been aroused in her. Looking around the class, hoping somehow to find her bearings, she found instead the other girls were also enjoying the spectacle, eyeing the punished girl with unconcealed lust. She knew the look, knew what it was like to feel hot desire raging and pulsing through her body, but she had only ever felt like that towards men. Now it was as if a whole new world had been opened up to her, and, like an explorer in a new world, she felt excited by the possibilities and yet gripped by the deepest of fears and a great disorientation.

The punished girl kept her eyes averted but held herself up, pressing her breasts higher. She glanced up at the other girls and tried to look defiant, but the blushes of embarrassment were clear to see.

'Bend over the punishment desk,' Mistress Shirer told the girl eventually. Disconsolately the girl turned away from the class and bent across the desk at the head of the class. She pressed herself low on its surface, so that her breasts were squashed flat, finding temporary solace in the coolness of the desk top.

Mistress Shirer unbuttoned the skirt and it fell around the girl's ankles. Slowly she pulled the white cotton panties down to the girl's knees. 'Part your legs,' she instructed and the girl obeyed.

The other girls craned forward in their seats, enjoying the view of the young naked backside so temptingly exhibited. The tight round arse-cheeks were pleasingly parted, hinting of the puckered arse-hole within. A mat of brown curly hair indicated the entrance to her sex, and was clearly visible at the top of her thighs. The girl turned her head back and looked at the class, her eyes welled with sorrowful tears, shamed by the terrible humiliations she had endured and was going to endure.

Mistress Shirer walked slowly round to her own desk, revelling in the sight of the girl exposed so deliciously on the punishment desk. The girl's breasts were still glowing with the afterburn of the spanking. From a drawer in her desk Mistress Shirer withdrew a long supple cane and she tested its mettle by swishing it through the air several times. The girl looked up beseechingly, terrified by the sight and sound of the wicked cane being played through the air.

Lucy stared at the girl, her eyes feasting on the beautiful pert backside and exploring the private places. It was as if she had only just discovered how beautiful and mysterious a feminine body is. The long silky thighs were stretched tight, every muscle extended and displayed for all to see.

Lucy was also stirred by the sight of the austere and attractive Mistress wielding and flexing the long bamboo cane. It was obvious that the Mistress was relishing the opportunity to degrade the recalcitrant girl.

'This is how I punish my naughty girls,' Mistress Shirer told the class, using one hand to position the unfortunate girl, pressing her down into the desk so that the arse-cheeks were raised temptingly higher.

The first blow whistled through the air and landed with a crack across the bare backside. The girl cried out, the stroke bit deeply into her flesh, a sharp spasm of pain seemed to connect up with the heat oozing from her punished breasts. A deep red line was etched across the white globes of her arse, a livid reward for her bad behaviour. Mistress Shirer paused deliberately before striking the next note of the painful litany.

The girls watched in awed silence, hearts pounding and minds racing. Lucy felt her head spinning; she was at once repelled by the painful public humiliation of the girl and attracted to it. Her eyes tried to take in the whole picture: the girl spread exposingly on the desk, her attractive young rear hoisted up, the stern black Mistress brandishing the cane and administering a painful and deeply sexual punishment. Mistress Shirer raised the cane high so that her skirt rode up, exposing long supple thighs clad in sheer black stockings. The picture was dazzling, a blindingly intense erotic tableau that drew Lucy's eyes like a magnet.

Stroke followed stroke and the punished girl's arse soon bore several distinct red lines deep in the flesh. She ached and cried, tears falling down her young pretty face. The pain was churning her insides, she felt a little sick, she was trembling.

Lucy turned away, checking her own behaviour by that of the others around her. She looked at the two girls in the aisle opposite and was shocked to see them caressing each other secretly. The small Indian girl, who looked no older than sixteen, had pulled her skirt up high and parted her legs wide, and Lucy could see that the plump girl was rubbing slowly between the dusky uncovered thighs. The Indian girl reciprocated by gliding her delicate little hand along the plump girl's thigh.

The Indian girl, careful not to attract Mistress Shirer's attention, shifted in her seat. She pulled her knickers a little way down and guided the other girl's hand into place. When she saw that Lucy was watching she smiled. With her free hand she gently lifted her skirt so that Lucy could see the plump girl fingering deep into the dark puffy folds of her pussy. The shock on Lucy's face was evident, and the Indian girl beamed delightedly, turning slightly to give Lucy a better view, and blew her a kiss.

Lucy blushed. She was aroused intensely by the view of the two girls masturbating each other, but didn't know how to respond to the smiles and the affectionate

21

kiss that had been blown to her. She turned back to the equally arousing sight of the girl being chastised by Mistress Shirer.

The girl's arse was on fire, the pain had become unbearable. The girl forgot everything, her whole life was concentrated on her naked backside, nothing else registered. Each stroke seemed to pump some strange sensation into her. The steady rhythm of correction assumed a singular importance, and without wanting to the girl began to raise her arse higher. The pain became pleasure-pain, her pussy was wet and aching.

Her breathing came in short gasps, the muted sobbing was replaced by the unwanted release of soft wordless moans. She lifted her arse higher still, trying to meet the downward stroke of the cane halfway. Her pussy was alive with pleasure, her tight bud was a molten burning centre of sex energy.

'Hurt me, harder,' she moaned softly. Her cheeks were crossed with the impression of the cane. At last the girl could hold herself no longer, she arched her back and let out a cry. She was oblivious to the cane and the searing pain, instead she was overcome by a wild cataclysmic climax. She gripped the desk and lifted herself as high as she could, stretched almost on to the tips of her toes.

The girl dived into an almighty screaming orgasm. She lost control as the last of the heavy strokes found her reddened arse. The caning stopped and she was sobbing uncontrollably, holding on to the desk with all her strength to stop herself collapsing to the floor. Suddenly she seemed to wince, she gasped audibly, and then let out a warm white jet of piss. She was too tired, or too overwhelmed, to do anything, she let the piss stream out and then the flow stopped to a trickle that cascaded down her thighs and on to her skirt and panties.

Mistress Shirer had stepped back and had not been soiled by the girl's piss. She seemed pleased that the girl had lost all control and had abased herself completely and utterly.

'Jenny can clear her own mess now,' she said calmly. 'The rest of the class is dismissed.'

Jenny had not been given permission to stand, and so she remained bent over the desk, her painful arse on display to all, wallowing in her degrading condition. The other girls filed passed her, eyes fixed on the alluring sight of her vulnerable backside.

Lucy followed the other girls silently, numbed by all that she had seen and felt. it was as if she had entered a new world where the perverse and obscene were considered normal. Every act and gesture was loaded with a sexual significance that she had previously been unaware of, or that had previously been absent altogether.

'I'm in room 2C,' the Indian girl told Lucy when they were outside the classroom. She smiled in a friendly innocently open way, totally at odds with the wanton behaviour that she had displayed earlier. 'Why don't you come to visit me later?' she continued when Lucy made no reply.

Lucy turned and fled, unable to cope with the encounter, unsure whether the invitation was sexual or social. She headed vaguely in the direction of her room, her mind reeling. Nothing was right with the world, everything had been turned upside down. She had been at the Institute for only a few hours and already her personality had been stripped bare. The hard wall of defiance and arrogance that she had so carefully constructed to protect herself had been demolished, leaving nothing in its place but uncertainty and fear.

She walked blindly down the long corridors, up and

23

down identical flights of stairs. She felt lost in more than the geographical sense. There was nothing for her to hold on to, no yardstick by which to measure herself. The other girls seemed totally corrupted by the erotic atmosphere of the place.

She felt enticed by the powerful sexual atmosphere that clung to the air like an early morning mist. For the first time she had found herself attracted by the possibilities of making love with other girls. The revulsion that she had felt for the idea before had vanished, and she wondered whether it had all been a massive negation of her true self. It occurred to her that she had previously denied the very thing that she was attracted to, simply because she had been unable to come to terms with it. It was a dangerous thought, she realised; her whole life was suddenly thrown open to question.

At last she found herself in familiar territory as she recognised the stairs leading up to her room. She bounded up gratefully, eager to find respite from the strange and cruel world around her. The room was empty and she flopped down on the bed with relief, tired by the enormous emotional strains of the day.

She closed her eyes tightly and tried to drown out the thoughts and images clamouring noisily in her mind. Repeatedly strong dreamlike images filled her with waves of disgust and desire. She saw Julie's hot mouth on hers, she saw Jenny being beaten on her lovely tits, she saw herself being touched by Julie, she saw the elegant wiggle of Mistress Shirer's walk, she saw Jenny letting out a long stream of piss.

The silence of the small room closed about her. With an effort she slowed her breathing, seeking calmness. Gradually she relaxed, letting the flood of thoughts wash over her, cascading through her mind until everything was still. All that remained was the heat in the tightness of her sex.

She changed position on the bed, so that her feet rested on the pillow and her head was at the foot of the bed. She lovingly caressed her breasts over the thin material of the shirt, cupping the large round orbs and playing her thumbs gently over the sensitive erect nipples. Taking the nipples between her thumbs and index fingers she gently squeezed, sending spasms of pure pleasure piercing through her body. Lazily she massaged and rubbed her tits, the ripples of pleasure connecting with the heat in her belly.

Slowly she pulled her knees up and apart, the skirt carefully covering her in case someone entered the room. She felt the panties press deep into her, damp again from the ferment of anticipation in her belly. She moved one hand down and began stroking the inside of her thigh, her fingers delicately kneading the responsive flesh. She pressed her fingers over the damp panties, exploring the entrance to the delicate folds of her pussy lips. With her other hand she continued the play on her breasts, making more urgent attacks on the hardened nipples, rousing herself expertly.

She traced the contours of the panties deep between her thighs, she liked to feel the soft material pulled deep up into her rear crevice, emphasising the shape of her buttocks. She lifted her bum a little and slipped the panties down, quickly pulling them off and hiding them neatly under the pillow. All the years in homes and institutions had taught her the art of concealing all. She resumed her position so that anyone entering the room suddenly would be met with the demure and innocent sight of Lucy having a quiet sleepy rest on the bed.

She spread her thighs, carefully arranging her skirt to

provide maximum concealment, and felt a cool breeze brush the entrance to her naked sex. She parted her cunny lips with her outer fingers and pressed the middle finger a little way in, finding the wet stickiness appealing. A surge of pleasure passed over her as her fingers began to tease and play with her excited pussy. She liked to make love to herself slowly, ensuring that every sensation was savoured, bringing herself to the edge of climax then drawing back a little to prolong the tension.

She began to dig her fingers deeper, pressing in and out rhythmically, ensuring that each thrust finished on her secret place. She swallowed the soft moans of pleasure, aware always of the possibility of capture. As she roused herself to higher levels of pleasure she began to writhe and lift herself up to meet the thrusting grasping fingers. Her pussy was sopping wet, her fingers enveloped in the sex honey. She tightened her muscles against the greedy fingers, forcing herself to work harder.

Unable to contain herself any longer, she arched her back and pressed fingers from both hands into her crack. She let out a long gasp of satisfaction and fell headlong into climax.

Afterwards she lay back breathing deeply, feeling wonderfully relaxed after the orgasm. Her mind had been filled with the erotic images of the day. The picture of Jenny was foremost in her mind. The sight of the girl being punished had excited her intensely, and she guessed that it had had a similar effect on the rest of the class. Without wanting to she wondered what it had been like to be punished so publicly. The pain and the humiliation must have been unbearable, but Jenny had been driven to an intense orgasm by the experience. Lucy couldn't understand the connection between pleasure and pain, yet it seemed that the entire Institute was based on the connection. She had never allowed anyone to punish her physically, and did not plan on it now. But still she was fascinated by all that she had seen.

Anne Young had been absolutely right, there was definitely something going on at the Institute. Belatedly she realised that all she had to do was report on the regime, even if only to list the incidents she had witnessed already, and she would get the money. The thought made her feel a little better, it gave her a link, however tenuous, with the outside world. Sitting restlessly she stared around the room. There was nothing in it to betray a hint of personality, everything was boring and functional. Listening intently for the sound of anyone approaching she stole across the room and sat on the other bed. Satisfied that it was safe, she opened the bedside locker and quickly examined the contents. The contents were disappointingly bland, mainly books and stationery.

She guessed that half the chest of draws was hers. The bottom two drawers were empty, the top two filled with clothes. The top drawer contained skirts and jeans and a pair of trainers. The second drawer was neatly filled with the neatly folded skirts, shirts and panties of the uniform.

Certain that the coast was clear, she carefully began to dig through the top drawer. She guessed that her roommate would keep all her private things there, safely isolated from the dour uniform and school things. She lifted the jeans and peered carefully underneath, then she pulled out a soft pink cardigan and checked through the pockets, which proved to be empty. She had almost given up when she felt something cold and hard right at the back of the drawer, buried deep behind the neat piles of clothes. It felt like a wallet and, very carefully, she prised it out.

It wasn't a wallet, though it was made of the same sort of material as a man's wallet. It was a long thin strip of stiff black leather, about twelve inches long. One end was shaped like a handle and the other was totally flat. She held it by the handle curiously, trying to work out what it was for. Only after swinging it through the air did she realise that it was some kind of instrument for punishment. Her first reaction was to put it away, but she held on to it, weighing it in her hand and playing it through the air several times.

She wondered what it was like to have it across her backside and shivered. Cautiously she started to replace it in its carefully hidden position but stopped.

Half apologetically, she smiled to herself in the mirror, but she was overcome with curiosity. It was as if she had no choice in the matter, she simply had to find out what it felt like. She turned her back and lifted her skirt over her waist. The sun fell across her bare buttocks that were reflected in the mirror. She straightened up and studied herself critically. Her bottom was pert and rounded, her silky thighs were long and smooth.

She held the skirt up with one hand and drew back the other, clutching tightly the leather strap. She let the strap whistle across and land squarely on her soft white arse-cheeks. She winced at the sharp sudden pain and let the strap fall to the floor. A thick red strip was etched on her backside, a perfect impression of the strap. The sudden pain was replaced with an aching stinging sensation, and then a hot golden glow seemed to spread over her bum-cheeks. It was not an unpleasant feeling in a strange sort of way.

She bent over to display her arse fully. The arse-cheeks were spread a little, offering a glimpse of the tight arsehole set in the darker rear cleft. She was a little surprised to find herself becoming excited again. She felt hot between the thighs, the damp heat merging imperceptibly with the glow from her behind. Bending a little more she used her free hand to rub the surface of her wound, feeling the raised weal like a message in braille inscribed on her flesh.

'What the fuck are you doing?'

Lucy was startled and jumped up immediately. She had become totally engrossed in her reflection and in masturbating herself once more. Burning a deep bright red with shame she brushed her skirt down, trying desperately to think of some excuse. Though she was freshly showered and clad in a short towelled robe, Lucy recognised the girl at the door as Jenny.

'Is this what you want?' Jenny sneered. She slammed the door shut and turned her back to Lucy, lifting the robe to display her reddened bottom.

'I wanted to see what it felt like . . .' Lucy admitted red-faced, her eyes fixed on the other girl's beautifully marked posterior.

'I'll show you what it feels like,' Jenny laughed menacingly. She stepped forward and picked up the leather strap from the floor.

Lucy watched silently, aware of what was going to happen and powerless to resist. She wanted it to happen, wanted to experience the feeling of being chastised; she simply had to see what it was like.

Jenny took Lucy by the arm and pulled her close. She pressed their mouths together and Lucy eagerly accepted a long searching kiss.

'Suck my aching tits,' Jenny ordered, stepping out of the robe and standing naked next to Lucy. She cupped her breasts and Lucy bent down to take the hardened nipples in her mouth, tasting each in turn, knowing

29

instinctively how to give pleasure. She flicked her tongue over the extended buttons then bit them gently.

Jenny pulled Lucy up and kissed her lovingly on the neck and mouth. Then Lucy bent over submissively and allowed herself to be positioned by the other girl, legs apart, skirt pulled up, arse raised high.

She felt on the verge of orgasm even before the first stroke was applied to her vulnerable backside. The pain was much more intense than when she had smacked herself, but the heat between her legs was also more potent. She couldn't see herself in the mirror, but she imagined the sight of her arse-cheeks being tanned a deep crimson colour and was further inflamed.

Jenny raised the strap high and brought it down with a heavy smack. Her breasts, still pink after the beating earlier, jiggled enticingly. She was enjoying the stimulation of beating another girl, revelling in her rare position of dominance. Her hot bum-cheeks were painful reminders of her own recent humiliation and now she was experiencing the exquisite pleasure of punishment from the other end. She was already planning what to do to Lucy once the spanking was finished.

Lucy was woken by an urgent nudge. It had been a difficult night for her, her mind was a ferment of doubts and images. She dreamed of money and sex, of pleasure and reward, and of the strange world that she had entered. Everything she had ever known was laid open to question, there was not an ounce of certainty left.

She opened her eyes and found Jenny standing by the bed.

'Turn over,' Jenny told her, smiling. Still half asleep, Lucy turned over onto her stomach. The covers had been drawn and she was naked.

The first stroke across the buttocks shattered the

early morning quiet and shocked Lucy to wakefulness. A tight pain was impressed across her soft white arse-cheeks by the hard black strap. Lucy gasped and tried to get up, but Jenny pushed her back and inflicted a second stroke. A searing aching pain suffused a raging lava of heat into her body. A third and fourth stroke were applied in turn, Jenny slowly gaining expertise in the use of the strap.

Lucy closed her eyes, trying to keep out the pain to no avail. She knew that if she tried she could fight back; she was bigger than Jenny and could certainly take the strap off her if she wanted. But the will and energy to do so were lacking. Instead she lay still and accepted her punishment, her arse-cheeks quivering under the repeated savage blows from the strap. She felt a wave of self-disgust rise up when she realised that she was becoming wet between the legs. Unable to resist the powerful desires she raised her backside up, meeting the swift downward swing of the strap. Each blow sent a spasm of pure joy deep into her pussy, the red heat from her arse-cheeks spreading a golden glow inside her. She let out delirious gasps and moans, the pleasure and pain were becoming indistinguishable.

Jenny studied the raised arse in front of her. She had inflicted a series of deep scarlet weals on the previously pure unblemished flesh. The buttocks were parted slightly and she could see that the crimson tan of the buttocks had spread down between the thighs and deep into the gaping sex, the rosebud just visible in all its feminine glory. She liked to feel the buttocks, tracing her fingers along the strap marks, following the contour of tight hot arse-flesh. She spread the buttocks and admired the puckered bumhole, noting that even here the strap had left its mark.

'Turn over,' Jenny ordered once more. Lucy

31

obeyed, turning over onto her back. She flinched a little as her aching wounds touched the sheets. 'I want you to call me Mistress,' Jenny told her in a whisper. She bent down and seized Lucy's mouth, pressing her tongue deep in a passionate and affectionate kiss. 'Just when we're together,' Jenny continued, whispering between kisses. 'This'll be our secret, our game.'

'Yes, Mistress,' Lucy answered, enthralled by the idea.

'Does your backside hurt?'

'It stings . . .' Lucy smiled.

'It stings, Mistress,' Jenny corrected.

'It stings, Mistress,' Lucy repeated.

'That's how it should be.'

'Yes, Mistress.'

Jenny gave Lucy one last kiss and stood up, she was naked under her skirt. She smiled and then climbed on to the bed, standing with shame over Lucy's face. 'Now you have to suck me off,' she smiled. 'I'm going to come in your mouth.'

'Yes, Mistress,' Lucy smiled back nervously. Jenny squatted down over Lucy's mouth, squirming herself into position so that sex and mouth were locked tight.

Lucy could hardly breath as the strong feminine smell of female sex enveloped her. She gingerly flicked her tongue over the velvety folds of Jenny's pussy lips, the soft curly hairs tickling her. Finding the entrance to the sex she pressed her tongue inside, tasting the salty taste of another pussy for the first time in her life.

Jenny began to wriggle, moving down hard on to the mouth clamped between her thighs. Lucy was searching with her tongue, lapping at the thick honey of the pussy juices, enjoying the cloying flavour of her Mistress.

As Jenny began to ride wildly, bucking her hips back

and forth, Lucy suddenly saw herself. It was as if she had taken a step outside of herself. She could see herself urgently sucking deep into another girl's pussy, her bare backside crossed with lash marks, her cunt hot and wet with desire. Her head spun with bewilderment and disgust and sick fascination.

Jenny was panting wildly, she clamped Lucy's head tightly with her thighs and cried out with release. Lucy came at the same time, arching her back, the fingers of one hand pressed deep into her quim, her face wet with a thin film of sweat and sex juices, her mouth drinking deeply from Jenny's sopping pussy.

As Jenny dismounted, Lucy opened her eyes and stretched deliciously. She felt alive, her body, especially her rear, tingling with a new feeling of vitality. There was no thought of rebellion or escape any more. She realised that she had so much to learn, and that a new self was emerging from the ruins of the old.

And it was still only the start of her second day at the Institute.

PARADISE BAY

Maria del Rey

Holidays in exotic places always hold the potential for erotic encounters. In the idyllic Paradise Bay, characters are brought together who complement each other perfectly in their lewdness. Martin, the voyeur, and Liza, his exhibitionist girlfriend meet Joanne, a powerful and beautiful businesswoman who is exercising desires of dominance over her pretty secretary. Revelling in shameful delights, they are not alone in their sexual games; other guests are also discovering that Paradise Bay is a haven for indecent amusement.

Martin dried himself casually, wiping away the cool, invigorating water. Frixos was hot and humid, and he woke every morning bathed in a sticky layer of sweat that made everything uncomfortable. The cold blasts of refreshing water had washed away the sweat, cleansing his body and clearing the darkness of mood that seemed to develop overnight.

Just as he finished pulling on his clothes he heard a sound coming from the bedroom. He padded barefoot across the light and airy bathroom, stepping casually on the damp towels that he had discarded, and pulled the door open an inch. Peering through the crack in the door he saw that a young woman had come into the bedroom. She was dressed in a thin white tennis skirt and matching white tee-shirt, casually carrying her tennis racket which she dropped on to the cane chair by the door.

She's got the wrong room, Martin thought. He made no move to enter the room, remaining rooted to his place by the bathroom door, staring in curiosity at the attractive young woman.

The young woman exhaled heavily. She was obviously tired out; her tee-shirt clung to her body, and dark patches of sweat were visible under her arms, down her back and between her breasts. She had long blonde hair tied in a single long ponytail. Her face was young but there was a sensuous quality to her, heightened by the way her full red lips were slightly parted. She wandered across the room over to the refrigerator, where there was a decanter with some glasses by the side. She poured herself an icy glass of water and then retraced her steps.

Martin watched her curiously. As she walked her breasts jutted tightly against the thin shirt, the dark patches of her nipples pressing visibly against the cotton garment. The short skirt, slit on one side to reveal a long elegant thigh, flapped gently over her round bottom.

She stopped by the dressing table and regarded herself in the mirror, putting the empty glass down. She bowed her head to one side and then pulled up her tee-shirt to wipe the sweat from her face. As she did so Martin caught a glimpse in the mirror of her firm round breasts, the tight nipples contrasting strongly with the pale white flesh of her chest. She wiped herself for a few seconds and let the tee-shirt drop again.

Martin felt his prick stirring, rising against the tightness of his shorts. The unexpected glimpse of the firm young breasts set his pulse racing.

The young woman turned away from the mirror and sat back on the bed, exhaling heavily once more. For a moment she seemed to be at a loss, sitting languidly on the bed, tiny beads of perspiration like jewels on her glowing pink skin. Eventually she bent down and pulled off her white sport shoes and ankle socks, letting them fall untidily on the floor. Next she removed the tee-shirt, pulling it high over her head so that her firm-fleshed breasts were naked in the bright sunlight streaming into the room.

She regarded herself in the mirror, sitting up straight, shoulders pulled back, chest pushed forward provocatively. The reflection appeared to displease her; she made a face at herself, twisting and turning, displaying herself from every angle.

Martin's prick was hard, pressing urgently against his clothes. From his vantage point he could see the woman's reflection completely, a vision of innocent loveliness captured in the long rectangle of the silver mirror. Her back was flawless, slender shoulders narrowing gently down to her petite waist. He was completely aroused by the view, excited by the look of her, and by the knowledge that she was unaware of his prying eyes.

She knelt on the bed, getting down on all fours and arching her back. She pouted seductively, blowing herself a kiss with her brilliant red lips and then laughing, her breasts swaying gently, the nipples tracing little circles in the air. Her short skirt was inadvertently pulled high around her waist, revealing her long supple thighs and a pair of snow-white panties pulled high into the cleft of her perfect backside.

From his place Martin could now see her pert backside and the beautifully proportioned pear-shaped breasts. She was close enough for him to discern a darker pattern in the panties, pulled tight between her arse-cheeks and soiled by a slightly damp patch at the entrance to her sex. Quickly he slid his clothes off, glad to let his raging hardness stand free.

She sat up on her knees and took her breasts in her hands, cupping them lovingly, covering the nipples coyly. She was caught up in a little game, posing seductively, enjoying the reflection of herself bathed in the golden rays of the sun. Her fingers began to play with the nipples, rubbing over the sore points of flesh, soothing and yet exciting herself. She pinched herself, forcing the tight points of flesh into erection, arousing herself at the same time.

She resumed her initial position, chest forward and shoulders back. But this time there was a difference. Her nipples were hard points of sensitive flesh, pressing forward invitingly. Her eyes were burning with a light that had been missing earlier, and her full lips were slightly parted. She lost the playful smile, and her expression was suddenly more serious, more intense.

She knelt down again, on all fours, unknowingly displaying her bottom to Martin. Very slowly, with cool deliberation, she slipped her hand down between her thighs. Watching her every movement in the mirror, she began to slide her palm up and down the inside of her right thigh, revelling in the feel of her muscular body. Her movements became concentrated higher up, just under the join in her thighs, where she pressed firmly with her fingers.

As she began to press her fingers inside her damp knickers, shuddering with pleasure when her fingers brushed against her cunny lips, Martin began to touch himself. He took his hardness in his hand, rubbing his fingers up and down the smooth pole of flesh. He imagined that the young woman's skilful fingers were touching him, caressing his firm hard prick.

She pulled her panties halfway down so that the thin garment was stretched between her thighs, almost as if it had fallen by accident. The pinkness of her sex was visible between the light patch of her pubic hair, the folds of flesh within seeming to glisten with the golden dewdrops of sex cream. Expertly she teased herself, playing her fingers tantalisingly across her pussy lips, threatening to enter but always withdrawing at the last instant. Her face was flushed, and her breathing had lost its rhythm as her eyes opened and closed with the dance of her fingers.

She cried out, gasping, when she pressed a finger deep inside herself, the force of penetration sending a ripple of pleasure echoing through her. Martin grasped his prick forcefully, rubbing himself, enjoying the vicarious pleasures on display. He closed his eyes momentarily, overcome with a shudder of pleasure, then looked again at the attractive young woman.

Her gasps of pleasure were clearly audible, a sighing accompaniment to the play of her fingers being forced into her sex. She had started with a single finger but was soon forcing three digits into her hungry sex, frigging herself with long slow strokes, bringing herself closer and closer to the moment of liberation. She switched hands quickly, managing to avoid losing the rhythm that had her pressing her backside in and out in rhythmic counterpoint to her fingers. She looked at the fingers of her free hand. The love juices were clearly visible: thick white drops of cream coated her fingers up to her knuckles. Without a thought she flicked out her tongue and lapped at her fingers, tasting herself, swallowing the drops of cream with evident relish.

Martin could hardly contain himself. He was using both hands to massage his prick, forcing tight fingers up and down the length of his hardness. His balls were aching, the pit of his belly was aflame with the swell of come ready for bursting. He was driven wild with desire by the glorious sight of the young woman masturbating herself with joyful abandon. All the time the pleasure was redoubled by the thought that he was invisible, that he was violating her space, invading her spiritually in some indefinable way.

'Oh Jesus . . .' she moaned loudly, her voice trailing into delirium. Silver trails of perspiration were beaded all over her body, and her thighs glistened with drops of sweat mixed with the thicker emissions from her pussy. At last, on the edge of elation, she turned her head back, eyes half closed with joy. Her fingers sought their target eagerly, blindly. She screamed once, with pleasure, with pain. Two fingers of her free hand were pressed forcefully into the tight dark bud of her arsehole, three fingers of the other hand attacking the rosebud in her cunt.

Swept along into the valley of orgasm, her body alive with an unbelievable energy sweeping her into nothingness, she turned and looked Martin in the eye. For a moment their eyes made contact, but then they each lost control. She froze, her body locked into position, swept into the abyss. Martin gasped once, he closed his eyes and sighed, his prick forcing thick jets of come over his fingers and on to the floor.

Martin cleaned himself up quickly before emerging from the bathroom. The orgasm had been amazing, his prick seemed to have squirted thick wads of jelly all over the place. His face seemed rather tired, as if the intensity of the experience had robbed him of all energy. He padded barefoot across the room and collapsed on to the bed.

'Well,' said Liza mischievously, 'that was pretty good wasn't it?'

'Absolutely amazing,' Martin admitted, his voice slightly hoarse.

'Good. I told you everything would be OK. By the way, the manager was asking questions again.'

'You didn't tell him anything?' Martin turned over on his side and faced Liza in concern.

'Don't worry,' she said reassuringly. 'Andreas was just interested in your plane. He was asking how much you bought it for, the running costs, that sort of thing. I don't trust him. He knows you've got money and he keeps sniffing around.'

'I can handle that. That's no problem. Just don't tell him anything else.'

'I told you,' Liza repeated, 'I didn't tell him anything.'

Alice watched the motorboat draw up to the ferry, the air thick with the shouts of the Greek sailors and the roar of the outboard motor. She looked on passively, too tired to feel any excitement. She had been unable to sleep the night before, tortured by the traumatic memory of what Joanne had done to her. It was not something that she had ever imagined possible. Not with another woman, and especially not with Joanne, whom she had always admired. Working for her had been as much a pleasure as anything else. She liked her, certainly considered her a friend, but that had been the full extent of her feelings.

But at the time, drawn insidiously by the simple sequence of events, she had felt powerless to resist. Every touch of Joanne's hand or mouth had seemed to inflame her, passing jolts of electricity through her body, until she had been completely mesmerised. She hadn't wanted it to happen, but once it had started she had let it go, surrendering herself completely.

She listened to the motor launch banging gently against the side of the ferry, the metallic bang echoing noisily through the hull of the old ship in contrast to the gentle lapping of the water against the bow. The steps down from the ferry to the launch looked precarious; the old wooden slats were fit to collapse and the lower steps were already wet and slippery.

'I hadn't planned on going swimming this early,' Joanne joked lightly, pointing to her black high heels and breaking the nervous silence that the two of them had shared from the moment they had left the hotel.

'I'll go first if you like,' Alice offered, edging forwards to the first step. She wasn't sure how to handle herself any more; she had lost the confidence that she had always displayed towards Joanne. The memory of all that had happened was still far too strong. Every time she closed her eyes she could feel Joanne's lips on hers, or remember the feel of Joanne's fingers exploring the soft folds of her pussy. The memories were strong and embarrassing and Alice felt guilty and afraid. But worst of all was the memory of the pleasure; the golden moment when she had climaxed had been like no other she had ever experienced.

'No, it's all right.' Joanne stepped forward and took Alice gently by the elbow. They looked at each other for the first time since they had made love. Their eyes met and gradually they smiled. It was as if an invisible spark had jumped from one body to the next, and the nervousness dissipated at once.

Joanne stepped down towards the launch, her heels clacking loudly against the old steps, adding to the cacophony that filled the morning air. A uniformed sailor helped her take the last step on to the launch, she jumped on to the deck and the boat rocked gently beneath her. She glanced up and saw Alice following, inching her way slowly from step to step.

When the half dozen passengers were aboard the launch, it cast off and headed noisily away from the old ferry which creaked its farewell. The launch jumped bumpily through the undulating water, a white spray rising up and falling away behind them.

As the launch drew closer it was possible to make out individual houses above the village, fine white structures dotted amongst the grey-black of the rocks. Far to the left of the village was Paradise Bay, the only hotel on the island, built around the sandy beach of a small inlet.

Alice turned and found Joanne looking at her. She smiled nervously and turned away, feeling exhilarated and afraid. Turning back to look at the ferry disappearing over the horizon, barely able to see the mainland in the distance, she knew that things would never be the same again. Things were going to change for ever, and she felt powerless to resist, completely mesmerised by a wordless bittersweet joy she didn't understand.

The sun was still low in the sky, a nebulous golden jewel shimmering like a mirage over the distant Aegean horizon, casting seeds of light that danced on the rippling surface of the sea. From his seat by the hotel pool, Martin had earlier watched the tiny fishing boats edge out across the bay and out into the wider sea, casting their tiny nets into the green-blue waters.

He liked being by the pool. It gave him a chance to look around, to watch everything and everyone. He wore dark mirrored glasses that gave nothing away, reflecting instead two pointed shafts of light, like a pair of lasers scanning the horizon. From his place he could watch the young women sunning themselves, their beautiful bodies almost naked, offering irresistible displays of their firm tanned flesh. He had watched a young married couple playing in the water, laughing joyfully and splashing noisily at each other, the woman emerging from the water like Aphrodite, her body glistening in the light, drops of water beaded over her like jewels.

All morning he had been in torment, aroused continually by the glorious bodies on display. Earlier one of the guests, a woman in her thirties, had gone for a swim. She wore a single-piece swimsuit made from a glossy material that clung tightly to her body. Her breasts were well covered, but the fullness of the shape and the largeness of her nipples were moulded into the material. As soon as he saw her Martin had become hard. She walked with poise and dignity; there was a seriousness about her, something a little stern, that he found immensely attractive. She walked to the edge of the pool, her firm breasts jigging lightly with every step, then stopped. For a moment she looked into the water with dark intense eyes, then she dived in gracefully, hardly raising a ripple on the silvery surface.

Martin had followed her with his eyes, tracing the shimmering vision as she swam under the water halfway across the pool. She resurfaced for a second, drawing a fast breath, then continued below the surface. She swam several lengths of the pool, always swimming under water, propelling herself with deft kicks of her long shapely legs. At last she stopped and sat in the water until she regained her breath, then pulled herself out. The water splashed from her body, leaving her dark skin glistening in the sunlight. The water had permeated the material of the swimsuit and it had become semitransparent, like an almost invisible second skin.

The woman became aware of her near-nakedness at once and looked round furtively, checking to see if she had been noticed. Martin had turned away at the right moment, avoiding her searching gaze. The poolside had been relatively empty. Coolly she headed slowly back to her room, all the time keeping her eyes lowered. Martin was fascinated. The dark mound of her pussy hair was clearly visible, indicating the entrance to her bulging and generous sex. The dark aureoles of her breasts, as big and as dark as ripe black cherries, had puckered from the shock of the cold water. As she disappeared from view he was able to admire the full-ness of her backside. The two round cheeks were almost bare and moved together seductively as she walked.

Martin had been hard all the time he had watched her, excited by the curves of her body and by the perfection of her face. He had wanted to take his prick in his hand, to close his eyes and express his admiration for her, to imagine her playing up and down his prick with her full generous lips. But, lying in the sunlight, out in the open, he had been unable to, and concealed the bulge in his shorts with a casually draped towel. The torment had been delicious, part of the strange game that he played.

Martin's thoughts were suddenly interrupted. He turned to find Andreas Karaplis, the hotel manager, silhouetted beside him, his tall thin frame blocking out the sun.

'May I join you?' Andreas asked, his voice betraying only the faintest hint of an accent.

'Sure,' Martin said politely, sitting back up in his seat. He smiled superficially, the dark glasses conceal-ing his irritation at being disturbed.

'A drink?' Andreas asked, waving a waiter over at once.

'A scotch, thank you, plenty of ice.'

'A scotch and an ouzo,' Andreas ordered, then turned back to Martin with a relaxed and friendly smile.

'This is a lovely place,' Martin murmured, feeling obliged to make at least some effort at conversation. All the time he scanned the poolside, on the alert in case some new woman should come into view.

'Thank you. Do you know Amanda Trevelyan?'

'The travel writer?'

'Travel writer and television star,' Andreas corrected with a short laugh. 'She's staying with us at the moment, you might meet her some time. Well, Amanda told me that it has taken thirty years of tourist development to achieve Paradise Bay. Can you imagine that? Thirty years of mistakes before we got it right!'

'I suppose she knows what she's talking about,' Martin said sourly, taking his drink from the waiter with scarcely a glance at the man.

'Oh she does,' Andreas continued blithely, ignoring the sullen remark. 'You said yourself that this is a lovely place. Have you explored the island yet?'

'No, not really.' Martin imagined that Andreas was doing his duty and playing the part of hospitable host, and he hoped that the single drink would be enough hospitality for the day.

'Oh you should,' Andreas urged enthusiastically. 'There is so much here for the discerning visitor. Up in the hills there are some very interesting archaeological sites, very interesting. There is a ruined temple to Diana. The frescoes there are unique, absolutely unique. And of course the village has a lovely atmosphere, unspoilt.'

'Yes, I'm sure we'll get to visit there soon.' Martin's rising irritation was plain. He finished his drink and turned away sharply, facing the pool once more.

'I can see you are tired,' Andreas said, preferring to ignore the discourtesy. 'Perhaps you have come here for a long rest?'

'Yes, that's right, a long rest. And some peace and quiet,' Martin said pointedly.

Andreas started to make another remark but was interrupted by the arrival of Liza. Martin's smile suddenly returned in relief.

'Hello again. Andreas stood up, offering his seat to Liza. 'Would you like a drink?'

'No, we've got to . . . er . . . go somewhere,' Martin said coldly, cutting off Liza's intended reply with a sharp glance.

'Yes, that's right,' Liza apologised. 'Another time perhaps.'

'Yes, definitely.' Andreas brightened at the prospect. 'One evening perhaps, I could show you round the old village.'

'Yes, yes,' Martin repeated impatiently.

He stood up and took Liza by the arm, ignoring the fleeting look of anger on Andreas's dark face. He led her away quickly past the poolside bar and towards the room, aware that Andreas was watching them go, his anger replaced with an unconcealed look of desperation.

'Well?' Martin asked expectantly as soon as he and Liza entered his room.

'I want you to know this wasn't easy,' Liza told him. She opened her bag and took out a pair of black silky panties.

Martin took them from her excitedly. For a second he fingered the smooth glossy garment, then brought it up to his face, breathing the pungent bouquet as if it were the most heavenly perfume. He walked across the room and sat back on the bed, not bothering to conceal the growing bulge in his shorts.

'I had to sneak into the staff quarters,' Liza added. 'I had to find the maid's room and then search through her things. God, that would have been hard to explain away.'

'But no one saw you.' Martin smiled, clutching the soiled garment close to his skin, a dreamy look in his light brown eyes. The room was full of blazing sunlight, focused in the mirror on the wall and then cast back in all directions.

'What did Andreas want?'

'Just being a pain in the butt.'

'Let me get changed,' Liza said, unbuttoning her white cotton shirt. It was hot, and the garment had started to stick to her soft smooth skin.

'Change in the bathroom,' Martin suggested, looking Liza directly in the eye.

'No, I'll change here,' she replied coolly, continuing to undo her buttons.

'All right, change here, but turn around,' he compromised.

Liza smiled. She knew Martin's ways. He loved to look at women, and she knew that for him there could be nothing more erotic than catching a secret glimpse of a beautiful woman undressing. But it had to be right; it was the essence of the moment that charged it with such erotic power. A fleeting glance, an unguarded moment: that was the aphrodisiac that made it so good for him.

She turned round and unbuttoned her shirt, knowing that he was spying her reflection in the mirror, feasting his eyes on her. It was strange; she knew that if she turned around and stripped off in front of him it would have little effect compared to stripping off in secret, trying to shield herself from his burning eyes.

She unbuttoned the shirt but did not remove it fully, letting it hang loosely, her breasts only partially covered. She unclipped her simple loose skirt and it fell to the floor around her ankles. When she stooped down to pick it up her pear-shaped breasts were fully revealed. For a second she caught his eyes in the mirror, watching her greedily, drinking in every image. She smiled at him mischievously, knowing that the look would disturb him, unsettling him in a way she didn't fully understand yet.

Martin smiled back nervously, doubt clouding his

eyes momentarily. His hand was rubbing up and down the bulge in his shorts, enjoying the feel of his hardness, working himself up to a greater level of arousal.

In a moment she had slipped off her panties and turned to face him, the white shirt hanging loosely on her shoulders. She was naked apart from the shirt and as she moved, the sunlight caught the shifting garment, revealing her firm breasts and smooth belly.

She sat on the bed beside him, careful not to touch him, but close enough so that he could feel the warmth of her body and breathe the faint scent that she was wearing. 'Lie back, right back, that's it,' she directed, pressing his shoulder down with the very tips of her fingers.

Martin lay flat on his back, holding the stolen panties close to his face like a powerful talisman. His prick was still hard, and the silver drops of fluid dripping from the glans had formed a damp patch in his shorts. She had calculated that the way her shirt shifted as she moved, as if blown by a non-existent breeze, would add to his excitement. He closed his eyes and lay back passively, stretched out completely on the bed.

Liza carefully edged his shorts down, releasing his stiff shaft of flesh. In an instant he was naked, his pale body bathed in the golden light playing through the room. His long hard prick looked delicious, the hard smooth flesh crying a single tear of silvery fluid. Her first instinct was to bend down and take the hardness deep into her soft receptive mouth, to taste the silver fluid on her tongue, to explore the sensitive dome with her lips.

'The maid enters the room,' she began, her voice soft and soothing. 'She is wearing her uniform. Frilly white cap. Black silk shirt with a white collar. Short black skirt with a slit. Black seamed stockings. Black high

51

heels. The uniform is smooth and glossy in the light. It looks like it's made of rubber or PVC.'

She waited for a moment, Martin had closed his eyes, she wanted him to picture the scene in his mind. She knew the image she wanted to project; she wanted him to see the maid in a tight black second skin, with an innocent angelic face and the body of a goddess.

'She doesn't see you, you are in the room next door,' she continued softly. As she spoke Martin's eyes were closed, but she could gauge the effect of her words by the way he shifted around on the bed. It was obvious that he was dying to take his thick hard cock in his hands. It twitched and flexed instinctively, the silvery fluid smeared already on to his belly.

'I've just come out of the shower,' Martin suggested eagerly, wanting to hurry the story along.

Liza complied. 'Your body is still wet,' she said. 'The water is dripping down your naked body. You go to the door to see what the noise is. You look out and see the maid. She is making the bed, she is on her knees at the foot of the bed. Her skirt is very short, you can see her long thighs, see the tops of the stockings, the dark suspenders.'

'I can see the suspenders are made of black rubber, pressing into her skin,' Martin added hoarsely, his hand moving towards his prick, touching it gently with his fingers but not taking it in his hand fully.

Liza wanted his obvious torment to grow so that the vivid picture in his mind, painted by her soft whispered voice would begin to drive him mad with desire. She moved his hand away from his prick gently, and then continued the story. 'I want you to see it all, the way the dark glossy uniform clings to the fullness of her body, the way that she moves, totally unaware that she is being watched by you. She bends down lower, humming a tune to herself. Her black panties are visible now, tightly pressed into the folds of her cunt, the dark hair peeking through.'

Without pausing Liza took the dark panties that he still held tightly. She brushed the knickers across his face for the last time. His body stiffened all over as soon as she took hold of his prick, using the dark silky panties to touch him where he was most sensitive.

'You walk into the room, she doesn't hear you. She spots that the bin by the desk has been knocked over. She crawls along the floor. You can see the skirt riding higher. The black panties are deep in her cunt. Your prick is hard.' She worked her hand up and down his hardness, wearing the panties over her hand like a glove. The feel of his prick under her fingers made her hot with desire. The story was affecting her as well as him.

'Her panties slip down . . .' Martin started to say, but his voice trailed off into a sigh of pleasure, jerking his pelvis higher to meet the downward stroke of Liza's fingers.

'The maid turns around and sees you,' she paused momentarily, knowing that Martin's fantasy and her story would diverge from here on. 'She looks at your hard prick, at the water dripping down your naked skin. You can see that her blouse is low cut, she has lovely dark tits.'

'No, I'm still in the bathroom . . .' Martin moaned, his face twisting with confusion.

Liza knew that the story was going wrong for him, as if his script had been replaced by another. From the way he caught his breath she was certain that the feel of her fingers must have been ecstatic. She lowered her voice a notch, bending down to whisper breathily in his ear. 'She smiles. You take her hand and put it on your prick. She smiles, she plays her hand up and down your prick. You move to the bed. She takes your cock into her mouth. She is moving up and down your cock with her mouth.' She was working her hand up and down rapidly, driving his prick harder and harder. From the pained expression on his face it was clear that he was nearing the end.

'She sits on me . . . I . . .'

Yes. She sits on your prick,' she improvised, working his words into her fantasy. 'Her cunt is warm and inviting, it feels like heaven.'

'No . . .' Martin gasped furiously, opening his eyes, a look of confusion etched on his face.

Liza saw that he was fighting back, trying to twist the story his way once more. She leaned forward quickly, knowing that she had little time. Urgently she slid her hand under his balls, searching with her fingers the space between his muscular buttocks.

'She's sitting on my face . . . Pissing on me . . . Pissing on me . . .' Martin whispered, wearing an expression of distant surprise, as if his fantasy had turned out strangely without his intervention.

Liza forced her middle finger up against his tight arsehole. In other circumstances she was certain that he would have resisted, but now he moved down, parting his thighs a little, so that her finger passed some way into his bumhole. He closed his eyes at once, fell back on to the bed, parting his thighs even more. 'She is riding up and down your prick,' she persisted, wanking him in the arsehole with one hand and his prick with the other. 'You are fucking her. She is fucking you. Up and down your prick. It's heaven. She is crying out with pleasure. Pleasure that you are giving to her. Pleasure that you feel as well.'

Martin cried out once, his body stiffened and then

relaxed. Thick wads of creamy spunk jetted out on to his belly; wave after wave of unbridled joy convulsed his sweating body. At the moment of release Liza had ensured that the image in his mind had been of the maid sitting over his lap, with him forcing his hard prick deep into her wet pussy.

THE PALACE OF SWEETHEARTS

Delver Maddingley

I know, for some Nexus readers, there's nothing more titillating than the thought of being surrounded by scores of naughty young girls barely into their first bloom of womanhood, and all keen to explore your mature talents.

Well, this is indeed the enviable situation our very lascivious hero, the Captain, finds himself in when he is employed as the caretaker at Cunlip College Finishing School for daughters of professional men. The Captain is a man of many tricks, and the lure of innocence finds him in many a sticky situation; not only in *The Palace of Sweethearts*, but in subsequent novels in the *Palace* series. Many readers have commented on the quality of the writing in this series of books, which is as fresh and delightful as the young ladies who befriend the Captain.

There are three books currently available in the *Palace* series with a new title, *The Palace of Eros*, due for publication in May 1994.

Overnight the thunderclouds had built up steadily, and by Wednesday morning the storms had broken. Rain lashed against the rattling windows of the Old Lodge, and the Captain felt a sense of emptiness and depression as he stood at the earthenware sink tackling the congealed grease of last night's meal. Outside, everything looked grey and sodden. The temperature had dropped like a stone. Had the long days of flaunted beauty and open-air sex finally come to an end? Officially banned from the main building of the college, what opportunities would he find for continuing to enlarge his circle of delightful young friends and for developing his growing intimacy with them? The rain poured down, and even his collection of erotic fiction failed to hold his attention. What was more, he had no waterproof clothing apart from his motorcycling leathers.

Around the middle of the morning, however, the clouds parted and the sun struck through, clear and brilliant. When he stepped outside, the long, wet grass clung to his ankles. The air was fresh, and all the clogged oppressiveness that had been thickening suffocatingly over the last week had been washed out of it. Breathing had become a rediscovered pleasure. And in

contrast to the coolness of the light breeze, the rays of
the sun when the breeze lapsed were as strong as ever.
The Captain went indoors to get dressed, inspired with
intimations of a new start. Intimations . . . 'All things
that love the sun are out of doors,' he declaimed aloud,
remembering a fragment of Wordsworth.

Patches of sunshine chased the shadows of the clouds
across the valley, and were chased by more clouds in
their turn. Through the open window the stream could
be heard, enlivened by the recent downpour, chattering
over its gravel bed below the plank bridge. Surveying
the sky, he reached the conclusion that although the
blue was gaining rapidly on the fleecy stragglers racing
across it, a dark bank of swag-bellied cloud looming up
on the left might still be the determining feature of the
day's weather. If he got a soaking in his overalls he
would feel miserable. He would venture forth in shorts
and T-shirt, easily discarded and easily dried.

As he crossed the plank bridge, he paused to enjoy
the sun sparkling on the laughing current, and noticed
the fluttering of a blue dress which immediately withdrew behind the oak tree downstream. A casual
approach seemed best under the circumstances. He
sauntered a few yards up the avenue, his lips pursed to
form a silent whistle, casting his eyes in idle rapture
from the dusty pathway up to the racing clouds and
down again. At precisely the right point he turned his
head towards the tree.

Even without seeing their faces, he knew by now who
these girls were: Susie Freemantle and Nikki Culpep-
per. Both wore their blue summer dresses. They stood
beneath the oak in a tight embrace. Susie's back was
towards the Captain. The hem of her skirt had been
lifted and her navy pants pulled down to her thighs by
Nikki, who was stroking her bottom. On catching sight

60

of him, Nikki put a finger of her free hand up to her lips, warning him not to let her friend know he was there. The Captain stopped in his tracks, fascinated, as the stroking continued and the caressing hand was slowly insinuated between Susie's delicious thighs.

The direction of the breeze favoured his overhearing scraps of their conversation. 'Ouch!' cried Susie. 'You're not supposed to go in there.'

'No, and I wouldn't have to, would I, if you'd only do as Melanie told you. You've got to do it with your own fingers, and you've only got till tomorrow night.'

'But it bleeds when I try to do it.'

'Good,' replied Nikki. 'That's what's supposed to happen. You must be nearly there by now. Just a little bit more and you'll be all nice and ready for him, and nothing's going to hurt any more. Let's have a nice kiss.'

Susie wriggled in her companion's arms. The position of their heads changed, and she became aware of the Captain's interested gaze. He waved to the girls and plunged into the dripping undergrowth, heading in light spirits towards the pool.

So early in the day he was not expecting any sport in that particular neck of the woods; he was happy just to commune with nature. All the same, as he drew near the expanse of water he exercised an automatic caution, moving with silent steps and remaining concealed in shady foliage.

His prudence was rewarded. On the end of the little jetty projecting from the opposite bank, resplendent in the dazzling sunshine, sat Anne Amory, her legs swinging in the water. As usual, her blonde curls were adorned with her fetching straw boater, which she now wore tilted back at a jaunty angle. Her bosom was not available for the Captain's admiration, as she sported a

61

voluminous bright red sweater. His eyes were thus drawn down to the pale, parted thighs, between which he could distinctly make out the line of pink dividing the dusting of fine yellow down. She splashed her feet in the water and blew a condomlike balloon of bubble gum.

At this moment her friend Carla emerged from the shadows to stand on the sunwashed, steaming lawn behind her. The dark, flat-chested girl was wearing nothing but a Walkman. She stood with her feet together and her hands clasped behind her neck. Her armpits sprouted little black tufts, and she swayed her slim loins, with their patch of black fur, in time with the music. Then she broke into an uninhibited dance, pirouetting, high-kicking, turning cartwheels and floating gracefully over the buttercups, daisies and dandelions, her trained limbs supple and expressive. The Captain recalled and silently articulated another snatch of Romantic poetry: 'Heard melodies are sweet, but those unheard are sweeter'. Wasn't that the ode in which 'loth maidens' were struggling to escape the 'mad pursuit' of men or gods? The idea of such a chase was most appealing – he would mention it to Melanie.

Real artistry informed the balletic display, which took on an increasingly erotic character as Carla's body swayed, gyrated and undulated. Her performance was wasted on Anne, who continued to sit with her back to it, noisily popping bubbles of gum. On the Captain, though, it was certainly not wasted. The tip of his penis had crept down to emerge from the leg of his skimpy shorts. A string of clear, sticky fluid snailed its way down the hairs on the inside of his thigh. Carla's skill was such that, as he watched with thumping heart, she seemed to be transformed from a naked girl with long legs and a little cunt into an open, inviting cunt supported by the flashing white flesh of a small body and its flailing limbs. It was the cunt that was dancing, in celebration of its own allure, in proclamation of its carnal hunger. The dance ended. Carla stepped on to the jetty and stood behind Anne, her legs apart. She removed the lightweight headset, and faint strains of Tchaikovsky drifted across the pool. 'Come and dance,' she said, stooping to lift Anne's sweater and let the sun fall on the snowy breasts.

But as her friend looked up, smiling, the sun went in and a chill breeze ruffled the surface of the pool. Heavy drops fell on the Captain's head and shoulders, shaken from the branches above. His manhood, uncomfortably pinched by the leg of his shorts, was cooled into detumescence. The spell was broken. Both girls were hurriedly dressing, and in no time had moved off, arm in arm, downstream.

Instead of following them, the Captain went the other way, seeking the shelter of the Palace of Sweethearts. Just as he reached the veranda, the rain began to fall in earnest. A powerful gale was blowing. Fortunately, the wind was coming from behind the building, so he could stand on the boardwalk, chilly but dry, as sheets of water bucketed over the roof and chased each other in shaking curtains across the field to the straining woods. He took out his key and went inside.

The shutters rattled intermittently, and when they were not rattling a steady dripping and splashing sound was indicative of the disrepair into which the pavilion had been allowed to fall. It seemed darker than usual, and this was not just because of the absence of sunshine. As he had guessed the night before, the large lockers had indeed been shifted to leave a clear space running the whole length of the room. They now stood along the walls, close to but not right up against them, obstructing the rays that entered through the chinks and spyholes. Because of this rearrangement, he no longer knew which locker contained the pornographic material with which he had hoped to beguile the time during the storm. He had examined only a few of them, all of which turned out to be either locked or empty, when a clatter of feet and babble of voices announced the arrival of a party seeking shelter. The Captain was glad he had locked the door; after all, the newcomers would be protected from the rain out on the veranda. He tiptoed round into the narrow space between lockers and windows, and applied his eye to the most suitable holes.

Half a dozen bedraggled girls, their bare legs spattered with mud, huddled there shivering in singlets and navy knickers. They had evidently been out for a run under the supervision of Miss MacDonald, who stood beside them in a soaking tracksuit, wringing the water out of her dark hair. The condition of their hair was indeed the immediate preoccupation of all of them, and its saturation, as well as the fact that they tended to stand with their heads hanging down and their eyes screwed up, made it a little hard to recognise them. But this, undoubtedly, was his lovely, freckled Gina, and the girl quivering next to her must be her friend Jane Jewkes, wielder of the famous salami.

Not without difficulty, Miss MacDonald had dragged the heavy top of her claret-coloured tracksuit over her head. The nipples that crowned her fine white breasts had gathered themselves into hard, glowing coals, a fierce orange-red among the surrounding goose pimples. 'Get out of those wet things, girls, everything except your trainers,' she ordered, lowering first the bottom half of her tracksuit and then the white silk briefs she wore under it. An innocent observer might have wondered why she found it necessary to remove this last garment. Beside the steaming flesh of her young charges, the Captain found it slightly incongruous that her pubic curls formed such a dry, fluffy bush on the mound between those athletic thighs. Naked and fanatical, she now devoted herself to helping the girls to peel off their drenched clothing. The chattering of teeth was punctuated by squeals of laughter.

The lurid untruths Melanie had told the Captain about Alexandra Fellowes, the young lady with the virginal reputation who had sex with her own brother, had stuck in his memory, and he recognised her even before Miss MacDonald rolled the navy-blue pants down over the girl's thighs. The familiar, ample bosom of cuddly Emily identified *her* readily enough as the vest was pulled over her head. Celia Prout was also known to him by now, but who was this handsome, snooty-looking sixth girl with narrow white belly, sodden black cunthair and long thighs?

'Off with that vest, Josie Greene!' the MacDonald's voice called out in answer to his silent question. The bottom of the clinging vest was raised, and the nipples, which had pushed out proudly through the thin and by now almost transparent material, were exposed in their full glory, hard, long and thick. In lifting her arms to remove the vest, Josie revealed the growth of dark hair adorning her armpits. Of course: Josie was the girl who had been fucked in the shower by Joker Jennings.

Briskly, Miss MacDonald lined the girls up in three pairs, one behind the other, and stood in front facing them at the end of the veranda. 'No towels to dry ourselves,' she shouted above the wind, 'so we'll do some exercises to get warm.'

The Captain moved along the line from peephole to

peephole, relishing the rippling of muscle under wet skin, the tensing and relaxing of buttocks, some lean and some plump but none of them excessively fleshy, and the jiggling of assorted boobs. On the whole the operation was being conducted in a good-natured spirit, but it was very plain that Gina and Josie, who formed the last pair, did not find each other's company congenial. At every opportunity the arm of one would swing round into the other's face, or an elbow would nudge spitefully into a breast.

For ten minutes or so the party was drilled in conventional exercises of the toe-touching, hip-swinging, arm-lifting kind, until they were all rosy and panting. The order was then given for the couples to turn inward, facing each other, and for each girl to raise her left leg and place it on her partner's right shoulder. For a moment they all stood looking at each other in disbelief. Jane and Celia, who occupied the middle position, then attempted the feat with some assistance from their neighbours, who had to hold them together in a lewd embrace, cunt jammed against cunt. Seeing that it was physically possible, Alexandra and Emily followed suit, while Miss MacDonald ensured that the two couples leaned lightly against each other for mutual support. She urged the reluctant Gina and Josie to complete the tableau. The result, of course, was disastrous, and all six girls collapsed in a gasping, giggling heap, although the giggles came only from Alexandra, Celia, Emily and Jane.

When they had recovered, the MacDonald consulted her watch. 'Right, girls,' she said. 'Twenty minutes left before that revision class you've all got. Just time for a quick competition. The rain's not going to stop, so we'll do it out there – the main thing's to keep warm. All know what an *orgasm* is, don't you?'

An embarrassed silence was taken to signify assent.

'Has anyone here never had one?'

Alexandra raised her hand, but quickly converted the gesture into one of scratching her ear when she realised she was alone.

'We're going to have an orgasm race,' Miss Mac-Donald continued.

'What's the prize?' Emily demanded.

'Dinner in my room.'

Celia sneered. 'In that case,' she said, 'they'll all cheat. Anyone can *fake* it.'

But Miss MacDonald was ready for that one. 'It's not the first to come, silly, but the last. Come down here – and you, Jane – and I'll show you how we're going to do it.'

The three of them stepped out into the rain. Jane Jewkes was made to stand with her feet apart and her hands raised above her head. Steadying her with one palm on the small of Jane's back and the other cupping a breast, Miss MacDonald helped her to bend backwards until first her hands and then her head touched the ground. The curve of her belly now formed a glistening dome, on one side of which her pink-tipped tits flowed back towards her armpits. On the other side a pouting pussy was offered to the rain, which saturated the black sponge of her pubic hair and trickled down the central runnel between the tensed thighs. Celia was then placed standing with her back to Jane, some eighteen inches in front of her and slightly to one side. She too was put through the backward-bending routine. Standing between her legs and grasping the concavity of her buttocks, Miss MacDonald manoeuvred her until her face hung directly underneath Jane's cunt. Once she was in this position, it was possible for the older woman to support and raise the nape of Celia's neck while the girl reached up to find a secure hold on Jane's hips. Miss MacDonald stood back. 'Just let your head hang right down,' she ordered. 'Now check whether you can pull yourself up and press your face back so that you can lick up her labia to her clitoris. Yes, that's fine. No, stop licking now or you'll have an unfair start.'

The other four girls were called down from the veranda, and the difficult operation performed by Celia was repeated by them in turn. Emily was positioned between Celia's legs, Alexandra between Emily's, Josie between Alexandra's, and finally, protesting loudly, Gina between Josie's. Thanks to the angle at which each girl had been placed relative to the one she was going to lick, they now formed not a line but an almost perfect hexagon. It only remained for Miss MacDonald to seize Jane by the armpits and lift her into position between the thighs of Gina, whose complaints died away when she felt the girls' hands on her hips and her breath on her groin.

This ingenious formation was evidently putting a huge strain on the poor girls, especially on the muscles of their legs; it was only the way they interlocked, and their powerful motivation, that allowed them to remain in place. As he watched the rain rebounding from their taut bellies, the Captain longed to sink his throbbing member into a moist sheath. The order was given: 'Lick!' Six eager tongues lashed into six reluctant clits – although in some cases the slavering Captain had the impression that the reluctance was quickly overcome. Who would be the last to succumb to this outrageous titillation?

Who succumbed last, or first, or whether indeed they all succumbed at the same moment, was impossible to say. What was clear, though, was that the first orgasm or orgasms caused convulsions that overthrew the whole cantilevered structure. The six girls sprawled on the wet grass, spending or spent, and the contest was declared a draw, with *tête-à-tête* dinners promised for all of them in the coming days.

Miss MacDonald clapped her hands. 'On your feet, my poppets,' she shouted. 'No time for a hot shower, I'm afraid. That'll be my reward, but you've got work to do. When we get to the bathhouse just grab your towels and take them up to your dorm to rub yourselves down before you put on dry clothes.'

Led by their popular and talented mentor, the girls gathered up the wet things they had left on the veranda and jogged off with stiff limbs down the Lower Field, heading to their right along the bank of the stream. The Captain locked the door behind him and followed them at a distance of some twenty yards, far enough behind for them not to sense his presence but close enough, even in the driving rain that quickly soaked through his T-shirt and shorts, to enjoy the view of their bouncing bottoms. Their vulnerable nakedness shone wetly, and on those of them whose hair was long the tresses were plastered down their backs. Bits of grass stuck to their thighs and buttocks from the collapse of their orgasmic circle, and the backs of their legs were splashed with mud as they ran wearily round the pool and up the avenue.

As they approached the building, the Captain dodged into the shrubbery and waited in increasing discomfort for a few minutes after they had all entered the door of the bathhouse. Then he let himself in quietly and looked around shivering. The girls had disappeared, but he could hear water running and saw clouds of steam issuing from one of the shower cubicles. This hint of luxury proved too much for him. He peeled his wet clothes off and advanced purposefully towards his unsuspecting quarry.

Before entering the shower, he stood for a moment waiting for his prick to stiffen while he admired the MacDonald's long back. The ridge of her spine as she bent forward to wash her hair divided the pale, muscular hardness that gave way below her waist to the tight, ripe cushions of her buttocks. Beneath them gleamed the athletic thighs, and between them the rift through which he could make out a dark mass of dripping hair.

This prospect had done the trick. As he stood on the tiled floor his penis had extended itself so far that the head, bursting out of his uncomfortably tight foreskin, almost touched the desired flesh. He stepped into the shower, delighting in the warm caress of the water, and pressed himself against the woman's back. She neither looked round nor straightened up. Instead, she reached a hand back through her parted thighs and grasped his tool. Her other hand followed, and eased open her dark-fringed lips. He entered her and started to fuck. It's got to be once only, he told himself, if I'm going to last the course at Melanie's party in the dormitory tonight.

Miss MacDonald lowered herself to a kneeling position, taking the Captain with her. Deliciously warm water streamed over his back, down between his buttocks and over his balls. One of his hands explored and briskly fondled the hanging breasts with their distended tips, and then slid along the smooth, hard stomach to find the sopping fur-pad. With thumb and middle finger in her groin channels, he squeezed the vulva hard until he could feel the pressure on the stem of the cock that filled it. Still holding her like this he pistoned in and out. His index finger ran upwards between her fleshy love lips and found the enlarged clitoris. He pressed the fingertip hard into this pip and rolled it from side to side.

He breathed thickly into her ear. Without turning for visual confirmation of the identity of her ravisher she murmured, as he pumped harder, 'Oh, Captain, do you call this netball?'

'I call it Physical Development,' he riposted. His wad of hot spunk shot straight up her womb at the very instant that her own ecstasy convulsed her limbs and left her howling into the white porcelain.

The temperature and humidity rose as the day wore on and gave way to an oppressive night. At eleven o'clock precisely, the Captain was waiting on the steps of the main entrance. The clouds had parted for a moment, and the scene was steeped in moonlight. He gasped as Melanie appeared in the doorway to welcome him. Her fair hair and pale limbs were lustrous in the strange light, and a sense of coolness was communicated to him as he took in the costume she had chosen for the dorm feast. It was of pale blue cotton material: a little, bust-hugging top with shoulder straps and a trimming of white lace above the bare belly, and high-cut knickers, loose round the hips but snug at the crotch, with lace at the waist.

She took his hand and led him into the building and up two flights of stairs to the room she shared with Emily, Honoria and Priscilla. Neither he nor the girls had any inkling that their activities and conversation were being monitored in close detail by the Principal, who was sitting up late in her study. Mary Muttock wore nothing but a lacy black negligée on this occasion, and her wet vagina was stuffed with about two-thirds of a solid rubber dildo, its straps hanging loose, which was

71

usually kept for demonstration purposes in Miss Mac-Donald's lab. Miss MacDonald was unaware of the Principal's habit of borrowing this instrument for her own pleasure, and of course neither woman had any idea of the part designed for it in the nuptial rites Melanie had planned for the following night. Concerning that occasion nothing was said now by Melanie, as it was meant to be a great surprise for the Captain.

Melanie's room-mates greeted him enthusiastically, and they all sat on chairs at the end of a bed on which the feast of cakes and fruit had been laid out. A bottle of Bulgarian Cabernet Sauvignon was passed round, and a second one. Eating and drinking gave the Captain time to admire these young ladies at close quarters. Emily attracted him more each time he encountered her. Tonight she wore a man-sized pair of striped pyjamas. Most buttons on the jacket were undone, and glimpses of her glorious bosom were freely bestowed whenever she leaned forward for the food. The punky Honoria also sported male attire, a rugby shirt of her brother's, maroon with a white collar. Priscilla sat there, demure in a white cotton nightie with wide openings under the arms through which the curves of her breasts could be seen. It seemed to be so contrived that the frills could easily be slipped down over the shoulders. Her long, black hair was tied back with a red ribbon.

The remains of the feast were cleared away, and the Captain followed his hosts to the Main Ward, as it was still called, which accommodated the younger girls in institutional austerity. There they moved between the iron bedsteads, selecting four playmates. At once, and without ceremony, they led them back to the smaller room. Not a bad selection, the Captain thought: Helen, Nikki, Anne and Carla.

Events now moved briskly. The four young concubines

were ordered to strip naked. Melanie took Anne to her bed, Priscilla took Nikki, Honoria grabbed Carla and Emily seemed happy enough to be left with Helen. The Captain moved from bed to bed, watching the couples as they sported on top of the covers, every now and then sitting beside them and assisting with judicious applications of finger or tongue. Throughout these proceedings, the older girls retained their nightclothes, although Helen soon removed Emily's pyjama bottoms. Prissy's nightdress slipped right down to her waist under Nikki's lustful scrabbling for her breasts, and Honoria's rugger shirt gathered itself up under her armpits. Melanie alone was still relatively untampered with, at least in this respect. Her pretty outfit was designed to attract and receive amorous advances without disturbing its general appearance – the close-fitting top encouraged the luxury of fondling through the material, and the knickers allowed the easy access at hip level of a hand which could slide down the front to the crotch or behind to the anus.

No sooner had all eight girls achieved their climax than they stood up, moved the bedside cabinets out of the way, and pushed the four beds together. At this point the Captain, as guest of honour, was brought more actively into the picture (a picture which, reduced to black and white, was affording Miss Muttock considerable diversion). Melanie, who as usual directed the operation, lay on her back. Next to her lay Honoria, then Emily, then Prissy. Their arms were stretched back above their heads. The four concubines were ordered to kneel straddling their chests, crouched so that their genitals brushed their mistresses' mouths while their own tongues could work the recumbent clits. The older girls then reached round with their hands to tickle the younger ones' breasts (although only

Anne had any real development there) and the pubic regions. At first the Captain saw no opening for himself, until Melanie demonstrated her idea. Pushing little Anne's head up from her crotch, she made her rise to an upright position. Our hero, who had already undressed, then mounted between Melanie's thighs, pulled aside the cute knickers and shoved his hard cock up her cunt. Cupping his hands round Anne's buttocks, he licked into her moist slit while fucking Melanie.

'Go steady!' cried the latter, her voice muffled by Anne's bum. 'Let's see if you can get it into all eight of us before you have to come.'

Inspired by this suggestion, he withdrew, and Anne changed places with Melanie. There is something poignant in the sight of an erect phallus prematurely withdrawn from a willing cunt, but in this case precautionary *coitus interruptus* was not the object. Glib with Melanie's spendings, the instrument was slipped with ease into Anne's small but elastic sheath. The pumping action was resumed, but only for a few strokes. Following exactly the same routine as with the first couple, the Captain bestowed his favours in rapid succession on Honoria and Carla, Emily and Helen, and Priscilla and Nikki. Each time he felt the semen gathering at the root of his prick, he drew out and took a breather before mounting the next girl.

It was while his tongue was nipped by Prissy's labia and his prick by Nikki's cunt muscles that he discharged, having just managed to service all the girls. As he came, he recollected for the third time that day some lines of Romantic verse:

A mighty fountain momently was forced
Amid whose swift half-intermitted burst

Huge fragments vaulted like rebounding hail
Or chaffy grain beneath the thresher's flail;
And, 'mid these dancing rocks, at once and
    ever,
It flung up momently the sacred river.

Instantly he was torn from Nikki's deep, romantic chasm and thrown on to his back. All eight of them were at him with hands and mouths, and no part of his body was spared their attentions. Nikki, delighted to have been the recipient of a tribute now running copiously down her thighs, insisted on kissing him and mumbling endearments into his ear. 'I'm really getting off on *Adventures of a Naked Girl*, mister,' she confided. 'Just love that bit when she's stretched out on the bough of a tree and the boy flops down on top of her.'

By now, the Captain's member was once more the dominant feature of this animated scene, its shining purple head straining towards the smoke detector above them. He thought there was something not quite right about that rather unexpected piece of technology; it had the appearance of an eye gazing down on them from the ceiling. The conflagrations raging below, however, would not require a sprinkling triggered by that dubious source to quell them.

As he lay glorying in the potency of his restored erection, the girls straddled him and shafted themselves one after the other, each bouncing up and down six times before surrendering the saddle to her successor. Melanie, Anne, Honoria, Carla, Emily, Helen, Prissy and Nikki all took his tower of strength into their vaginas and exercised it furiously while he played with their nipples. A second round began, and he had got as far as the lewd young Helen with her dark-ringed eyes and corrupt grin when his pent-up reservoirs burst open and poured another mighty fountain into a canal too tight to contain it. But before the surplus had time to spill into his pubic hair he was asleep.

Miss Muttock plucked out the dildo and slumped back in her chair. Then she too slept.

The Chronicles of Lidir

THE DUNGEONS OF LIDIR

A Saga of Erotic Domination

Aran Ashe

Imagine a dungeon of beautiful young slaves only too willing to please you, lest your wrath should bestow itself upon their tender flesh. In Aran Ashe's four books known as the *Chronicles of Lidir*, we can find loving descriptions of exquisite violation which are rarely surpassed. The mythical principality of Lidir is home to both the good and the wicked.

The prince is summoned away leaving his gorgeous, copper-haired betrothed, Anya, in the care of Ildren, taskmistress of the castle. Ildren's lusts are notorious for their perversity. In this extract, we find her taking great pleasure in her intimate inspection of the fresh arrivals to the dungeon. And by the look of things, Anya will not be spared her dignity. Never mind, she's a girl who cannot help enjoying every moment of humiliation.

In addition to *The Chronicles of Lidir* the reclusive, but prolific, Aran Ashe has written a novel of Edwardian decadence entitled *Choosing Lovers for Justine* and is planning a long-awaited new series of books along the same theme as the *Lidir* stories.

The Taskmistress stood on her balcony. Far below her, the cherry orchard lay transformed into a gently swelling sea of green with rolling pink-white spindrifts scintillating in the morning sun. Today, Ildren was feeling lyrical. Spring was really here at last, and spring had never smelled so sweet. And this particular spring day would be presenting Ildren with a rare treasure in the person of a very special spring-fresh creature, a slave whom Ildren had not even met and yet, paradoxically, a slave who was now pivotal to Ildren's calculations. She closed her eyes and stood there, drinking in the perfumed air, soaking up the morning sun. Life seemed so exhilarating. All the blackness and the pain had dissolved away; her confidence was back. But now, she thought, to business: a Taskmistress has her duties, be it spring or be it winter; the Taskmistress must prepare for this very special, very close investigation . . .

She selected from her wardrobe a freshly laundered deep red robe and a matching pair of slippers; she would not wear her boots today. But what about her jewellery? She settled for a pendant, a gold clasp fastened round a polished, large and heavy black stone. This pendant, on a suitable chain, could be worn around the neck so it dangled down between the breasts to provide some weighted stimulation to a wearer so inclined. Ildren liked the way the rounded weight rolled back and forth across her belly and caused the chain to swing across and on occasion catch upon her nipples. For underwear, she chose something very simple – a well-oiled, very thin and very long piece of leather cord, knotted closely round her waist at one end, with the excess length left dangling very casually; she liked the feel of the cool supple cord just brushing against her inner thighs in unpredictable tickles manifesting themselves at inappropriate times.

And now – what equipment would she need for the inspection? She would need to think about it; she would need to browse. Strictly speaking, it wasn't essential that the new slaves be examined in detail. A single glance would normally suffice. She had only to look at a slave to know approximately how he or she would respond to training. True, there were exceptions, the unpredictable ones that Ildren found so delightfully interesting, and the intractable ones, as their impatient lordships liked to put it, that provided the challenge. Yet even without these minor fascinations and tricky little problems, Ildren loved these inspections; the innocent, beautiful creatures filled her with delight, especially when the examination was both meticulous and prolonged – which was where the equipment was required. The nature of the instrument did not seem to matter. Ildren had found that what counted was its presence rather than its specification. Inanimate as it might – in most cases – be, it nevertheless constituted a third party at the examination, an implied threat, to be introduced at any point where a bondslave might be feeling vulnerable.

So, as Ildren opened drawers and rummaged through

the cupboards of her storeroom, she wasn't searching for anything in particular. She would use whatever provided inspiration when it came to hand. For example, the item she had just picked up held for her a curious fascination. It had a basic quality of roundness yet it wasn't round in detail. it was made of wood, a dense black wood, ebony perhaps, and was very smoothly carved and polished. It was large, too large for one hand really, and yet the palm seemed to fit so naturally around it, with the middle finger fitted along the smooth and shallow groove beneath. It was a sculpture of a man's part – a very large pair of ballocks with a small retracted cock. This was what made it so unusual – most of Ildren's sculptured pieces were fiercely erect. As it stood, it wasn't any use – no part of it could be conveniently applied or easily inserted – but then neither was it ornament, for she kept it in the drawer. Ildren could never understand the secret of its fascination, and yet, even as her eyes roamed around for something a little more practical, she found herself moulding her palm around it and absent-mindedly pulling at the end.

Then she spotted, in the same drawer, the very things she needed – a broad-bladed spatula of wood and a wooden drumstick with a bulbous end. Two finds in one go – this was so auspicious. She slipped them quickly into the pocket of her robe and set off straight away, with the leather cord tickling so deliciously up against her person, out into the corridor, down the stairs, beaming at the guards and servants as she passed them and wishing them 'good day'. And now, she surprised herself by deciding on impulse to take a detour through the stables. It would be an opportunity to see how the preparations for the Prince's departure were progressing. She liked to see the grooms and stablehands busying about their work; perhaps one of their lordships might be entertaining a slave or two in one of the stalls, in which case Ildren might be able to offer some advice or even casual assistance.

But as she crossed the courtyard, she realised something was amiss. There seemed to be hardly anyone about and no activity at all. Ildren challenged the only person she could find, a stableboy sitting kicking his heels, on a barrel by the door.

'Boy!' The lad fell off the barrel. 'Think yourself lucky it wasn't the Prince that caught you idling.'

The boy rubbed his elbow and looked about him uneasily before replying in a very uncertain tone, as if he didn't want to contradict. 'But Taskmistress – the Prince is gone . . .'

Ildren was taken aback. Her mind was working quickly. 'Gone . . . But are you sure of this, my child?' Her voice was softer now, more encouraging, for this could be good news, even better than she could have hoped for – much better than her wildest dreams.

'Yes. Two hours since.' The boy was gaining confidence now. 'They had to leave two days early on account of the river.' The Taskmistress's eyes widened. 'Soon it will be in flood,' he pronounced with authority, as though he himself had sat upon the bank, looking askance at the other side, with the water lapping around his toes and working up towards his ankles.

Now Ildren was dizzy with exhilaration; she knew that fate was on her side. She wanted to pick that urchin up and kiss him like she'd kissed the cat, but the timid creature only backed against the stable wall. She had to content herself with blowing him a kiss before continuing on her quest. The boy looked mystified and then a little worried.

*　*　*

83

Ildren leisurely climbed the broad stairs to the Great Hall, thinking. With the Prince gone, how could she possibly fail? She turned into the west wing, along the corridor and through into the Bondslaves' House, smiling at the houseguards and resisting the sudden temptation to peek beneath their loincloths. Unless directed, they never seemed to move a well-oiled muscle, Ildren mused; they seemed a different breed entirely from the castle guards. She had once witnessed one of these hulking creatures carrying four bondslaves, two under each arm, from here to her apartments, and even then, even at a brisk trot, Ildren had scarcely been able to keep up with him.

The conversation died as the Taskmistress swept through the sea of beautiful women in golden chains and purple cloaks, leaving a trail of bowed heads in her wake. Today, with three new slaves requiring close investigation, she did not really have the time or even the inclination to dally with the others. Marella was waiting for her over at the far side. That woman really ought to lose some weight; she never stopped wheezing these days.

'Good morning, Taskmistress. The slaves are ready.'

'Good. Bring them in. No . . . take them straight into the examination room. I think we shall need some privacy. Wait!' Marella had something in her hand. 'What's that?'

'A note, Taskmistress . . . just an errand for one of their lordships; I am supposed to deliver it before noon . . .' Marella slipped the folded piece of vellum into her pocket. 'But what with one thing and another, and having to wait so long for your arrival . . . well, it's almost noon now, Taskmistress.' She started wheezing.

Ildren frowned. She did not like the servants being

cheeky. But today, she would let it pass, and though she always liked to maintain an interest in their lordships' little schemes, other matters were much more pressing. 'Then you had better take it now, Marella.' Marella turned to go. 'But first of all, bring me the slaves if you please – as I requested some while ago.'

The examination room was set out according to Ildren's specification. It had a soft, deep carpet, two chairs, a low upholstered bench and stool, a wooden bar supported at waist height – very convenient for quick examinations – and, in the middle, a circular table closely covered in soft leather and of a height such that the Taskmistress could if necessary reach the centre without having to resort to acrobatics. She would use this table today, when the pace would be more leisurely. While she waited, Ildren lifted her robe and sat upon the table, running her fingers over the softness of the leather, spreading her thighs, feeling the softness kissing her person, reliving past pleasures, daydreaming . . .

'The slaves, ma'am.' Ildren got up quickly and adjusted her dress.

'Thank you Marella. That will be all.'

The taskmistress closed her eyes for a moment or two to clear her mind completely. Then she looked upon the slaves – the sweet fresh nubile bodies, with their eyes downcast in innocence, their hands held limply at their sides, and those breasts so softly trembling – those full and nervous breasts with tender fleshy nipples – and then the feeling came, that delicious feeling, the heavy weight that blocked her throat at first then sank so slowly down to swell her breast and press against her heart, then slid again to drop into her belly, making Ildren catch her breath and spread her thighs to let the

85

weight bed itself lower. For there, on the right, was the very girl she needed for her plan. There, looking even more dejected than she could have dared to hope, more soft, more pliable, more pink and fresh and so much more delicious, was innocence personified. She could tell it straight away; she would not even need to check.

Now Ildren was drowning in the waves of honeyed wanting. The weight inside moved again; she wanted it to sink and sink between her thighs to swell her so she could not close her legs. Ildren felt so drugged with desire that she could not move. She could not speak. She could hardly even breathe. All she could do was caress that innocent body with her eyes. At last, she forced herself to drag her eyes away.

The other two girls looked as if they might be sisters, one a little taller, with dark hair, the other with even darker, curlier hair and slightly fuller breasts. But both were from the same basic mould and both of them quite delectable, with those sensuous lips that were always so attractive in a slave. Neither one would disgrace the Prince's bedchamber, and very soon now, given that innocent body which was the centrepiece of Ildren's melodrama, there was sure to be a vacancy in the royal bed. Their training to that end would bring Ildren much joy and satisfaction. She could tell it at a glance. She would probably wish to train the two of them together.

'Introduce yourselves, my darlings,' Ildren murmured in her most seductive voice. No one spoke at first; then the taller one answered in a whisper:

'Lianna, ma'am.'

'Lisarn,' the darker one chipped in quickly, then added, 'ma'am,' and curtsied.

So, Ildren had been right; they were sisters. But both of these beauties were eclipsed by the soft sweet treasure standing so forlornly beside them, on the point of tears. She was too afraid to speak. Her long pale golden hair was swept round over her left shoulder so it draped across her breast, where it broke into glass-like open curls which danced across the surface then curled around to frame the nipple, which shook very gently with the tremors of her breathing. Her breasts, though not large, seemed so full for so young a body, as if her tightly gloving skin had not expanded fast enough to keep pace with her burgeoning womanhood; the pressure of their substance filled them to the tips. The caps had inturned ends, as if the centres of her nipples were attached inside by threads which held them back against their growth and needed to be cut. Her belly formed a rounded oval, with faintly softened curls below, and her hips were already full; she had the narrow waist, but the perfectly proportioned fullness for her size, and the warm softness that Ildren knew men desired. And not only men . . . This girl was perfect, like a soft bronzed-pink peach – her upper arms, her belly and thighs, her whole body, seemed to be covered in a fine golden haze, an aura almost, a soft, soft down which Ildren would take such delight in brushing with her fingertips and tongue. Yes, this girl was the one. And this examination would be so sweet a pleasure for the Taskmistress, behind the mask of sternness which Ildren must now draw down to conceal the fire of lust that burned right through her belly.

'You! On the end – yes. No! Keep your eyes down!' The blonde girl cringed back as Ildren took a step towards her. Her eyes had flashed deep blue.

'What is your name?' Ildren snapped.

'F . . . Fawn, ma'am, if . . . if it should please you.'

It surely did. The Taskmistress felt queasy. The oily thong was tickling her between the legs, just when she needed it least – no, most. 'On the table, Fawn.' The girl tried to look around the room whilst keeping her eyes downcast. The other two slaves looked very frightened. They would have their turn. 'Quickly!' Ildren could see the tears begin to well as Fawn took nervously shuffling steps towards the large round table. Then of course she did not know what to do, or how the Taskmistress wanted her positioned on the table. In the end she stood beside it, half facing Ildren, the tears rolling silently down her face, with the edge of the table pressing against the back of her upper thigh, lifting one cheek of that perfect bottom, pushing it out and making Ildren almost pass out there and then. 'Turn round; bend over the table,' she said suddenly. She had to touch that bottom *now*. Otherwise she would die. 'Lie flat. Move back. Press those breasts flatter to the table.' She wanted the bottom curved up stronger, tighter. 'Stand on tiptoes. Oooh yes.' Ildren could not stop the exclamation of desire. She brushed her palm shakily over the curve, down one side then, allowing her fingertips to kiss the softened inner surface, brushed upwards over the other. The skin felt tight and yet so soft and downy. The bondslave quietly whimpered. 'Up . . . higher on your toes.' Ildren's voice had nearly failed her. She brushed again; it felt so heavenly. 'On your back . . .' Ildren's knees were buckling, from suppressed desire, and the cool cord tickling her precisely *there*. 'Head in the middle, feet over the edge. Do not look at me. Look straight up.' Fawn suddenly looked terrified; Ildren smiled. 'Hands by your side. Keep your head still. Thighs together tight. Tighter! Now do not move a muscle.'

Ildren had no idea how she had managed all those words; the weight inside was moving up again to choke her. The girl was trembling, as was Ildren beneath her velvet robe. Her nipples were stiff – deliciously stiff, she could not help it and she would not have it other- wise. She wanted to kneel down beside the table and have Fawn's soft feet, those delicate toes, slip beneath her robe and up her belly and tickle her nipples tenderly, brush the soft young toepads back and forth across her stiffly poking tips; but regrettably, she could not permit herself such self-indulgence while she was on duty. This was Ildren's rule.

The Taskmistress now positioned the other two girls – or had them position themselves – with care and precision. She knew that little details such as this were so important at this early stage; with a suitably intensive course of training, the first twenty-four hours could condition a slave for life. This was why Ildren was so certain she would be able to bring her wayward lover – the Prince's harlot – very soon, and very firmly, back again to heel.

All three girls were evenly spaced on their backs around the table. They formed a perfectly symmetrical pattern, touching each other only at the head, so they were aware of each other's presence, and could hear each other's breathing, but because their eyes were directed straight towards the ceiling, at the painting (again to Ildren's specification, it was of a slave in chains, on a table just like this one seen from above, with her thighs held wide apart whilst the long red tongue of a smooth green snake licked out to taste her fleshpot), they could not see each other and therefore could not know what was taking place beside them, other than on the basis of the sounds – usually soft ambiguous moistened sounds or sighs or tender womanly moans – which might, under Ildren's orches- trations, drift across at intervals.

In fact, Ildren was very pleased indeed with this

room layout; it was most effective when, as now, there were several slaves available for examination. Three, she had found, was the ideal number since, with this spacing, both access and awareness were enhanced. The impassioned resonances with three slaves under simultaneous stimulation were always very deep and moving. Nobody felt left out – least of all, Ildren.

She began with Lianna, the taller of the dark-haired girls, by merely standing in front of the girl with her velvet robe just brushing Lianna's knees. The girl, in looking directly upwards at the lewd scene above her head, couldn't see Ildren at all; she could merely feel the tickling. She might well have been imagining the worst – that Ildren actually had a snake concealed about her person. On this occasion, of course, the Taskmistress did not, for she wanted the girl to remain on the table throughout the examination. She waited until Lianna's eyelids flickered and her pupils momentarily darted from side to side; this was the signal for Ildren to proceed.

'Part your thighs, my dear.' This utterance to a new slave would always make Ildren's belly quiver. Lianna spread a little, revealing a dark brown bush and, peeping to invitingly, a pair of soft pink prominent lips. 'Wider!' Ildren's sudden shout made all three women jump and the blonde begin to whimper once again. 'Get those legs apart. Your Taskmistress requires good extent.' And now Lianna was straining to keep her legs held very wide indeed. Ildren could see the muscles standing tense upon her inner thigh. She stroked those firm smooth muscles tenderly, very softly, and very near the top, to counterpoise the straining tension in that skin, using the tips of the fingers of both hands, while she watched the velvet lips expand. 'Bear down, my sweet, tighten your belly, make those lips swell for me . . .' Ildren gently brushed the curls away from them but did not touch the flesh; it was much too soon for that. 'Good,' she said. 'Now, keep bearing down. Do not stop.' Lianna held her breath and pushed while Ildren's belly overturned to witness the rippling and the tightness – that wantonness spread so lusciously before her – and the polished, blood filled lips. 'And keep those legs apart.' And now the Taskmistress was impaled upon a sudden urge – an urge to wet her fingers and to smack them very hard against Lianna's swollen lips while that slave was made to keep very tight and open to the smacking – but once again she denied herself yet another delight and somehow managed to unhook her squirming belly from the pleasure of that urge. Instead, she quickly dipped a fingertip into the gently rolling navel atop the tense round surface – she just could not resist that at least – before moving to the sister and instructing her as follows:

'Turn over, Lisarn; turn on your belly.' Lisarn looked stunned. 'Quickly now. Your Taskmistress must examine you very fully,' Ildren explained, although this didn't seem to help the girl relax. 'Turn your head – lie on your cheek. Good. Now – what must a girl do next? Hmm?' Ildren watched the soft pale cheek suddenly flood with pink. Ildren was ecstatic – Lisarn must know precisely what was needed. The girl hesitated, then very slowly, very self-consciously edged apart her thighs. Ildren's head was swimming beneath the luscious waves of pleasure as she watched the sweet creature spreading so slowly and so delectably, exposing just for her the tightly swirling flesh within the secret groove and the full soft furry peach of love below it.

'Very good, my darling. Very, very good,' she managed in a deep and husky voice, for this slave clearly now was full of promise. She could tell this from the way Lisarn had spread so very wide, without having to be told, and from the way she had closed her eyes – not tightly, out of shame, but with the heavy-lidded expectancy of pleasure; her lips had parted very slightly, and most significantly of all, perhaps, the girl was trying to arch her back to lift and push that sweet peach back – to offer it to Ildren. This creature possessed a quality of lewdness which Ildren needed to encourage. Therefore, she brought across a cushion and, from behind and between Lisarn's legs, pushed it underneath the girl, not lifting her belly first, but merely pushing firmly, applying her weight to slide it underneath her. This action was important, for by this means the cushion was compressed and would press very firmly against that belly, stretching the skin back from the mound, thereby imposing a tightness round the peach which would stir the girl's desire. Ildren placed her fingertip low down on the flat part of Lisarn's back and drew it round and round. Lisarn arched her neck and moved against the cushion. Ildren reached very carefully in between the girl's legs and, taking great care not to touch her anywhere else, not even to brush against her curls, very precisely fitted her longest fingernail beneath the hood of flesh and nervously – very ticklishly – lifted it back to make the hard little nub poke out and, in touching briefly against the back of Ildren's fingernail, deposit a dab of stickiness there. Lisarn emitted a low murmur of half-pleasure.

'Good, my child,' Ildren said, touching the hub once more only, then sucking her fingertip. 'Now keep this delicious nubbin pushed out very firmly. Your Taskmistress loves to see a woman's nubbin at attention.' But Ildren was careful not to touch that nubbin again even though she dearly would have loved to, for a slave's pleasure must be administered very slowly, in precisely measured doses, sometimes, as with this very promising one, over several days. She tenderly stroked Lisarn's back again, then spread her bottom cheeks, and the delicious creature's belly shook. How Ildren loved this lewd little bondslave. She wanted to take the oily thong that dangled from her waist and push the end very firmly up into that whirlpool of temptation whilst she worried the syrupy nubbin to distraction . . . But according to her rule, such a thing was not allowed.

When the Taskmistress moved round the table to where Fawn lay, her mask of duty almost dissolved away; her belly nearly melted. Her loving heart reached out to that soft sweet thing with liquid lines of sadness drawn across her cheeks, and though she should never have done it, she no longer cared about the rule, for even Ildren's rules were not totally inflexible. That would be too cruel. Ildren reached across and kissed the teardrops, then brushed her moistened lips against the girl's, which felt hot; her lips were burning, making Ildren want to take her there and then. She had to wrench herself away to deny herself that pleasure which, she supposed in retrospect, only served to emphasize the purpose of the rule.

'Look into my eyes,' she said. Fawn's deep blue eyes seemed full of fear and longing. Ildren must hone the fear to a keener edge, must make the longing deeper and make the slave's pleasure, when it finally came, that much more profound. For the Taskmistress had decided that, of all the three, Fawn would be the only one to be permitted her deliverance that day.

She knelt above the girl, produced the spatula, held it up and watched her eyes widen first to uncertainty, turning very quickly into terror as Ildren waved it with a flourish. Ildren then held up the drumstick. Fawn's eyes darted from side to side, then looked imploringly at Ildren. Ildren's very breath was taken by her soft blue liquid gaze, and the slow wave of anticipation that disturbed the smoothness of her belly. She very lovingly ran her palm over that tight and frightened belly, then brushed it with her fingers, then quietly climbed off the table and returned to Lianna, whose thighs were still spread very wide and whose belly was pushed out so temptingly but whose eyes were still directed straight upwards, so she could only try to guess by feel alone the nature of the cruel device now being applied between her legs.

It was, of course, the spatula – what else could it have been against those luscious lips? The Taskmistress was using it to *develop* them, as she put it, vibrating it from side to side, slowly at first then faster, trying to find the critical vibration – there! The girl had suddenly gasped. Ildren knew these resonances from Lianna's thickened fleshy lips would be drilling up inside her; her nipples were stiffening up. Ildren decided to kneel beside her, so she could pull and stretch her nipples while she worked her to the brink. When Lianna gasped again, a much stronger gasp, Ildren changed the pattern of stimulation by pressing the spatula to one side of Lianna's lips, then very suddenly flicking it, so the lips shook, then applying it to the other side, very firmly, and flicking once again, and doing this pressing and flicking until the girl's hips jerked upwards from the table.

'Is your pleasure very near?' Ildren asked her very sweetly. Lianna murmured indistinctly; the meaning nonetheless was clear.

'May your Taskmistress split you now? Examine that pip of love?' Lianna shuddered as if the hand of pleasure, instead of flicking at the lips of lust, had closed inside her belly. Ildren pressed two fingers just above the hooded flesh, then placed the edge of the spatula along the line of join and carefully twisted it from side to side, as if the flesh were a pink and tight-lipped oyster. Against the murmurs, against the shudders, the lips split smoothly open. The hood was carefully teased back, exposing the burning pearl of lust, while Ildren drew the edge of the spatula very lightly, very cruelly and as slowly as she possibly could across the polished nubbin. She could feel the belly beginning to squirm beneath her palm. It was clearly time for her to move on to the sister. But first, she planted a single kiss upon that deliciously squirming belly as she drew the spatula down again before delicately spreading apart the lips (which had now gone very much softer, like leaves of moistened dough) to keep the fleshpot fully open, like those widespread thighs, and instructed Lianna to keep bearing down to maintain her tiny point of loving pleasure very firm – and very full of wanting.

Moving round them to the promising one, as Ildren tended to think of Lisarn, who still lay belly-down, the Taskmistress found that she could not look upon the split and tightly rounded bottom, with that fleshy peach beneath it and the lustful pip still peeping out, without a feeling of light-headedness, and now, as she reached out to touch it, a slamming breathlessness against her breast which threatened to stop her heart completely. Ildren laid her right palm against the left cheek of Lisarn's bottom in such a way that the side of her little finger lay snugly in the crease and, though the firm resilient cheek felt cool against the palm, her little finger could very definitely taste the woman's heat. Ildren drew it lightly downwards in the groove, then kissed its pad against the hot little mouth of very silken twisted skin. Lisarn's breathing sounded clear and very carefully controlled, as if she did not trust her body to breathe correctly without her instigation. Ildren loved to hear that sign of tense pleasure in a woman's body; it was the first step on the slow ascent to delirium. She fitted the palm now to the other cheek and this time brushed her thumbpad very softly back and forth across the tightened rim. 'Do you like that, my sweet?' she whispered, touching repeatedly in that spot. 'Does it stir those naughty feelings? Does it make this delectable bottom mouth feel very, very lewd? Would it like a cock pushed up it?'

It was necessary for the Taskmistress to use rude phrases such as this; her duties required her to excite the slaves to the point of wild abandon. Even at this stage, so early in their training, she needed to nurture that inner quality of lickerishness which their lordships prized so highly. She might have done it anyway, however, simply because it gave her pleasure. She loved it; she loved the effect it had. And now, she was very pleased to see the tried and trusted combination of suggestiveness and stroking of the slavish bottom mouth was working – making the slave's peach of love pulsate.

It was time to produce the drumstick; she would beat the tiny little drumskin to distraction. Ildren spread the cheeks to make the drumskin tight and, holding the stick quite lightly, swung it down to tap precisely in the centre. Lisarn jerked in pleasure; the mouth contracted and then pushed out more strongly then before as if reaching to kiss the instrument of punishment. 'Now, I want you to hold these cheeks apart for me . . . would you do that my darling? Hmmm?' Ildren tapped again; the bondslave caught her breath so sweetly. 'Now stretch very tight and hold still.' Ildren reached underneath, into the soaking peach, and closed her fingertips round the pip; she held it, gently rotating now and then, as the mood took her, but keeping the flesh lips at all times open while she tapped upon the drum, until Lisarn began to move her hips slowly in a circle, then more urgently back and forth, attempting to push down, to spread herself more fully and to slip her nubbin between Ildren's very lightly touching fingers rather more positively than Ildren cared to sanction at this juncture.

Ildren had other plans; she needed to see how that little mouth might close around and suck upon the drumstick bulb. 'Open, my sweet,' she said, carefully rotating the end against the tightened whirlpool, 'let this instrument of pleasure twirl round inside your body.' Ildren encouraged her by once again working her fleshy tip, which now felt dangerously hard between her softly sucking fingers. Therefore, when the bondslave drew breath very sharply, she paused – partly to wet the bulb and reapply it. Ildren knew that time was on her side; eventually, yet curiously just at the point when Lisarn's body went tense, the bulbil slipped in smoothly. So now, as Ildren milked upon the nubbin and the Lisarn's breath came in nervous little jerks and random tremors shook her body, Ildren could test the gripping of that mouth, not pushed out now so much as pulled, as she twirled the stick until the girl gave out a long low grunt – a growl almost – and her body went rigid.

'Very good, my darling,' Ildren coaxed her. 'Do not move. Hold back that pleasure . . .' And yet Ildren could not resist one final little squeeze of love upon the slippery nubbin before she laid her palm across the bottom, with her fingers to each side of the stick, and very slowly drew out the stub – and she too felt a delicious shiver as the lifted rim of rubbery flesh very briefly touched against her fingers. But before moving on, the Taskmistress gently cupped one hand between those outspread thighs and held her slave, whispering words of tender reassurance, while Lisarn's tight little body leaked slowly through her fingers and onto the table top.

As a direct consequence of these prolonged but as yet inconclusive investigations into these young women's bodily needs, the Taskmistress was quite drunk with desire, even before she slid open the slim broad drawer beneath the table, folded back the soft yellow cloth and removed the set of gold chains. Fawn, the blonde young creature watching her (illicitly but not unnoticed), was not, as might have been suspected, paralysed with fear. Her fear was real enough and certainly well-founded, and yet by now the fear had been tempered by so many soft sweet moans, so many sounds of moistness and of pleasure, and by the all-pervasive heat of female wanting which enveloped her in a cloud of heavy-scented seduction, a sea of lust in which the young girl's innocence was slowly drowning. Her deep blue eyes were being swallowed up by blackness as Ildren lay beside her, washing her body with her eyes, caressing her softness, wanting to brush her lips across the smoothness of Fawn's thin-skinned tight-filled breasts, wanting to suck upon the nipples till the tiny retractions yielded to her tongue. She lifted the bondslave's left hand, kissed the inside of her wrist and fastened the chain around it, then made her raise her right leg whilst Ildren likewise kissed the ankle – again on the inside, merely brushing her lips against it – and slipped the chain around, then kissed her belly, with a soft kiss like baby's breath across the misted skin. Ildren's heart was thumping when that tender belly arched to allow her to slip the chain beneath it and to fasten it around.

'Open your thighs, my darling. Lift your knees. Submit your body to my caress.' And Fawn was balanced so invitingly with legs uplifted, open, gently angled above her while Ildren's hand cradled her head and Ildren's robe was parted. The Taskmistress took her own long and fleshy nipple and brushed it back and forth across the full warm lips and watched the searching pools of eyes and waited, brushing all the time, until the full lips parted and the long deep violet tube slipped in to suckle while Ildren's fingertips whispered downwards over the belly, between the balanced thighs, through the pale golden silken curls to touch at last the small lips, flushed hot now with desire, and very gently to part them – to open out their tenderness and feel the burning heat, the soft wall of moistness and the tight constriction that could barely kiss the tip of Ildren's little finger and, moving up, the hard and wanton pip of lewdness which belied that innocence.

'Rock, my sweet . . .' As the bondslave took her suck, her delicately balanced open thighs, one higher than the other, gently swayed in rhythm with the delicious drawing down through Ildren's nipple, and in sympathy with the soft, liquid pulling of three wet tips-of-fingertips which formed a tiny sucking mouth around the little nubbin. And when at last the belly tightened to a hard little knot and rippled with waves of wanton girlish shudders and the tongue around her nipple tried to burrow underneath it to nip it from her bosom altogether, Ildren held the young girl's head very tightly to her breast while the length of silken hair cascaded down across her belly and she whispered, as the shudders came again to make those hot tight lips contract so strongly round her fingertips: 'Let your pleasure overflow, my precious; have no fear; your Taskmistress will keep you safe.'

Which was surely very true, for the Taskmistress would be taking very great care to keep her special bondslave very safe and very fresh indeed . . . until the morrow.

AMAZONS

Erin Caine

Many Nexus authors prefer to specialise in writing about particular aspects of sexuality. Here's one who is happy with a variety of themes. From the Amazon forest to British suburbia, this collection of erotic tales by Erin Caine has one thing in common; they all celebrate the powerful sensuality of the larger, more voluptuous woman.

Erin's a no-holds barred writer and her explicit use of language is sometimes shocking, but always arousing. She has written three books for Nexus so far. They are *Amazons*, *Knights of Pleasure* and *Castle Amor*.

These days, the tabloids are so full of sightings of Elvis Presley and man-eating goldfish from Mars that I was pretty blasé when I first heard about Carmichael. Frankly, I didn't think there would be much mileage in this particular 'sensational exclusive'. Ever the hard-nosed reporter, I suspected he was fabricating the whole thing to drum up publicity for his god-awful museum. But my editor's instincts told him we should take the bait, so I packed my bucket and spade and headed for the coast.

Neil Carmichael was the owner and curator of a poky little private museum, one of the more surprising features of a kiss-me-quick seaside town in the North-East. It was one of those horrible unstructured museums which seem to have grown in fits and starts since the mid-nineteenth century, accumulating vast quantities of junk in the process and finally getting stuck somewhere in the 1950s, when the last thing museums were supposed to be was exciting. A few dusty fossils here, a moth-eaten badger there: all in all, the stuff of rainy autumn afternoons. Not very exciting.

But it did boast the famous Carmichael collection of anthropological artefacts, which had been put together by the present curator's great-grandfather, a professor of anthropology and the creator of the museum. It seemed the old boy had been fascinated by the sexual habits of the remoter South American tribes, which at that time had scarcely been touched by civilisation. One room contained case after case of what you might call up-market porn. You know, arty stuff: fertility statuettes of men with huge erect phalluses and fleshy women with pendulous breasts and distended bellies; carved and painted groups depicting men and women copulating in all 69 positions, and a few more besides; carved ivory dildoes; implements used in the ritual defloration of virgins . . . it all came as quite a shock to the system after glass cases full of stuffed cormorants.

Anyhow, it was Carmichael senior – the horny old devil – who was the immediate reason for my visit. His great-grandson claimed he had been clearing out a storeroom in the museum and had come across a small box of the Prof's personal effects, catalogued by his son. Among these objects was a diary – a diary of such sensational content, apparently, that Carmichael had got on the phone to my editor faster than you can say 'cheque-book journalism'.

Carmichael turned out to be a tall, middle-aged man with a slight stoop and greying hair falling limply across his high forehead. He greeted me eagerly.

'Good afternoon, Mr Stokes! I'm so very glad you could come.'

'Well, if what you've got is anything like as juicy as you say it is, the journey will have been well worth it, I replied, wondering if it would yet turn out to be a wild-goose chase.

'I am certain you will not be disappointed,' he assured me with a knowing smile.

Carmichael led me into his private apartment, which was attached to the museum, and went off to make a pot of tea. Whilst I was waiting, I had a good snoop round and found plenty more stuff which was no doubt too near the knuckle to put on display in the museum – boy, some of these things would really make your maiden aunt wet her knickers.

There was an old painting, showing a man impaling a woman on his immense penis. He had thrust his cock violently into her cunt, running her through, and you could see it emerging from her mouth, floods of semen spurting from its glistening head. The woman's eyes were full of an inexplicable ecstasy, and the brown tips of her swollen breasts were as hard and wrinkled as brazil nuts. I felt drawn into the picture, imagining my own penis growing and swelling to that immense size. The woman appealed to me too: nut brown and exotic, and broad and firm and juicy as a ripe fruit. I imagined my penis piercing her, just as the point of a sharp knife pierces the skin of a peach, releasing an outrush of sweet juices.

Carmichael returned, bringing tea and a dusty brown cardboard box. He blew off the dust, opened it and took out an oilskin-wrapped parcel. Within the fragile covering lay a green leather bound volume, battered and stained but still intact.

'My great-grandfather Edwin's diary,' explained Carmichael, placing it almost reverently in my hands. 'He began it in 1885, just after the death of his beloved Marietta.'

'Marietta?'

'My grandfather was the product of a short-lived union which ended in an acrimonious separation. Edwin never sought a divorce from his wife. But for the next twenty years he had a passionate affair with a rich society woman who took an interest in his work and helped to support him financially in his academic projects. Her name was Marietta. As far as I can see from

105

letters and extracts from the diary, she behaved appallingly towards him, but he was utterly fascinated by her in spite of it all.'

Carmichael indicated a passage near the beginning of the diary, which read as follows:

'JANUARY 25th, 1885: Dreamed of Marietta again last night. Although she is no more of this earth, I still see her so vividly in my dreams. I can recall every detail of her bountiful body as though she were even now with me, blessing me or chastising me according to her whim. She was so wondrous that even now my member leaps up in homage as I recall sinking between her powerful thighs, feeling her immense softness bearing down upon me, engulfing me, crushing me.

'I dreamed, too, of the divine lash with which she imposed her will upon me: sweet instrument of longed-for chastisement. How skilfully she whipped me into lusty wakefulness, until my nether cheeks burned and bled and my virile member pulsated with the desire to enter her.

'Now that she is gone, how shall I live without my Marietta, save by losing myself in my work? I am lost; and utterly alone.

'It is for this reason that I have determined to accept Pemberton's offer to lead his expedition to the Amazonian jungle. I am, besides, intrigued to know what fate has befallen the white explorers who have disappeared in this part of the world over the last decade. And who knows? Perhaps I, too, shall not return . . . Then I shall at last be reunited with my beloved Marietta: my demon, my damnation.'

I glanced up at Carmichael, already intrigued.

'The expedition was organised by the Royal

Geographical Society but funded by the wealthy explorer Sir Henry Pemberton,' he explained. 'A puzzling number of explorers had disappeared in a small and very remote area of the Amazon basin, you see, and of course the Victorians, being what they were, they couldn't rest easy until they had found out exactly what had happened to them. Professor Carmichael was appointed leader because of his special interest in the anthropology of the area. His companions were Pemberton, the expert in tropical diseases Dr Murray Hope, and Sydney Tait – a hack journalist from the *Pictorial News* whose editor had bought him a place on the expedition in the hope of turning up an exclusive story.'

I carried on reading, skipping over the pages which described the elaborate preparations for the expedition and the party's eventual embarkation at Southampton. I took up the story again at the end of their long voyage to South America.

'MARCH 6th: Since we left England so long ago, we have all been tormented by dreams which I know are born of intense sexual frustration. I am ashamed to report that I and my companions have had recourse to the comforts offered by the local women. I know well enough that I should be channelling all my energies and enthusiasms into the pursuit of our academic quest, but how can I concentrate those energies when my mind is forever full of Marietta, Marietta, Marietta? I am but flesh and blood, alas.

'Last evening, Tait – a seedy individual with an irritatingly nasal voice and a strong Cockney accent – indicated to the rest of our party that he had located a local bordello, and suggested that we should visit it. To my surprise, our blond Adonis, Dr Hope, was all in favour of the enterprise – which he assured us would purge our minds of distractions and, far from weakening our bodies, strengthen them for whatever ordeals might lie ahead. After a few initial doubts, Pemberton consented to go along with the will of the majority.

'The bordello – officially an inn – was situated in a low, wooden building next to the local military barracks. By seven in the evening it was already seething with life: gay, riotous music pouring out of the windows and half-dressed girls tumbling out into the reeking dusk on the arms of drunken soldiery. The madam was a handsome half-caste woman with dark glossy hair and fiery eyes. She exchanged words – and money – with Tait, whose grasp of Spanish is obviously better than his command of the English language; and then led us into a back room, where four young women awaited us.

'Three were small, doe-eyed native girls, naked and sly beneath gaily coloured woven blankets cast about their shoulders. They were unquestionably pretty in a girlish way, with their upturned breasts and the catlike grace of their slender bodies; but Tait knew me well enough by now to guess that this was not to my taste, and he and the madam had chosen well for me. My own young woman was a tall mulatto with a strong and statuesque body and breasts whose vast, downy softness contrasted sharply with the hardness of her muscular arms and thighs. Such was her haughty pride in her charms that she made no concessions to false modesty: from the first, she stood erect and unashamed before me, in the full, glowing magnificence of her naked flesh.

'My companion's name was Arancha, and she was undisputed mistress of the games we played all night. She motioned to us to undress, and pulled the blankets away from her giggling companions. They at once fell silent and quickly knelt on the ground before us, bowing their heads in complete submission. Arancha immediately set about them energetically with a length of coarse hemp rope, yet although her assaults raised scarlet welts on their coffee-coloured skin, they did not move or make the slightest sound during their ordeal.

'This novel spectacle at an end, I and my companions were much excited and eager to have sexual congress with our women. Such summary behaviour, Arancha would not countenance. Although – strong as she was – we could have overruled her by force without the slightest difficulty, not one of us could summon up the strength of will to say her nay when she commanded us to go and stand with our backs against the wall. Before we had quite realised what she was doing, she had chained us all there by our wrists and ankles, at which point we were truly at her mercy, and even I began to have doubts about what would now transpire.

'Arancha's willing handmaidens got to their feet and came towards us, clearly invigorated by their ordeal. Battle was joined. Each of us found himself attacked with vigour and the greatest thoroughness, feeling the stinging fury of a length of coarse rope upon his naked flesh. The pain was not, I admit, extreme; but it was skilfully administered. Unlike the stoic Indian girls, and to our eternal shame as true-born Englishmen, we were unable to hold our tongues for long, and were soon singing an unmelodious song at the tops of our voices. It was not until the beating had ceased and the sharp pain had turned into a dull throbbing pulse that I realised that every one of us had emerged from the experience more aroused than he had begun it. My own member was iron hard and those of my companions equally so.

'Arancha then signed to her handmaidens and all

four of the women advanced towards us again, this time with smiles on their faces. They rubbed themselves up and down our helpless bodies in an indescribably lewd manner. It was infinitely more painful for me to feel Arancha's tawny globes gliding down my naked body, and know that I was powerless to reach out and touch them, than it would have been for me to endure another dozen of her beatings with a length of rope. I groaned piteously, and could have wept openly as she brushed a stubby brown nipple across my lips, alas too swiftly to allow me to seize it between my teeth or take it into my mouth.

'At last, at long last, Arancha knelt before me and took my penis into the warm, inviting cavern of her mouth – working upon it so skilfully that she prolonged my agony and ecstasy for what seemed an eternity, even though I was now at fever pitch and was convinced I would pour forth my jism the very second my cock entered her mouth. She left me drained and utterly exhausted.

'My companions and I returned to the fazenda in the early hours of the morning, weary and sore but greatly recovered in spirits. I only pray that we shall all prove adequate to whatever other tests face us in the coming weeks and months.

'Tomorrow, we begin our final preparations for our perilous journey into the heart of the Amazonian rain forest.

'MARCH 8th: Today, we attempted to engage native bearers to guide and accompany us on our quest – with little success. The entire native population appears to have an utter dread of the area which we intend to explore and there is much wild-eyed babbling about 'mighty women'. We are quite confounded by it all.

'A number of the locals recognised the likenesses of the missing explorers which we showed them, but not one of them had ever been seen again once he left Manaos. Even Hope, with his expert knowledge of local dialects and customs, is unable to prise any more information out of them, or induce the fellows to accept our generous terms and accompany us on our expedition.

'In the end, we were able to take on only one guide, a half-breed fellow called Perez who knows the area like the back of his hand but is, I suspect, not entirely honest. I should not be at all surprised if he were to lead us off up some obscure tributary and then sneak away at the dead of night with half our possessions, leaving us to the mercy of jungle beasts and worse. He seems to have struck up a crude rapport with Tait – which also does not surprise me.

'I find I am still troubled by dreams of an erotic nature, but am heartened by the knowledge that my fantasies now feature the woman Arancha as well as Marietta. I think perhaps I am over the worst of my loss, and that there is hope of rebuilding my life anew.

'MARCH 12th: Up to now, our canoes have made excellent progress in navigating the turbid waters of the Amazon, although we have had to get out and carry them overland in several instances, to bypass dangerous rapids. I have revised my view of Perez somewhat, as he has proved to be a knowledgeable and resourceful guide. Occasionally we have glimpsed parties of Indians spying on us from the riverbank, but he assures us that they are merely curious and will not harm us. For my part, I cannot quite empty my mind of the persistent rumours of cannibalism and head-hunting in these regions.

'For the next stage of our journey, into the interior, we must abandon the canoes and move onward on foot, through the steamy rainforest.

'MARCH 25th: Today, we found poor Unwin's remains – bleached perfectly clean, with not a scrap of flesh on them – and gave them a Christian burial. We were only able to identify them because his gold pocket-watch and engraved signet ring were lying near the body. One thing troubles me greatly: all the bones of the skeleton had been neatly arranged in a heap, with the skull placed carefully on the top – obviously the work of some human agency. Hope says the poor fellow's neck was broken, very skilfully and by someone – or something – immensely strong.

'MARCH 27th: I am writing this in circumstances which are almost beyond belief, and I do not know if I shall even live to complete this entry in my diary, let alone find some means of transmitting its contents to the outside world. And if my words should eventually reach the eyes of others, can I hope that they will be believed?

'The steamy heat of the jungle almost overpowered us in the early stages of our journey. Only Perez seemed not to notice it, and strode along cheerfully, hacking away at the undergrowth with his machete and leaving us trailing in his wake. In the very heart of the jungle, one might easily believe one had wandered into some great Gothic cathedral, with the canopy of overarching branches looming tens of feet above and the constant, interweaving cries of birds and insects forming hypnotic canticles and counterpoints in the sun-mottled twilight. But I have never felt myself to be in a more godless place in all my life.

'The very next evening after finding Unwin's remains, the sounds of strange pagan music came to our ears, and we hardly knew whether to forge ahead or run away. At length, Perez – who was a few yards in front of us – signed us to keep silent and crept forward towards a gap in the trees. He squatted down on his haunches and beckoned to us to advance on all fours and follow suit. I tremble now as I recall what I saw in the clearing beyond.

'We found ourselves looking out onto a group of simple, circular huts made from branches and leaves. Beyond the huts I could see the ruins of many magnificent stone buildings – some almost overtaken by the swiftly encroaching jungle vegetation, and all built in the strangest architectural style I have ever seen. They gleamed fantastical in the sulphurous light cast by hundreds of flaming torches. The buildings were vaguely European in character, one might even have said classical – and yet every visible surface or pinnacle was decorated with the most explicit sexual imagery: fornicating couples (animal and human), heavy-breasted women and everywhere the image of the erect phallus. Indeed, in the very centre of the clearing stood a mighty stone phallus fully twenty feet high, with many life-size phalluses branching out from its base at about waist height (these reminded me very much of representations of the Roman god Priapus).

'But all this was as nothing, compared with what was happening within the jungle clearing. Had I not had four other witnesses with me, I should almost have thought I had caught a fever and was hallucinating. For was I not gazing at dozens – nay, a whole tribe – of enormous women, none below six feet in height and all of them massively, breathtakingly formed!

'"Amazons!" breathed Pemberton, obviously as

entranced as I by this utterly unbelievable vision. "Incredible!"

'But these were in no way recognisable as the Amazons of classical folklore – the one-breasted warrior women. Warriors they might well be, but one-breasted they were certainly were not. In fact, they had particularly well-formed breasts, succulent and heavy yet curiously buoyant upon their oiled and well-muscled chests.

'As I feasted on their imposing beauty, I began to notice an interesting fact about them. They were clearly not of Indian stock: their huge stature and almost European features, and their pale skin, suggested a more distant heritage. They resembled no one race in particular, and I could not for the life of me imagine how they had come to be living deep in the heart of the forest. Strangely enough, we saw no native menfolk with them.

'They were entirely naked except for the most amazing ornaments which glittered brilliant green against their tanned flesh, and which I immediately realised were made of the most exquisite emeralds, valuable almost beyond the dreams of avarice. How much more priceless did they seem to me when they adorned the luscious bodies of these Junos of the rainforest.

'But my lust was tempered with another emotion: fear. For the Amazons were not alone. They had with them several white men, chained together like slaves – and I at once recognised one of the miserable captives as Sinclair Radford, the Scottish anthropologist who had disappeared eighteen months previously whilst making an expedition into the interior.

'The three white men were also naked, their bodies unadorned save for elaborately jewelled harnesses

114

enclosing their genitals, as though this was the portion of their bodies which the women sought above all to enslave.

'As we watched, dumbstruck with desire and apprehension, one of the women – a veritable giantess with beautiful udderlike breasts and haunches as broad and solid as those of a prize mare – stepped forward and began to issue orders in a language which was instantly familiar to all except Perez and Tait.

'"Great Scott!" gasped Hope. "I'll be damned if she isn't speaking in Latin!"

'He was correct. Of course, it was rather a bastardised version of that noble tongue, but entirely comprehensible to anyone with a modicum of education. And yet surely the Romans had never ventured as far as South America! Fame and fortune would undoubtedly await any scholar who could decisively prove such a connection. But my attentions were drawn back to the fearsome array of beauty before me.

'"Prepare them for the mating ceremony!" ordered the awesome giantess, whose dark chestnut hair hung to her waist in oiled ringlets, each spangled with dozens of multifaceted gems. She continued: "They have had sufficient time to recover since the last mating. The priestesses have pronounced the phase of the moon propitious. Let the ceremony commence."

'"It shall be done, O Queen." Other women stepped forward from the waiting throng and at once the three captives fell to their knees, weeping and begging for mercy. They seemed exhausted and I heard Radford crying "No more, no more, I beg of you."

'Their hard-hearted captors were unmoved. The white men's harnesses were removed, exposing their still-flaccid genitalia. I was amazed: how could any red-blooded Englishman resist the prospect of sexual congress with these magnificent women? Already my own prick was iron hard and ready for anything, and I took it out and stroked it lovingly as I watched. As I glanced out of the corner of my eye, I could see that my companions were equally excited by what they saw.

'Three of the women knelt down and began to fellate the white captives in the most delicious way, teasing their pricks with the tip of the tongue, tickling their balls and then taking their balls right into their capacious mouths. At last, the three pricks slowly began to stiffen, and the men's eyes began to glaze over with reluctant lust. They were moaning piteously.

"Administer the elixir," commanded the Queen.

'A broad-hipped wench whose nipples were decorated with gold and emerald stars brought forward a glass vial, which she forced between the three men's lips in turn. The effect was almost instantaneous and quite astonishing. Within seconds, all three had immense erections and were moaning now with mingled fear and lust.

'I then discovered what the stone phalluses in the centre of the clearing were used for. One at a time, six of the women processed towards it and, parting their buttocks with their hands, lowered themselves slowly down onto the thick stone shafts, until at last their cunts had swallowed up the entire length. Then they worked themselves up and down on the stone pricks, whilst massaging their heavy breasts. Beads of sweat stood out on their oiled flesh as their excitement mounted. Gasping with pleasure, they brought themselves to orgasm one after the other, and when they stood up the stone pricks were inundated with love juices.

'The men were released from their chains only to face another form of capture. Two women held each man down, flat on his back, whilst a third sat down on his prick, soaking it with the juices from her already sopping cunt.

'"I don't believe it!" exclaimed Pemberton in a hoarse whisper. "Here are three white men, actually being taken by violence, against their will, by a tribe of Latin-speaking Junos. Not to mention an elixir which induces instant potency! And those gems . . .!" He had grasped hold of his erect prick and was now masturbating furiously, and I wondered if the wealthy aristocrat was more excited by the sight of the myriad precious jewels than by the sight of so much oiled flesh.

I too was rubbing at my prick, deeply aroused by the vision before me and imagining I was being held down by two radiant Junos, whilst a third merciless beauty with glistening thighs pumped up and down on my cock, making the white seed fountain forth from my loins in spite of my feeble protests.

The three men came with loud cries, and lay panting on the ground.

'"They must have a short period of rest," announced the Queen. "Give them nourishing foods and then more of the elixir. They have much work to do before the ceremony is over."

'It was at that moment, when our guard was at its lowest and we had all but forgotten the danger, that the trap was sprung for us. Before I had a chance to take stock of what was happening, a strong hand was clapped over my mouth and a glittering blade pressed against my throat.

'"Do not struggle," hissed a female voice, in Latin. "It will be the worse for you."

'Within moments, all five of us had been trussed up like chickens, picked up and slung over the broad shoulders of ample warrior maidens, who took us into the clearing and presented us to the Queen. The look of

117

despairing recognition on the face of the unfortunate Radford was in sharp contrast to the sheer delight with which the Amazonian queen greeted us. She patted and pinched our flesh as though we were horses or cattle, examined our teeth and was thoroughly satisfied by the sight of our still-erect penises, which we had not had time to cover up when we were caught.

'The Queen insisted that we be stripped naked, and proceeded to a minute inspection of our every secret place. She showed little interest in Perez, apparently because he is not a white man, and said that he could remain our servant for the time being.

'I thought that we should perhaps be ravished there and then, but our captors proved to have other plans for us. Since our capture this morning, we have been held prisoner in one of the village huts, whilst two of the mighty women stand guard outside. We have lost all our weapons and our clothes have been taken away; and I am beginning to despair of escape.

'And yet I cannot deny my growing fascination for this lost tribe of mighty women. Where are their men-folk? Why do they prize white men so highly for sexual purposes? Where do their priceless jewels come from? And why is it so fearsome to serve their carnal needs?

'APRIL 5th: Since being kidnapped and brought here, we have learned many secrets from our captors: secrets which have convinced me that they will never permit us to leave this place alive.

'It appears that the women refer to themselves as the "Children of the Moon", and worship a moon goddess similar to the Roman Diana. They are descended from an ancient race which – I surmise – must have intermarried with Roman settlers (perhaps adventurers, drawn here by the legends of untold wealth) to found a new

118

civilisation. Although the grandeur of this lost era has long departed, the women still retain their ancestors' enormous appetite for sexual gratification.

'I would assume that the women's unnatural size is attributable to a genetic mutation, as another curious characteristic of their race is that many of the menfolk are puny or sterile. The men are therefore relegated to secondary duties – mere drones fit only to perform menial chores and wait upon their Olympian mothers and sisters. The women prize their great strength and pale skins, which is why they have gone to such lengths to capture Europeans for the purpose of sexual satisfaction and procreation – not just the dozen or so explorers we knew about, but a steady stream of white settlers who inadvertently wandered into the area over the years. From time to time, the women even mount raiding parties specifically to capture suitable males for breeding stock.

'We now know that no man who has been brought here has ever escaped or been allowed to leave. The sexual appetite of the women is quite remarkable, and they value their captives only for as long as they continue sexually potent. Even with the aid of their miraculous elixir, which can restore potency within moments, a man's strength will eventually fail him. Once this happens, he is offered a stark choice: a life of terrible servitude and hardship in the emerald mines, or honourable death: in which latter case, after he has been drugged and fellated by the High Priestess, she swiftly and skilfully breaks his neck. His mortal remains are then feasted upon in the most reverential manner (they are believed to induce fertility) and his bleached bones are finally laid to rest. Despite Tait's feeble attempts to keep our spirits up, we are all disconsolate. Having lost first Marietta and now my liberty, I for my part would seek out death immediately – were it not for my perverse longing to taste sexual union with these terrifyingly beautiful women.

'APRIL 6th: this is the Lord's Day, and yet a day of rites so pagan I can scarcely recall them without shame – and desire.

'Early in the morning, one of the women came to take me to the Queen. For a moment, I looked into her dark, fathomless eyes and thought I saw Marietta, come back to me.

'"Marietta . . .?" I cried out foolishly, though I knew it was not she.

'She laughed, but not mockingly. I thought I caught a glimpse of desire in her eyes as she replied, "Aminta, priestess of the Moon." She is certainly very reminiscent of Marietta, though only in an impressionistic way. How I long to lie with her, to feel her strength as she slakes her lust upon me.

'I was taken to the Queen's residence, which is situated in one of the old Roman buildings. Its fine mosaic floor – depicting an orgy of copulating nymphs and satyrs – is still intact, and the building retains some of its original grandeur. The Queen was lying on her back on a marble bench, naked save for a huge emerald which guarded the door to her most secret place. She did not speak to me, but signed to her henchwoman to proceed.

'"The Queen desires the seed of your loins," announced Aminta.

For a moment I just gaped at her.

'"You mean – I am to lie with the Queen?"

'"The Queen lies with no man. You will bring forth your seed and I shall place it within her, according to the rites of the goddess." She handed me a small bowl,

120

which I realised – with shock – was carved out of a single massive emerald.

'Despite my great desire for sexual release, I found myself unable to masturbate immediately, before the Queen, as was required of me. My terror of failing to perform ended, alas, in that very inability to do as I was bidden! I thought for a moment I would be killed for my abject failure, but I had not reckoned with the ingenuity of the Amazonian women.

Aminta clapped her hands and two women brought in the strangest contraption I have ever seen. It was a machine, clearly very old: made of bronze, cast in ornate shapes and decorated with erect phalluses – a sort of pump, I deduced, operated by an elaborate handle which produced a powerful vacuum suction.

'"Sit," commanded Aminta.

'As soon as she began to handle my penis, I felt the beginnings of the rigidity which had so far eluded me. She slipped my stiffening shaft into a little leather pouch, and tightened the bronze sleeve around it. Then she begun to turn the handle. Immediately I felt an incredible suction, arousing me to fever pitch. The sensation seemed to go on for ever, and I felt myself drowning, drowning in Aminta's laughing eyes . . . At last honour was satisfied as I delivered up my seed. As my semen spurted forth, Aminta collected it in the emerald bowl, took it to the Queen and inserted in her regal quim by means of an exquisite jewelled spoon.

'APRIL 8th: We have lost Perez and Tait. It was as I suspected. The two had been in league ever since they clapped eyes on the wealth of jewels. I cannot say I blame them for wishing to escape from this lost world of fear and subjugation (though I am daily more enslaved by the woman Aminta) but their greed was utterly reprehensible.

'They attempted to escape this morning, with a bag full of jewels – the weight of which of course slowed them down in their escape. Perez got away into the jungle (where he will no doubt be eaten by a jaguar or hunted down by the Amazons), but poor misguided Tait was caught clean between the shoulder blades with a priceless emerald-headed arrow, the irony of which would no doubt have escaped him.

'APRIL 9th: Pemberton, Hope and I have taken the place of poor Radford and his companions as the sexual slaves of the Amazons. Those poor fellows, utterly worn out by their duties, have been consigned to the emerald mines, beyond our powers to help them. I can only wonder how long it will be before we too are faced with the choice between slavery and death.

'At moonrise last night, the Amazon women held a fertility festival, at which we three were initiated with great ceremony. The Amazon men had prepared jewelled harnesses for us, very like the ones which Radford and his companions had worn.

'We were led out into the clearing in the torchlit darkness. It was surprisingly chill, and I began to shiver in my nakedness. Fear turned my blood to ice as I saw six mighty Amazons waiting for us in the clearing, greedily stroking each other's breasts and kissing each other's cunts in preparation for the mating ritual which was to follow. Weird music filled the air – reed pipes and drums beating a mesmeric rhythm.

'"Prepare them for the mating ceremony," commanded the Queen.

'Three women came forward and took off our harnesses. Although I had long yearned for sexual congress, my penis was slow to respond, chilled by fear and the knowledge of what had happened to Unwin and

Radford. The woman charged with arousing me was full-breasted and heavy-thighed, toweringly beautiful and all-consuming as she pressed herself against me, exploring every crevice, every fold of my yielding flesh. Her greedy lips drew out my sex until it began to respond, to rise, to swell. She parted my thighs and drew her tongue deliciously from my arse to my stones, lingering over them until they were taut and about to explode.

'"Mate with them!" came the command.

'And the women were suddenly upon us, flinging us to the ground and using their weight and strength to hold us there. We did not resist. How could we? their softness engulfed us. The wetness of their well-prepared cunts swallowed us up. All too soon I felt the semen rising, spurting – and I fell back, exhausted.

'Suddenly, I felt a glass vial pressed against my lips and a few drops of liquid forced into my mouth. It was bitter, but I swallowed it with difficulty. Immediately I felt as though my entire body had been consumed with fire, as though I were floating off on a cloud of flame into the heavens and the whole world was in my penis, and my penis was itself the whole world. All at once I was light as air and so aroused I was amazed to discover that I was again ready for sexual union, though it was but moments since I had come to orgasm in the woman's belly.

'I opened my eyes and the world seemed brighter, warmer. I looked up straight into the eyes of Aminta. Her huge, oiled torso was bearing down on me, her massive breasts threatening, weighing, touching, then squashing against me. A thick nipple brushed my mouth and I parted my lips to welcome it, sucking greedily and losing myself in the fleshy folds of her breasts. Aminta lowered her cunt onto my prick, straddling me with her powerful thighs, and rode me like

123

fiery Pegasus across the heavens. Never before had I felt such intensity of pleasure, seen such colours, experienced such an outpouring of joy as the semen spurted forth from my loins and into the belly of Aminta.

'I heard her whisper soft and low, as though she were speaking to me from a very long way away:

'"Carmichael, I wish to have you for myself alone. It is forbidden here, among the warrior women. I will help you run away . . ."

'And as I lapsed into unconsciousness, I could think of only two things: Aminta and freedom.

'APRIL 10th: Although I feel I owe a debt of loyalty to my companions, Hope and Pemberton steadfastly refuse to countenance any thoughts of escape. They know, as I do, that to remain here means certain death, if not immediately, then in a year or two's time when they are worn out and superseded by some younger, more virile men. Perhaps it is some lingering effect of the elixir, but they seem blinded to the need for action by their desire for continued congress with the Amazon women. They would rather live with their fear and enjoy the delights of love which the elixir produces, than attempt escape and perhaps attain freedom once more.

'I have to admit that my chances of making a successful escape seem pitiful. Yet Aminta continues to assure me that she is willing to help me and to escape with me, even though it means leaving all that she has ever known. Last night, she came secretly into the hut and took me silently on the floor whilst the others were asleep. I knew then that I must accept the risk and try to escape with her.

'It is dark now, and storm clouds are gathering over the moor. Soon we shall make our bid for freedom. I shall very likely die in the attempt, and so I bid whoever is reading this a fond farewell. Reader, pray for my soul: and for the lost souls of Unwin, Radford, Hope and Pemberton, and countless others led astray into the ranks of the eternally damned, trapped forever in the deadly toils of the mighty Amazon women.'

The diary ended there. I closed it slowly and thoughtfully, and looked up into the curator's watchful face.

'It's one hell of a good yarn,' I told him. 'Real *Boy's Own Paper* stuff, you might say. But I reckon that's about as far as it goes. He had quite an imagination, though, your great-grandad; I'll give him that. Hoped to make a bob or two out of his "memoirs", did he?'

'Wait a moment, Mr Stokes,' said Carmichael, raising his hand as though to prevent me from uttering further blasphemies. 'The story does not quite end there. You see, this museum was set up by my great-grandfather *before* his last expedition: he never returned here. In fact, nothing more was seen of him at all. He simply disappeared. That is, nothing more was heard of him until two years after the date of that last diary entry.'

'So what happened then?'

'According to my grandfather's notes, which you will also find in the box, that diary which you are holding arrived here, by post. It was postmarked Manaos. There was no letter with it. But there was this photograph.'

He handed it to me. I had to admit that it was a remarkable snapshot of the professor. The old boy was standing amid the jungle greenery, completely naked save for an amazing jewelled harness worn over his genitalia. But it wasn't the Professor your eye was drawn to: it was his companion. Fully six feet six, broad-shouldered, big-bosomed and heavy-hipped, she was smothered in jewels which accentuated the opulence of her exotic body. You could lose yourself in that body. Her dark hair hung to her waist in oiled and jewelled ringlets.

'And there was this, too.'

He handed me a huge, beautifully cut green stone, which glittered in the shaft of dusty sunlight coming through the curtains. There was no way this was some cheap piece of green glass.

'It's a perfect emerald. A masterpiece of nature and the jeweller's art. And if you look at the photograph, you will see where it comes from.'

I looked, and I had to admit the guy had a point. The cut and polished jewel was a dead ringer for the one old Carmichael was wearing in his harness, hanging like a medallion over the end of his prick.

'My God!' I had to admit it: I was seriously interested now. 'So how much is this baby worth, then?'

'I haven't had it valued yet – but hundreds of thousands of pounds, undoubtedly.'

'I'm impressed.'

'And there is one thing which I think will interest you.'

Carmichael bent down and took a small glass vial out of the cardboard box. It looked empty. It's significance was not lost on me.

'Come on – surely you're not telling me that wonder sex-elixir stuff really existed?' I protested. 'It's just got to be an old wives' tale – hasn't it?'

'The elixir was contained in this vial. I am sure of it. Sadly, either my great-grandfather used it all up, or it has evaporated away with the years. If only I had enough of it to get it analysed, to learn what the active ingredients are . . .'

'Jeez! A perfect emerald *and* the sexual wonder-drug of the century. You'd be in the money – no doubt about it. But if there's not enough to analyse . . . where are you going to get more from?'

'Why, can't you guess, Mr Stokes? I shall go back to its very source. Naturally, I shall need to mount a proper expedition. And I might well need a good press-man with me, to cover the news angle. Of course, I don't know what we might find there. It could well be dangerous. But think of the rewards . . .'

There was a wild look in that man's eye. And you'd better believe it: I was beginning to catch some of that wildness myself. You see, I'm nobody's fool: and he just didn't sound like a crazy man to me.

Maybe it's the exclusive of the century. Maybe I'm just chasing after rainbows. But either way, we're leaving for Manaos on Friday.

A MAN
WITH A MAID

Anonymous

And now to a genuine pearl of Victorian erotica. What follows is an extract from *A Man with a Maid 1*, the first book in this trilogy of 19th-century chastisement stories by an anonymous author.

The Victorian era was an age of discovery and invention. We know how creative our forefathers were in the use of machinery and new-fangled equipment. It seems their capacity for the use of gadgetry extended to the boudoir. The spurned gentleman, Jack, has lured his quarry – the capricious tease, Alice – into his snuggery so that he can make her 'voluptuous person' recompense him for earlier disappointment.

The most innocuous objects of furniture are employed as mechanisms of punishment and restraint as Jack gleefully submits Alice to his wanton desires.

Devotees of Victorian erotica will find many titles amongst the Nexus list to their liking. But be warned, the language is very explicit. I was obviously wrong to think that gentlemen were well-behaved in those days!

During the ten minutes' grace that I mentally allowed Alice in which to recover from the violence of her struggles, I quietly studied her as she stood helpless, almost supporting herself by resting her weight on her wrist. She was to me an exhilarating spectacle, her bosom fluttering, rising and falling as she caught her breath, her cheeks still flushing, her large hat somewhat disarranged, while her dainty well-fitting dress displayed her neatly 'crummy' figure to its fullest advantage.

She regained command of herself wonderfully quickly, and then it was evident that she was stealthily watching me in horrible apprehension. I did not leave her long in suspense, but after going slowly round her and inspecting her, I placed a chair right in front of her, so close to her its edge almost touched her knees, then slipped myself into it, keeping my legs apart, so that she stood between them, the front of her dress pressing against the fly of my trousers. Her head was now above mine, so that I could peer directly into her downcast face.

As I took up this position, Alice trembled nervously and tried to draw herself away from me, but found herself compelled to stand as I had placed her. Noticing the action, I drew my legs closer to each other so as to loosely hold her between them, smiling cruelly at the uncontrollable shudder that passed through her, when she felt the pressure of my knees against hers! Then I extended my arms, clasped her gently round the waist and drew her against me, at the same time tightening the clutch of my legs, till soon she was fairly in my embrace, my face pressing against her throbbing bosom. For a moment she struggled wildly, then resigned herself to the unavoidable as she recognized her helplessness.

Except when dancing with her, I had never held Alice in my arms, and the embrace permitted by the waltz was nothing to the comprehensive clasping between arms and legs in which she now found herself. She trembled fearfully her tremors giving me exquisite pleasure as I felt them shoot through her, then presently murmured: 'Please don't, Jack!'

I looked up into her flushed face, as I amorously pressed my cheek against the swell of her bosom: 'Don't you like it, Alice?' I said maliciously, as I squeezed her still more closely against me. 'I think you're just delicious, dear, and I am trying to imagine what it will feel like, when your clothes have been taken off you!'

'No! No! Jack!' she moaned, agonizedly, twisting herself in her distress, 'let me go, Jack; don't . . . don't . . .' and her voice failed her.

For answer, I maintained her against me with my left arm round her waist, then with my right hand I began to stroke and press her hips and bottom.

'Oh . . .! don't, Jack! don't!' Alice shrieked, squirming in distress and futilely endeavouring to avoid my marauding hand. I paid no attention to her pleadings and cries, but continued my strokings and caressings over her full posteriors and thighs down to her knees, then back to her buttocks and haunches, she, all the while, quivering in a delicious way. Then I freed my left hand, and holding her tightly imprisoned between my legs, I proceeded with both hands to study over her clothes the configuration of her backside and hips and thighs, handling her buttocks with a freedom that seemed to stagger her, as she pressed the front of her person against me, in her efforts to escape from the liberties that my hands were taking with her posterior charms.

After toying delightfully with her in this way for some little time, I ceased and withdrew my hands from her hips, but only to pass them up and down over her incurving sides; thence I passed to her bosom which I began lovingly to stroke and caress to her dismay. Her colour rose as she swayed uneasily on her legs. But her stays prevented any direct attack on her bosom, so I decided to open her clothes sufficiently to obtain a peep at her virgin breasts, and set to work to unbutton her blouse.

'Jack, no! no!' shrieked Alice, struggling vainly to get loose. But I only smiled and continued to undo her blouse till I got it completely open and threw it back onto her shoulders, only to be baulked as a fairly high bodice covered her bosom. I set to work to open this, my fingers revelling in the touch of Alice's dainty linen. Soon it also was open and thrown back – and then, right before my eager eyes, lay the snowy expanse of Alice's bosom, her breasts being visible nearly as far as their nipples!

'Oh! . . . oh! . . .' she moaned in her distress, flushing painfully at this cruel exposure. But I was too excited to take any notice; my eyes were rivetted on the provokingly lovely swell of her breasts, exhibiting the valley between the twin-globes, now heaving and fluttering under her agitated emotions. Unable to restrain myself, I threw my arms round Alice's waist, drew her closely to me, and pressed my lips on her palpitating flesh which I kissed furiously.

'Don't, Jack!' cried Alice, as she tugged frantically at her fastenings in her wild endeavours to escape from my passionate lips; but instead of stopping, my mouth wandered all over her heaving bosom and to her delicious breasts, punctuating its progress with hot kisses which seemed to drive her mad to such a pitch that I thought it best to desist.

'Oh! my God!' she moaned as I relaxed my clasp and leant back in my chair to enjoy the sight of her shame-faced distress. There was not the least doubt that she felt most keenly my indecent assault, and so I determined to worry her with lascivious liberties a little longer.

When she had become calmer, I passed my arms round her waist and again began to play with her posteriors then, stooping down, I got my hands under her clothes and commenced to pull them up. Flushing violently, Alice shrieked to me to desist, but in vain! In a trice, I turned her petticoats up, held them thus with my left hand and with my right I proceeded to attack her bottom now protected only by her dainty thin drawers!

The sensation was delirious! My hand delightedly roved over the fat plump cheeks of her arse, stroking, caressing, and pinching them, revelling in the firmness and elasticity of her flesh under its thin covering, Alice all the time wriggling and squirming in horrible shame, imploring me almost incoherently to desist and finally getting so semi-hysterical, that I was compelled to suspend my exquisite game. So I dropped her skirts, to her relief, pushed my chair back and rose.

I had in the room a large plate glass mirror nearly

eight feet high which reflected one at full length. While Alice was recovering from her last ordeal, I pushed this mirror close in front of her, placing it so that she could see herself in its centre. She started uneasily as she caught sight of herself, for I had left her bosom uncovered, and the reflection of herself in such shameful dishabille in conjunction with her large hat (which she still retained) seemed vividly to impress on her the horror of her position!

Having arranged the mirror to my satisfaction, I picked up the chair and placed it just behind Alice, sat down in it, and worked myself forward on it till Alice again stood between my legs but this time with her back to me. The mirror faithfully reflected my movements, and her feminine intuition warned her that the front of her person was now about to become the object of my indecent assault.

But I did not give her time to think. Quickly I encircled her waist again with my arms, drew her to me till her bottom pressed against my chest, then, while my left arm held her firmly, my right hand began to wander over the junction of her stomach and legs, pressing inquisitively her groin and thighs, and intently watching her in the mirror.

Her colour rose, her breath came unevenly, she quivered and trembled on her legs, as she pressed her thighs closely together. She was horribly perturbed, but I do not think she anticipated what then happened.

Quietly dropping my hands, I slipped them under her clothes, caught hold of her ankles, then proceeded to climb up her legs over her stockings.

'No! no! for God's sake, don't, Jack!' Alice yelled, now scarlet with shame and wild with alarm at this invasion of her most secret parts. Frantically she dragged at her fastenings, her hands clenched, her head thrown back, her eyes dilated with horror. Throwing the whole of her weight on her wrists, she strove to free her legs from my attacking hands by kicking out desperately, but to no avail. The sight in the mirror of her struggles only stimulated me into a refinement of cruelty, for with one hand I raised her clothes waist high, exposing her in her dainty drawers and black silk stockings, while with the other I vigorously attacked her thighs over her drawers, forcing a way between them and finally working up so close to her Mont Venus that Alice practically collapsed in an agony of apprehension and would have fallen had it not been for the sustaining ropes which alone supported her, as she hung in a semi-hysterical faint.

Quickly rising and ripping her clothes, I placed an arm-chair behind her, and loosened the pulleys, till she rested comfortably in it, then left her to recover herself, feeling pretty confident that she was now not far from surrendering herself to me, rather than continue a resistance which she could not but see was utterly useless. This was what I wanted to effect. I did not propose to let her off any single one of the indignities I had in store for her, but I wanted to make her suffering the more keen, through the feeling that she was, to some extent, a consenting party to actions that inexpressibly shocked and revolted her. The first of these I intended to be the removal of her clothes, and, as soon as Alice became more mistress of herself, I set the pulleys working and soon had her standing erect with upstretched arms.

She glanced fearfully at me as if trying to learn what was now going to happen to her. I deemed it as well to tell her, and to afford her an opportunity of yielding herself to me, if she should be willing to do so. I also wanted to save her clothes from being damaged, as she was really beautifully dressed, and I was not at all confident that I could get her garments off her without using scissors to some of them.

'I see you want to know what now is going to happen to you, Alice,' I said. 'I'll tell you. You are to be stripped naked, utterly and absolutely naked; not a stitch of any sort is to be left on you!'

A flood of crimson swept over her face, invading both neck and bosom (which remained bare); her head fell forward as she moaned: 'No! . . . No! . . . Oh! Jack . . . Jack . . . how can you . . .,' and she swayed uneasily on her feet.

'That is to be the next item in the programme, my dear!' I said, enjoying her distress. 'There is only one detail that remains to be settled first, and that is, will you undress yourself quietly if I set you loose, or must I drag your clothes off you? I don't wish to influence your decision, and I know what queer ideals girls have about taking off their clothes in the presence of a man; I will leave the decision to you, only saying that I do not see what you have to gain by further resistance, and some of your garments may be ruined – which would be a pity! Now, which is it to be?

She looked at me imploringly for a moment, trembling in every limb, then averting her eyes, but remained silent, evidently torn by conflicting emotions.

'Come, Alice,' I said presently, 'I must have your decision, or I shall proceed to take your clothes off you as best as I can.'

Alice was now in a terrible state of distress! Her eyes wandered all over the room without seeming to see anything, incoherent murmurs escaped from her lips, as if she was trying to speak but could not, her breath went and came, her bosom rose and fell agitatedly. She was endeavouring to form some decision evidently, but unable to do so.

I remained still for a brief space as if awaiting her answer; then, as she did not speak, I quietly went to a drawer, took out a pair of scissors and went back to her. At the sight of the scissors, she shivered, then with an effort, said, in a voice broken with emotion: 'Don't undress me, Jack! . . . if you must . . . have me, let it be as I am . . . I will . . . submit quietly . . . oh! my God!!' she wailed.

'That won't do, dear,' I replied, not unkindly, but still firmly, 'you must be naked, Alice; now, will you or will you not undress yourself?'

Alice shuddered, cast another imploring glance at me, but seeing no answering gleam of pity in my eyes, but stern determination instead, she stammered out: 'Oh! Jack! I can't! Have some pity on me, Jack, and . . . have me as I am!! I promise I'll be . . . quiet!'

I shook my head, I saw there was only one thing for me to do, namely, to undress her without any further delay; and I set to work to do so, Alice crying piteously: 'Don't, Jack, don't! . . . don't!'

I had left behind her the arm-chair in which I had allowed her to rest, and her blouse and bodice were still hanging open and thrown back on her shoulders. So I got on the chair and worked them along her arms and over her clenched hands onto the ropes; then gripping her wrists in turn one at a time, I released the noose, slipped the garments down and off it and refastened the noose. And as I had been quick to notice that Alice's chemise and vest had shoulder-strap fastenings and had merely to be unhooked, the anticipated difficulty of undressing her forcibly was now at an end! The rest of her garments would drop off her, as each became released, and therefore it was in my power to reduce her to absolute nudity! My heart thrilled with fierce exultation, and without further pause, I went on with the delicious work of undressing her.

Alice quickly divined her helplessness and in an agony of apprehension and shame cried to me for mercy! But I was deaf to her pitiful pleadings! I was wild to see her naked!

Quickly I unhooked her dress and petticoats and pulled them down to her feet, thus exhibiting her in stays, drawers, and stockings, a bewitching sight! Her cheeks were suffused with shame-faced blushes, she huddled herself together as much as she could, seemingly supported entirely by her arms; her eyes were downcast and she seemed dazed both by the rapidity of my motions and their horrible success!

Alice now had on only a dainty Parisian corset which allowed the laces of her chemise to be visible, just hiding the nipples of her maiden breasts, and a pair of exquisitely provoking drawers, cut wide especially at her knees and trimmed with a sea of frilly lace, from below which emerged her shapely legs encased in black silk stockings and terminated in neat little shoes. She was the daintiest sight a man could well imagine, and, to me, the daintiness was enhanced by her shame-faced consciousness, for she could see herself reflected in the mirror in all her dreadful dishabille!

After a minute of gloating admiration, I proceeded to untie the tapes of her drawers so as to take them off her. At this she seemed to wake to the full sense of the humiliation in store for her; wild at the idea of being deprived of this most intimate of garments to a girl, she screamed in her distress, tugging frantically at her fastenings in her desperation! But the knot gave way, and her drawers, being now unsupported, slipped down to below her knees where they hung for a brief moment, maintained only by the despairing pressure of her legs against each other. A tug or two from me, and they lay in snowy loads round her ankles and rested on her shoes!

O that I had the pen of a ready writer with which to describe Alice at this stage of the terrible ordeal of being forcibly undressed, her mental and physical anguish, her frantic cries and impassioned pleadings, her frenzied struggles, the agony in her face, as garment after garment was removed from her and she was being hurried nearer and nearer to the appalling goal of absolute nudity! The accidental but unavoidable contact of my hands with her person, as I undressed her, seemed to upset her so terribly that I wondered how she would endure my handling and playing with the most secret and sensitive parts of herself when she was naked! But acute as was her distress while being deprived of her upper garments, it was nothing to her shame and anguish when she felt her drawers forced down her legs and the last defence to her cunt thus removed! Straining wildly at the ropes with cheeks aflame, eyes dilated with terror, and convulsively heaving bosom, she uttered inarticulate cries, half-choked by her emotions and panting under her exertions.

I gloated over her sufferings and I would have liked to have watched them – but I was now mad with desire for her naked charms and also feared that a prolongation of her agony might result in a faint, when I would lose the anticipated pleasure of witnessing Alice's misery when her last garment was removed and she was forced to stand naked in front of me. So, unheeding her imploring cries, I undid her corset and took it off her, dragged off her shoes and stockings and with them her fallen drawers (during which process I intently watched her struggles in the hope of getting a glimpse of her Holy of Holies, but vainly), then slipped behind her; unbuttoning the shoulder-fastenings of her chemise and vest, I held these up for a moment, then watching Alice closely in the mirror, I let go! Down they slid with a rush, right to her feet! I saw Alice flash one rapid stolen half-reluctant glance at the mirror, as she felt the cold air on her now naked skin. I saw her reflection stark naked, a lovely gleaming pearly vision; then instinctively she squeezed her legs together, as closely as she could, huddled herself coweringly as much as the ropes permitted – her head fell back in the first intensity of her shame, then fell forward suffused with blushes that extended right down to her breasts, her eyes closed as she moaned in heartbroken accents: 'Oh! Oh! Oh!' She was naked!!

Half-delirious with excitement and the joy of conquest, I watched Alice's naked reflection in the mirror. Rapidly and tumultuously, my eager eyes roved over her shrinking trembling form, gleaming white, save for her blushing face and the dark triangular mossy-looking patch at the junction of her belly and thighs. But I felt that, in this moment of triumph, I was not sufficiently master of myself to fully enjoy the spectacle of her naked maiden charms now so fully exposed; besides which, her chemise and vest still lay on her feet. So I knelt down behind her, forced her feet up one at a time and removed these garments, noting, as I did so, the glorious curves of her bottom and hips. Throwing these garments onto the rest of her clothes, I pushed the arm-chair in front of her, and then settled myself down to a systematic and critical inspection of Alice's naked self!

As I did so, Alice coloured deeply over face and bosom and moved herself uneasily. The bitterness of death (so to speak) was past, her clothes had been forced off her and she was naked; but she was evidently conscious that much indignity and humiliation was yet in store for her, and she was horribly aware that my eyes were now taking in every detail of her naked self!

141

Forced to stand erect by the tension of the ropes on her arms, she could do nothing to conceal any part of herself, and, in agony of shame, she endured the awful ordeal of having her naked person closely inspected and examined!

I had always greatly admired her trim little figure, and in the happy days before our rupture, I used to note with proud satisfaction how Alice held her own, whether at garden parties, at afternoon teas or in the theatre or ball room. And after she had jilted me and I was sore in spirit, the sight of her invariably added fuel to the flames of my desire, and I often caught myself wondering how she looked in her bath! One evening, she wore at dinner a low-cut evening dress and she nearly upset my self-control by leaning forward over the card table by which I was standing, and unconsciously revealing to me the greater portion of her breasts! But my imagination never pictured anything as glorious as the reality now being so reluctantly exhibited to me!

Alice was simply a beautiful girl and her lines deliciously voluptuous! No statue, no model, but glorious flesh and blood allied to superb femininity! Her well-shaped head was set on a beautifully modelled neck and bosom from which sprang a pair of exquisitely lovely breasts (if anything too full), firm, upstanding, saucy, and inviting. She had fine rounded arms with small well-shaped hands, a dainty but not too small waist, swelling grandly downwards and outwards and melting into magnificent curves over her hips and haunches. Her thighs were plump and round, and tapered to the neatest of calves and ankles and tiny feet, her legs being the least trifle too short for her, but adding by this very defect to the indescribable fascination of her figure. She had a graciously swelling belly with a deep navel, and, framed by the lines of her groin, was her Mont Venus, full, fat fleshy prominent, covered by a wealth of fine silky dark curly hairs, through which I could just make out the lips of her cunt. Such was Alice as she stood naked before me, horribly conscious of my devouring eyes, quivering and trembling with suppressed emotion, tingling with shame, flushing red and white knowing full well her own loveliness and what its effect on me must be; and in dumb silence I gazed and gazed again at her glorious naked self till my lust began to run riot and insist on the gratification of senses other than that of sight!

I did not however consider that Alice was ready to properly appreciate the mortification of being felt. She seemed to be still absorbed in the horrible consciousness of one all-pervading fact, viz that she was utterly naked, that her chaste body was the prey of my lascivious eyes, that she could do nothing to hide or even screen any part of herself, even her cunt, from me! Every now and then, her downcast eyes would glance at the reflection of herself in the faithful mirror, only to be hastily withdrawn with an excess of colour to her already shame-suffused cheeks at these fresh reminders of the spectacle she was offering to me!

Therefore with a strong effort, I succeeded in overcoming the temptation to feel and handle Alice's luscious body there and then, and being desirous of first studying her naked self from all points of view, I rose and took her in strict profile, noting with delight the arch of her bosom, the proudly projecting breasts, the glorious curve of her belly, the conspicuous way in which the hairs on the Mount of Venus stood out, indicating that her cunt would be found both fat and fleshy, the magnificent swell of her bottom! Then I went behind her, and for a minute or two, revelled in silent admiration of the swelling lines of her hips and haunches, her quivering buttocks, her well-shaped legs! Without moving, I could command the most perfect exhibition of her naked loveliness, for I had her back view in full sight while her front was reflected in the mirror!

Presently I completed my circuit, then standing close to her, I had a good look at her palpitating breasts, noting their delicious fullness and ripeness, their ivory skin, and the tiny virgin nipples pointing outwards so prettily. Alice colouring and flushing and swaying herself uneasily under my close inspection. Then I peered into the round cleft of her navel while she became more uneasy than ever, seeing the downward trend of my inspection. Then I dropped on my knees in front of her, and from this point of vantage, I commenced to investigate with eager eyes the mysterious region of her cunt, so deliciously covered with a wealth of close curling hairs, clustering so thickly round and over the coral lips as almost to render them invisible! As I did so, Alice desperately squeezed her thighs together as closely as she could, at the same time drawing in her stomach in the vain hope of defeating my purpose and of preventing me from inspecting the citadel wherein reposed her virginity!

As a matter of fact, she did to a certain extent thwart me, but as I intended before long to put her on her back and tie her down so, with her legs wide apart, I did not grudge her partial success, but brought my face close to her belly. 'Don't! Oh, don't!' she cried, as if she could feel my eyes as they searched this most secret part of herself; but disregarding her pleadings, I closely scanned the seat of my approaching pleasure, noting delightedly that her Mont Venus was exquisitely plump and fleshy and would afford my itching fingers the most delicious pleasure when I allowed them to wander over its delicate contours and hide themselves in the forest of hairs that so sweetly covered it!

At last I rose. Without a word, I slipped behind the mirror and quickly divested myself of my clothes, retaining only my shoes and socks. Then, suddenly, I emerged and stood right in front of Alice. 'Oh!' she ejaculated, horribly shocked by the unexpected apparition of my naked self, turning rosy red and hastily averting her eyes – but not before they had caught sight of my prick in glorious erection! I watched her closely. The sight seemed to fascinate her in spite of her alarmed modesty, she flashed rapid glances at me through half-closed eyes, her colour coming and going. She seemed forced, in spite of herself, to regard the instrument of her approaching violation, as if to assess its size and her capacity!

'Won't you have a good look at me, Alice?' I presently remarked maliciously. 'I believe I can claim to possess a good specimen of what is so dear to the heart of a girl!!' (She quivered painfully.) After a moment I continued: 'Must I then assume by your apparent indifference that you have in your time seen so many naked men that the sight no longer appeals to you?' She coloured deeply, but kept her eyes averted.

'Are you not even curious to estimate whether my prick will fit your cunt?' I added, determined, if I possibly could, to break down the barrier of silence she was endeavouring to protect herself with.

I succeeded! Alice tugged frantically at the ropes which kept her upright, then broke into a piteous cry: 'No, no . . . my God, no!' she supplicated, throwing her head back but still keeping her eyes shut as if to exclude the sighs she dreaded, 'Oh! . . . you don't really mean to . . . to . . .' she broke down, utterly unable to clothe in words the overwhelming fear that she was now to be violated!

I stepped up to her, passed my left arm round her waist and drew her trembling figure to me, thrilling at the exquisite sensation caused by the touch of our naked bodies against each other. We were now both facing the mirror, both reflected in it.

'Don't, oh! Don't touch me!' she shrieked as she felt my arm encircle her, but holding her closely against me with my left arm, I gently placed my right forefinger on her navel, to force her to open her eyes and watch my movements in the mirror, which meant that she would also have to look at my naked self, and gently I tickled her.

She screamed in terror, opening her eyes, squirming deliciously: 'Don't! Oh, don't!' she cried agitatedly.

'Then use your chaste eyes properly and have a good look at the reflection of the pair of us in the mirror,' I said somewhat sternly: 'Look me over slowly and thoroughly from head to foot, then answer the questions I shall presently put to you. May I call your attention to that whip hanging on that wall and to the inviting defencelessness of your bottom? Understand that I shall not hesitate to apply one to the other if you don't do as you are told! Now have a good look at me!'

Alice shuddered, then reluctantly raised her eyes and shame-facedly regarding my reflection in the mirror, her colour coming and going. I watched her intently (she being also reflected, my arm was still around her waist holding her against me) and I noted with cruel satisfaction how she trembled with shame and fright when her eyes dwelt on my prick, now stiff and erect!

'We make a fine pair, Alice, eh?' I whispered maliciously. She coloured furiously, but remained silent.

'Now answer my questions: I want to know something about you before going further. How old are you?'

'Twenty-five,' she whispered.

'In your prime then! Good! Now, are you a virgin!'

Alice flushed hotly and painfully, then whispered again: 'Yes!'

Oh! My exultation! I was not too late! The prize of her maidenhead was to be mine! My prick showed my joy! I continued my catechism.

'Absolutely virgin?' I asked. 'A pure virgin? Has no hand ever wandered over those lovely charms, has no eye but mine seen them?'

Alice shook her head, blushing rosy red at the idea suggested by my words. I looked rather doubtingly at her.

'I include female eyes and hands as well as male in my query, Alice,' I continued, 'you know that you have a most attractive lot of girl and woman friends and that you are constantly with them. Am I to understand that you and they have never compared your charms, have never, when occupying the same bed . . .' but she broke in with a cry of distress. 'No, no, not I, not I, oh! How can you talk to me like this, Jack!'

'My dear, I only wanted to find out how much you already knew so that I might know what to teach you now! Well, shall we begin your lessons?' And I drew her against me, more closely than ever, and again began to tickle her navel.

'Jack, don't!' she screamed, 'Oh, don't touch me! I can't stand it! Really I can't!'

'Let me see if that is really so!' I replied, as I removed my arm from her waist and slipped behind her, taking up a position from which I could command the reflection of our naked figures in the mirror, and thus watch her carefully and note the effect on her of my tender mercy.

147

STEPHANIE'S CASTLE

Susanna Hughes

And how she's changed! Transformed from a hesitant career woman in the first book of the *Stephanie* series into a jet-setting seductress, our leading lady is summoned to the luxurious Italian lakeside home of Devlin, the man who changed her life and awakened her taste for sexual sophistication. She can sample at leisure the delights of having free run of the castle and its bevy of good-looking slaves. That is, until the conniving Gianni arrives and subjects her to experiences of submission where she has no control.

Stephanie's Castle is the second book in the series. The following books are *Stephanie's Revenge* and *Stephanie's Domain*. *Stephanie's Trial* is published this month. Susanna Hughes is the author of *Melinda and the Master*, and specialises in novels of sophisticated decadence suffused with a hint of the darkly perverse. What I like about the *Stephanie* series is the detail lavished on the trappings of elegance: the clothes, the gardens, the perfume and the all round luxury!

Upstairs it felt hot. Devlin had gone off to take a telephone call somewhere in the depths of the castle, leaving Stephanie on the terrace where they had breakfasted. She sat on one of the loungers sipping what had become the accustomed champagne, and debated whether to go and change into her bikini to take advantage of the sun. The Italian sun had almost reached its zenith but a cooling breeze from the lake made the temperature tolerable. For the time being Stephanie was content to relax, enjoy the magnificent panorama laid out in front of her and wait for Devlin to return.

The Devlin who finally came back on to the terrace was a very different man from the one who, happy, buoyant and relaxed, had left Stephanie some half an hour before. This Devlin suddenly looked old and tired, the worries of the world settled on his shoulders. He tramped across the terrace, his whole demeanour suggesting his anxiety.

'What on earth's the matter?' Stephanie asked, genuinely concerned.

'I'm afraid something has come up. Business. I've got to go to the mainland right away. I'm sorry . . .'

'Anything I can do?'

'No, no . . .' Though his eyes were looking at her she could see his mind was somewhere else entirely.

'When will you be back?'

'Probably after lunch. I'm sorry. It's unavoidable.'

'Don't worry about me. I'll sunbathe. It's so hot.'

'If you want lunch, they'll bring you anything you want.'

'Thank you.'

'And make yourself at home. There are no locked doors for you.' He looked reluctant to leave her.

'Devlin, go. I'll be fine. There are no more secrets, are there?'

'No. You've seen it all.' Devlin smiled weakly but the worried frown soon returned. 'If you want Bruno, dial 5 on the phone.'

'And I don't expect him to say hello, right?'

This time he did not manage a smile. She saw one of the servants waiting with a large briefcase as Devlin shuffled off, clearly totally absorbed in whatever problem had suddenly cast a shadow across his world. Surely, Stephanie thought, with such obvious wealth, it could be nothing too disastrous.

She watched from the terrace as Devlin climbed aboard the motorboat and turned round to see if she was still on the terrace. He waved distractedly when he saw her and she waved back as the boat pulled away from the jetty, then sped over the almost still waters of the lake, leaving a foaming white wake.

One of the servants poured her a glass of champagne. She had never drunk so much champagne in her life and it felt good. It was, she decided, her favourite drink. The maximum of intoxication with the minimum of alcohol, though she would have been intoxicated enough without any. The secrets of the castle were revealed. Most of the questions answered. She remembered that she had not

153

asked Devlin about Venetia and made a mental note to do so when he returned.

Taking her champagne she sat on one of the loungers in the full sun, feeling the sun on her face. In the distance she could still hear the faint roar of the motorboat's engines carrying Devlin to the mainland. What the problem was she could not imagine but, to be honest with herself, she was glad of the chance to be on her own and let her mind digest what was happening to her. She thought of going up to her room and lying in the sun on her terrace, as she wasn't yet ready for lunch, but for the moment she had no inclination to move.

As she lay with her eyes closed against the sunlight she let her mind wander back to the cellar and its occupants. Remembering the feelings she had felt as she lay on her back drowning in Dolly's flesh, she could not help an involuntary shiver of pleasure. She got up and walked into the house, telling the servants she'd have lunch in an hour. But as she walked to the staircase and mounted the first few steps she stopped, reversed her direction and headed instead for the small wooden door hidden behind the tapestry drape. The cellar was pulling her back. She had felt the same with the masked man on the plane, a force like a magnet, invisible, but impossible to resist. She wanted more, though more of what specifically she had no idea. More of something.

The cellar door had been left unlocked. Was that Devlin anticipating her needs? She grasped the rope at the side of the stone steps and walked down into the dimly lit cellars. She wondered, as she rapped twice on the door to the cells, whether Bruno would let her in on her own, but when the door swung open he seemed almost to be expecting her and stood aside immediately to let her in.

She said nothing to him and walked up and down the

corridor looking into the cells more carefully this time. One of the women, a tall blonde beauty with long hair and long slender legs, particularly caught her eye. Stephanie noticed thin red marks on the top of her thighs and imagined she had been whipped. Of all the slaves this woman looked the most discontented. But Stephanie did not feel in the mood for a challenge of another lesbian experience. As she contemplated the tall blonde she realised that what she actually wanted was cock. She wanted to be fucked. That was what she had missed this morning. She wanted a hot live cock deep inside her cunt. As she thought about it the need grew and became urgent.

There was no way to compare the cocks of the male slaves, as they all wore the hard leather pouches. She would have to go on general appearance and hope for the best. She could, of course, have Bruno strip the pouches off but that would have taken too long and she was in a hurry. In the second cell was a stocky, hairless and reasonably attractive man in his late thirties. He had a good firm body and short dark hair with an alert and open face.

'Number two,' she ordered. Bruno opened the cell without question.

The man assumed the position she had seen Dolly adopt with Devlin, kneeling with his head down. Stephanie went over to him and stroked his hair gently, very much as Devlin had with Dolly. He did not look up, and she took his chin in her hand and forced his head up so he had to look into her eyes. His name-tag read: *Adam*. She could not tell what was in his mind, whether it was fear or anticipation or disinterest. Whatever it was she suddenly laughed out loud. She continued to laugh as she took her dress off for the second time this morning.

Bruno still stood in the doorway of the cell. Stephanie considered sending him away but decided against it. There was no point. In fact, the short riding crop tucked into the belt of his tunic had given her an idea, an idea that excited her more than she would have imagined possible after this morning's activities. She removed her bra and saw that her nipples were already hard. It was as though she had saved them earlier, not wanting Dolly to finger them, so that they would be fresh and alive now. She stripped off the stockings wanting to be completely naked this time, and then stood in front of the kneeling man.

'Pull my knickers down,' she ordered.

He reached up and found the waistband, pulling the french knickers down to her ankles and she stepped out of them. He bowed his head again as though he were not allowed to look at her naked body.

'Put your head up again, Adam,' Stephanie said, allowing annoyance to enter her voice. He obeyed at once. She stepped forward slightly and pushed her pubis into his forehead, feeling its hard bone against her fleshy mound. His mouth, in this position, was between her thighs and she could feel his hot breath on her cunt. She pressed her pubis into him rhythmically, as though she were fucking his forehead.

'You're very lucky, Adam. You're going to fuck me. A straightforward fuck,' she lied.

She got on to the bed, which was identical to the one she had lain on in the other cell. For the second time that morning she lay on her back, bent her knees and opened her legs. For the second time her cunt felt incredibly hot and wet. She knew that a lot of her excitement was in this power that Devlin had given her, this ability to command whatever she desired. She had always been turned on by words, had always wanted her lovers to talk to her and her to them, always loved being told that she was going to be fucked or sucked or buggered and now she realised that her voice – hard and strange – issuing unequivocal orders was turning her on as much as anything else.

She noticed Bruno's eyes had not left her for a moment.

'Fuck me then,' she said impatiently.

Adam stood up, looking pathetically down at the hard leather pouch chained over his genitals. Stephanie had forgotten about that.

'Get it off him, Bruno. Quickly.'

Taking a key Bruno roughly spun the man round and removed the little padlock from the thin chains that held the pouch in place. Suddenly freed from the constriction that had lasted for god knows how long, Adam's cock sprang into a rigid erection.

'Come on,' Stephanie said, wanting no further delays, the level of her arousal increasing every moment.

The man did not need further bidding. There was to be no foreplay. He fell on Stephanie and in one movement his cock was buried inside her. It was not the size of Devlin's of course, but it was good to feel the base of a cock grinding up against her clitoris again, a feeling no woman would ever achieve with Devlin. He was thrusting madly, violently as though he hadn't had sex for weeks. Stephanie took his hair in both her hands and held it tight. She moved her mouth to his ear and whispered in the most menacing tone she could muster: 'Stop now.'

He obeyed immediately, though she could feel his penis pulsing involuntarily inside her.

'Bruno, use you whip.' This was her idea. Bruno took the whip from his belt and in one fluid, practised motion, striped it across the man's buttocks. His penis bucked into Stephanie. Calling for the whip, hearing herself saying those words, had brought her to the edge of orgasm.

'Again,' she ordered, holding herself back, wanting to stay on the edge and in control and not be plunged into the abyss of a climax. Again the whip came down and Adam's penis drove into her propelled forward like a pile-driver. She ordered the whip again. His penis bucked. She clung to his hair and screamed with pleasure as Bruno's strokes fell on Adam's naked arse and she lost control, allowing herself her orgasm and feeling it course through her body unleashed at last. How many strokes landed before he came she did not know or care. But she knew she was ready for his spunk and felt it jet out into her seconds after the whip drove his cock into her again. She had never felt spunk so hot. It felt like liquid fire. She heard herself scream with pleasure as his spunk spurred her orgasm to a new intensity.

It was minutes before she realised she was still grasping his hair. She let go and had to stop herself apologising as she could see it had brought tears to his eyes. How silly to think of saying sorry, she scolded herself. Why should she care? It was an attitude she intended to get used to.

During the aftermath of her orgasm Bruno must have left the cell, as he now offered her a white towelling robe. She extracted herself from the man and put it on. With a movement of his hand Bruno indicated that she should follow him, which she did, not bothering to look back into the cell as she left.

At the far end of the corridor, opposite the entrance, was another stout wooden door. This opened on to what looked like a conventional suite of rooms, decorated with the same lavish style as the rest of the castle, except, of course, for the absence of windows. Light was provided by a series of tastefully arranged spotlights, big lamps and by the lights illuminating every picture. The rooms had a strange feeling, a feeling of secrecy and decadence.

Obviously anticipating Stephanie's needs, Bruno showed her to a large marbled bathroom. She showered and towelled herself dry on one of the large stock of fresh white bath towels neatly folded on the heated towel rails. As in her own room, the bathroom cabinet was stocked with expensive toiletries and Stephanie selected a moisturiser and annointed her body with it. The cool liquid felt good on her skin.

Pulling on the towelling robe again, Stephanie walked back into the corridor of the suite. Bruno had gone. She wandered through the other rooms. There were two large bedrooms, each with king-sized beds, one with a mirror on the ceiling above the bed. Both rooms had televisions and video recorders but there were no tapes that she could see. Presumably this was where Devlin's 'friends' brought the slaves for various sexual athletics, perhaps preferring not to be seen with them above ground. Or perhaps their appetites could not wait to be satisfied quickly once they had seen the opportunities laid before them.

The remaining room in the suite was less conventional. It had the same stone walls and floor as the cellar outside and the lights were harsher and brighter, though they could be dimmed. But it was what the room contained that fascinated Stephanie. Months before, before her affair with Martin, before sex meant anything more to her than simple fucking, she had come across the first of many books, a book on the more outré sexual dimensions. It had fascinated and enthralled her. She had bought other books and read them all with an equal relish. It was as though she had stumbled into a secret world, a world that existed behind closed doors, a world she had never suspected or dreamt of. But she had known that it was a world she would, sooner or later, want to explore. And that had led to her affair with Martin. Martin had shown her around that secret world. It had scared her, she had to admit it, but it had also thrilled her. It had given her sexual pleasure she would never have dreamt possible.

Now, as she stood in this room, the impact of reading that first book came flooding back to her. The room contained everything she had read about. There was every conceivable piece of sexual equipment, handcuffs, leather straps, ball gags, chains hanging from the ceiling and from the walls, punishment frames, a stock and a wooden rack. There was every type of whip, crop and paddle, and every size of dildo. A strong pulley, threaded with nylon rope attached to padded cuffs, hung from the ceiling. Three large wardrobes stood against the further wall. Stephanie opened each in turn to find them full of leather and rubber clothing, high-heeled shoes and a selection of wigs. There were drawers of bras, panties, suspender belts, corsets and stockings, all neatly arranged by size.

It was all here. Bondage, rubber, tranvestite, sado-masochism. It was all here in this room. Every fantasy could be catered for. In this room it would be possible to bind a man or a woman, dressed in rubber, leather, or whatever, in any position one cared to imagine. And do to them whatever one cared to do. There would be no escape. The illustrations in the books she had bought had always been line drawings, not photographs; drawings of men and women tied in extremis. Because they were drawings they had not appeared real; in this room the bondage would be only too real. The thought sent a chill through Stephanie. Then she thought of what Devlin had said about the slaves. They were all thieves. And in this room they would get their punishment. Of that she was certain. The frisson of fear she had felt as she contemplated these devices turned to a little knot of excitement. She would not like to be on the receiving end of any of this equipment. Or would she?

In a sense Martin had tortured her. Not physical pain, admittedly, but he had put her into bondage. She walked over to the pulley tied off on a cleat screwed into the stone wall. She unwound the white nylon rope from the cleat and let it loose. Immediately from the centre of the room the other end, attached to the leather cuffs, descended. She went over to where they hung at head height and inspected them. Fitting one on to her wrist she felt the thick padding inside the leather, very much like the cuffs that had held her last night. She tightened the strap on one wrist and stood with her hands high above her head, as high as she could reach. She closed her eyes and felt the strain in her shoulders. Could she imagine herself standing there bound and naked, not able to bring her hands down to relieve the pressure, waiting helplessly to be whipped or handled or fucked in any way her tormentor wished?

She brought her hands down and unbuckled the cuff. Her hands were trembling slightly. The stretching had loosened the towelling belt and as she pulled the belt free to retie it, the robe fell open and she glimpsed her naked body. Both her nipples were puckered and rigid, as hard as she had ever seen them.

The sun was high in the sky and heat radiated in a shimmering haze from any surface not protected by shade. Stephanie had changed into the bikini that Devlin had provided, a costume definitely not capable of withstanding exposure to water. Cut high on the hip, it

161

showed off Stephanie's long legs and tight curved bottom while the spangled tiny bra did little to conceal her breasts. The wrap, designed to be worn with it, was no more than a thin veil of chiffon. Coming down to the main terrace Stephanie had ordered a light lunch of lobster and salad and had decided against more champagne. She sipped ice-cold mineral water instead and had been tempted by the offer of ice cream after the salad. The melon ice cream the waiter had brought was unbelievably delicious, but she avoided the temptation to gorge herself on it. As she had thought on the plane, the main problem this weekend was to know where to draw the line. From where she sat the view over the lake was breath-taking, framed by the cascading flowers, the sun reflected off the almost still water. The heat of the sun made her body feel calm and relaxed.

The secrets of the castle were hers now. It was extraordinary that Devlin seemed to trust her implicitly with all this. He had been true to his word: there had been no locked doors, either physically or metaphorically – she had been able to go and do whatever she had wanted. Had Devlin not been so obviously distracted by his long telephone call Stephanie would have thought him quite capable of deliberately leaving her alone to see what her reaction would be, to see what she would do or perhaps to draw her deeper into the web.

The waiter brought her a steaming cup of espresso coffee. She left it to cool and walked over to the parapet of the terrace and looked down to the lake below. She could not see the stone steps leading down to the jetty as they were completely covered in the twining bourgainvillaea and jasmine but she could see the jetty itself and the water of the lake softly lapping at its wooden supports. She could hear the noise of the water from here too. Whatever Devlin imagined she would feel standing here on his terrace, the beauty of the castle and the island all around her, her mind able to dip into the memories of the morning in the cellars and the pleasures of last night, Stephanie had to admit her reaction was rather curious: she felt strangely at home.

After a second cup of coffee she decided to go upstairs to her terrace and lie out in the sun. Devlin would be back soon she thought, so this was her chance for a little sunbathing. Back in the bedroom she noticed the underwear she had discarded in the cell this morning had been washed and neatly folded in a precise pile on one of the chests of drawers.

Outside she positioned one of the loungers to catch the full sun and lay, feeling the heat boring down on her body. She closed her eyes. Quite unexpectedly, in her mind's eye, she saw herself strapped into the leather cuffs in the punishment room of the cellar suite, hoisted by the pulley on to tiptoe naked and helpless. She opened her eyes again to free herself of the image then, in a matter of seconds she was asleep. Dreams swarmed into her head, dreams that were so realistic as to be more memories than dreams. She saw Devlin kneeling between her legs, his huge cock erect, his banana finger already inside her. And then her sleep deepened and there were no dreams at all.

Only a few minutes later she awoke, feeling unusually refreshed. But she was hot, the delicate bikini streaked with her sweat. She walked into the bedroom to find some suntan lotion as she could feel her skin was already taking colour. In the bathroom cabinet, as she had come to expect in the castle, there was an expensive oil which she massaged into her face. Looking in the bathroom mirror she could see that even after such a brief exposure her face and arms were browning. She rubbed the thick white cream into her cheeks and forehead, looking at herself intently as she did so. Her eyes stared back at her, looking strangely knowing after the last eighteen hours. Her brown eyes were bright, the whites very white. Trying to be objective, she had to say she thought she looked very good. Sex obviously suited her. At least this sort of sex.

She went back into the bedroom and examined herself in the full-length bedroom mirror. The cut of the expensive bikini, despite the sweat, complemented her body perfectly. She had no idea what it cost but it was certainly more than *she'd* paid for an entire outfit. She felt good in it. She felt good in all the clothes that Devlin had given her. She loved the feeling of these beautiful materials made with the minutest attention to detail. All the clothes he had given her in the suitcase felt as if they had been made for her. They felt comfortable and elegant, and she knew they suited her. She felt at home in them. She had to say she loved the life here at the castle too. But then, who wouldn't? London, her job seemed to be in another world. Effectively, of course, it was another world, and one she had no desire to think about until it was absolutely necessary. And that time was not now.

The scent of bourgainvillaea drifted in from the terrace on a light breeze. All she had to think about now was Devlin. And herself. He would be back soon so in the meantime she could enjoy the sun. Why she was lying in a bikini on what must be the most private terrace in Italy, she thought suddenly, she could not imagine. But if she was going to lie naked then she would need her skin oiled against the burning sun. She smiled to herself as she walked over to the phone on the bedside table. She had to dial five, she remembered Devlin telling her. Her smile broadened as she heard the phone ring twice before it was answered.

'Bruno, bring one of the men to my room right away.'

She heard him hang up by way of reply.

The pleasure she took in issuing these orders was out of all proportion to the orders themselves. It was the sensation of being in command, a pleasure she had never experienced before, that she enjoyed. It was a pleasure Devlin had given her, created for her. There was no question in her mind that being able to command, in the way she had this morning in Devlin's cellar, had affected her deeply. She could hear her voice – that strange hard voice she had never heard herself use before – and remember what she said, what commands she issued. It was a part of the sexual experience, an integral part she knew, that had done more than given her an endless stream of orgasms. It had, in some way, defined her sexuality. Of course, Devlin was responsible. She had allowed Devlin to use and abuse her, she had enjoyed the game of 'rape'. But that was only the other side of the coin, the flipside. In a strange way, tied and held down on the bed last night, helpless as she was physically, she had still been in control. She had given Devlin his pleasure. The game he had begun she had hijacked. She had started wanting to please Devlin, certainly, but something else had taken over: all that eventually mattered was that she had pleased herself. Ironically, she thought with delight, the more she pleased herself, the more she seemed to gratify Devlin.

She wondered if Devlin would get a report of her activities while he'd been away. No doubt the servants had tracked her movements but she did not know how he could get information from Bruno; he did not look as though writing was one of his talents. Not that she wanted secrecy. She wanted Devlin to know precisely what she had done. She could always tell him herself.

165

The knock on the door pulled her out of this reverie. 'Come in.' She heard her hard cold voice again.

Bruno entered, followed by a man dressed in a one-piece nylon work suit elasticated at cuff and waist and with a long zip running from neck to crotch. Bruno immediately indicated, in effective sign language, that the garment should be removed. Under it the man was naked save for the hard black leather pouch chained tightly around his genitals and, of course, the name disc on the chain around his neck. The disc read: *Paul*.

'Out on the terrace, please.' Stephanie made a mental note not to use the word 'please' again in these circumstances.

She stepped out into the sun and the two men followed. She pulled the thin shoulder straps of the bikini bra down over her breasts. She watched Paul's eyes staring at her tits, the nipples already hardening under his gaze.

'What's your real name?'

'I'm not allowed to say, madam.' His voice was reedy and uncertain.

'You're allowed to tell me.'

Bruno shook his head vigorously and put a finger to his lips, presumably to indicate the need for silence. But Stephanie was not prepared to obey Bruno, just as she had not listened to Susie on the plane. Stripped to the waist, her firm tits hardly bouncing on her chest, as she walked over to him.

'I don't want to have to tell Mr Devlin that you have not cooperated with me, do I Bruno? He wouldn't like that, would he? What would he do if he didn't like it, Bruno? What would he do if I told him you had refused me?'

For half a second Bruno stared into Stephanie's eyes with a look bordering on contempt. But the thought of

Devlin's displeasure was too powerful a totem to ignore, as it had been for Susie. Bruno dropped his eyes to the floor and studied his feet.

'So your name is . . .' Stephanie returned to the slave picking up the metal name tag in her hand.

'Norman, madam.'

'See,' she said looking at Bruno. 'That's wasn't too difficult, was it, Norman?'

'No, madam.'

'I have much more difficult things for you to do in a minute. How long have you been here, Norman?'

Bruno's head came up again as if to intervene but Stephanie was already looking at him defiantly and he quickly thought better of it.

'Four weeks, madam.'

'Oh, so you'll be quite experienced then.'

'If you say so, madam.'

'So polite. I like that.'

Stephanie pulled the bottom of the bikini down over her thighs and, bending over, pulled it off her ankles. As she bent down, her arse nudged against Norman's thigh. His eyes had followed every movement and as she bent over he could see clearly the long slit of her sex, and the lips of her cunt covered in curly black pubic hair.

The terrace was equipped with a double-sized lounger, a lounger of the usual design and length but of double width which could accommodate two people lying side by side. 'There's sun-tan oil in the bathroom, Norman,' said Stephanie, lying down. 'Bring it here. You're going to rub it in for me.'

Norman immediately disappeared inside. Stephanie stretched out, her legs open, her arms above her head. Almost at once she could feel the sun on her sex. It was a strange feeling. In England she had never sunbathed in

167

the nude. She looked over to Bruno who still studied her feet, apparently showing no interest in her. He looked hot, his black costume more suited to the cool of the cellar than the heat of the sun.

Norman returned with the oil.

'You can start on my back,' Stephanie told him, rolling on to her stomach. Norman knelt by the side of the lounger, squeezing the thick cream on to her shoulder blades and then starting to massage it all over her back with both hands. He had strong hands and a firm touch and Stephanie closed her eyes to enjoy the sensation of the cold cream being worked into her already warm skin. Once he had finished her back he squirted more cream on the top of her thighs and started to work on the back of her legs. Stephanie opened her legs again as he massaged her buttocks, knowing he was seeing every detail of her labia and puckered arse.

'Right down there, Norman.' This would be torment for him, she knew. His fingers spread over her arse and then down till she could feel them edging against her cunt. He started to move his hand away, down her thighs and calves.

'No, back where you were,' she teased. His penis must be straining hopelessly against the pouch now, unable to come to full erection, or find any release. His fingers kneaded the oil into the bottom of her arse again; they could not help brushing the lips of her cunt.

'All right, that's enough.'

With relief she could almost feel, his hands moved back down her legs to her knees and calves. She had considered getting him to massage her cunt properly but decided she wanted to relax; she was not going to go short of sex in the next few hours, that was certain.

She turned on to her back and looked straight at

Norman. Her breasts were quivering slightly from the movement and she could see his eyes looking at them hungrily.

'Do you think I have a good body, Norman?'

'Yes, madam.'

'I let one of the slaves fuck me this morning, Norman.'

'Did you, madam?'

She could hear the edge of excitement creeping into his voice, reflecting a slim hope that she might just be planning the same fate for him.

'Get on with it then. Do my front.'

He squirted cream on to her navel and worked it all round her chest without actually touching her breasts. His hands creamed down to the triangle of pubic hair without touching that either. Then he worked on the front of her thighs and down to her calves and feet. Stephanie closed her eyes again, letting herself go to the delicious feeling the massage and the warmth of the sun were producing.

Since her remark about fucking the slave, Norman's touch on her flesh had changed. It was softer, more sensitive. He was no longer trying to keep himself detached, to view her as an inanimate object in order to keep his desire in check. Now it felt like foreplay.

'Take his pouch off, Bruno,' she ordered, opening her eyes to watch Norman's reaction. The slim hope was growing bigger, she knew. But Bruno was shaking his head vigorously. His eyes said this was the last straw and definitely not allowed. In the cellars he had not hesitated to remove Adam's pouch, so clearly there was some problem about doing it above ground. If it was a house rule it was an extremely silly one, Stephanie thought.

'I'm going to ask you to do it once more, Bruno.'

He shook his head again.

'How do you think Mr Devlin is going to feel when he knows that his favoured guest, whom he has brought all the way from London, has been assaulted by one of his servants?'

Bruno shook his head from side to side in extreme agitation.

'Yes, Bruno. I've heard that even men who've had their cocks cut off get randy. But trying to assault me! Trying to get your hands up me! Not very nice, is it? I can't imagine what Mr Devlin will say. Let's put it this way, I don't think you're going to be working at the castle much longer, do you?'

The defiance in Bruno's eyes changed to fear. He came over to where Norman was still kneeling and taking a small key from the many on his keyring, he unlocked the padlock that held the pouch in place and pulled it away. Norman's penis, creased and reddened by the constriction, immediately sprung to full erection.

'You've forgotten to do my breasts, Norman. You don't want my breasts to get sunburned, do you? As she said it she saw his erection swell again. She could see what he was thinking. Why else would she have had his pouch removed? She could feel his excitement as he squeezed the cream on to the palm of his hand and applied it to her breasts. He wasn't sure yet, though. He daren't allow massage to become caress as he felt the supple firm flesh and the tight rigid nipples under his hands. He could not prevent his erection nudging into her side as he stretched across her body to reach the furthest side.

Stephanie moved on to her side and looked down at his penis. It was already weeping a tear of fluid and had left a little wet trail where it had rubbed along her side.

She smiled to herself. If she were to take him in her hand now it would only be a matter of seconds before he came. She put her hand down under his cock and found his balls. She weighed them in her hand as if trying to estimate how much they held. She squeezed them not at all gently and Norman moaned. Then she let them go and laughed.

'Bring me some mineral water, Norman.'

Norman got up immediately and went into the bedroom hoping, no doubt, this was just a temporary delay. Stephanie watched his erection bobbing along in front of him as he walked. Bruno did not move. he stood as usual his arms crossed over his chest, his forehead wreathed in sweat, a look bordering on hatred smouldering in his eyes.

The water was ice cold and Stephanie sipped it before putting the glass, already wet with condensation, against Norman's penis.

'It must be very hot, Norman.'

'Yes, madam.'

'Do I make you hot, Norman?'

'Yes, madam.'

'Why is that, Norman?'

'You are very attractive, madam.'

'Would you like to fuck me, Norman?'

He hesitated, perhaps fearing that if he said yes it would provoke punishment.

'I asked you a question, Norman.'

'Yes, madam, I would.'

'A little more oil between my shoulder blades,' she ordered, turning on her stomach and putting the water down on the terracotta tiles. He knelt again and resumed the massage.

'That's enough,' she said. He stopped.

Stephanie lay still. Norman waited, his erection

throbbing inches from her oiled flesh and the object that would give him release. He did not move. She knew that the temptation to throw himself on her, to bury his cock deep into that hairy open cunt was almost unbearable.

Laying on her stomach, her face turned away from the slave, Stephanie could not help but smile. Her body felt pampered, smothered in the rich oil and basking in the sun. She could feel Norman's tension and was enjoying it immensely. Occasionally over the next half an hour she moved around on the lounger and watched his greedy eyes search out every detail of her cunt and thighs and breasts. Not for a moment did his erection flag. If she cared to look she could see the engorged veins. He was uncircumcised and his foreskin still covered most of his glans. How he would love to reach down and pull the foreskin back, or better still, have her do it. Well, that was never going to happen and his disappointment was going to be complete.

The game was over. Her mood changed. She wanted some time alone before Devlin came back.

'Take him back, Bruno,' she said.

Norman said nothing but his eyes pleaded with her. He would get no relief in the cellars. This woman, with the hard cold voice, was not going to give him any comfort. He got to his feet. Bruno handed him the worksuit which he clambered into while Bruno picked up the leather pouch. They left. Stephanie noticed they used the little door that the men had used last night. It must be some sort of passage directly to the cellars.

Stephanie relaxed. Experimentally she ran a finger between the lips of her cunt. She was not surprised to find a wetness there. The knot of her clitoris felt hard too. But, without too much difficulty, she restrained herself from harder contact. Masturbation on this island would be like drinking water while sitting in a vat of wine. And in any event she thought she could hear the faintest hum of engines on the lake in the far distance. Devlin as on his way back.

She walked over to the parapet. Sure enough, in the distance, a dark speck was heading for the island. It did not take long before the speck became the definite shape of a boat cutting across the placid water leaving a white trail behind it. She watched, fascinated, as the boat got closer. She watched the wake of the boat, churned up by the propellers, gradually die away until the calm water re-established itself as though never disturbed. It was like watching the condensation trails of jets high in the sky as they gradually faded away.

She pulled on the diaphanous wrap. Though it was obviously intended to be worn with the bikini underneath, Stephanie had no intention of putting the costume on again. She slipped into a pair of high-heeled sandals and walked down through the castle to the jetty to await the boat's arrival. As the boat got closer she could see Devlin was sitting aft with another man. They were talking intently. She had expected Devlin to be alone. She pulled the transparent wrap around herself more tightly and thought of running upstairs to change, but then dismissed the idea as pointless and even faintly ridiculous. After what she had experienced already on the island modesty seemed distinctly out of place. It was a decision she would regret.

WILD

Andrea Arven

Science Fantasy and erotica seem to inhabit similar realms of our imagination. Both genres operate in the hyper-real as opposed to the down-to-earth. Both involve the attention to the detail of elements such as clothes, technology and design. In a way, both subjects are fetishistic. Andrea Arven's books combine the best of these two worlds to take the action-packed adventure story into the domain of the sexual.

Imagine *Mad Max* where the central characters are women; highly-sexed, beautiful women who inhabit a land of extreme danger and startling tropical splendour and you'll be on the right track. In this sequel to *Wicked*, heroine, Fee Cambridge, her pirate lover and personal assistant are embroiled in a plot to recover virtual reality discs which can take the fantasies of the user and turn them into reality. In this extract, handsome pirate, Will, has survived an attack on his life by warrior Amazenes who want him as the sacrificial prize at their unholy bacchanalia. *Wanton* – the third and final book in the trilogy is published in April 1994.

Will opened his eyes and saw he was under water. He wouldn't move his body just yet, he decided. He couldn't for the moment remember why but he was sure deep within himself that it as a very bad idea.

His eyes moved slowly. Even his eyeballs hurt in the green aqueous light. It was all green, humming and green. Ripples of liquid light danced up the walls. Plants hung in riotous confusion dripping from some height above him. He could hear water, its rich moist tinkle.

He was alive. He could see. He could hear. Will moved his body very slightly and pain knifed horrifically through him. He was certainly alive.

Later on someone bent over him. He was lifted slightly, that hurt too, and they gave him drink and spoonfed him liquid food. They washed his face and he slept again.

He came round again and knew he was in a building with a lot of water in it. He could hear the water and there was a funny smell in the air. The building didn't have much of a roof because the weak sunlight flooded gently down through a mass of vines and growing plants. He saw the ripples of light again and knew them for reflections. Shortly he would work out what had happened to him, why he was here, where he was, but at the moment his memory could rest sealed off. He knew he was safe. He knew he was being looked after. That was enough.

There were two of them and one was horrific, her body a dance of colour that was wholly inhuman. He didn't know if it was tattoo, or liquid crystal, or if she was an alien. But both tended him with gentleness and soon he knew that strength would begin to flow back into his big exhausted body.

They fed him. They washed him. They lay with him in the night and kept him warm.

'Wing,' said Will.

'You are awake. You know me.' Wing clapped her hands. 'You have been so ill but now you are truly better.'

'Where am I?'

'We are nowhere. It is a ruined bathhouse but the water is good. If you feel strong enough you must use the hot springs. It will help.'

'What happened?'

'Ash saved you. She fought the Amazene. She tricked them over the poison. We brought you here. We are safe, Wolf. Quite safe. No one comes here. No one knows we are here.'

'Ash?'

'That is not her name but that is what she calls herself.'

'The snake lady.'

'Yes.' Wing looked sad. 'She saved you.'

'Good. I will thank her. Did Janine get away? The Townsister.'

'Yes, she got away.' Wing looked steadily at Will.

'Good. I hope she's safe. She was real trouble.'

'Are you hungry?'

'Yes, I think I am.'

Wing laughed. 'I will feed you. And I will tell Ash you are back with us in your own mind. She will be so happy.'

They changed his bedding. They helped him to lie in the hot water and feed on its mineral strength, letting his tortured muscles recover. They fed him and they continued to warm his bed in the night, one each side of him, their naked bodies pressed close to his. For in this warm empty paradise none of them wore any clothes. It had a primeval innocence at first, but as Will's health and strength returned, the innocence began to slip away.

He became bored lying on his back all day in the warm filtered sunlight buzzing with insects. He levered himself from his bed and went out of the ruined building, through its mock-classical columns, to see how the world went on. Out there he squatted painfully and let the heat of the sun penetrate his aching muscles. He must start taking some exercise and loosen up. It was just that he was so tired and there was a voluptuous pleasure in being waited on by the two women, though one of them never spoke and hardly touched him except when it was necessary. He wondered who the snake woman was, whether she wanted to go to the Town. For himself, he felt he could stay here forever.

His tanned body was the colour of stone and it blended with the columns of the building. He sat still and when the two girls came back from wherever they had been, they did not see him. Their heads were close together and they were chattering, laughing, though he could not hear the words or the joke. Will kept still, watching.

They had been gathering plants. They put them

down and sat on the grassy ground, stretching and relaxing. Above them the little cliff reared and its vegetation cast speckled shadows. The snake woman rolled suddenly and her body flickered brilliantly, inhuman in its uncertain shape. Wing went over and knelt by her and Will saw Wing bend over the supine girl and lay her lips on hers. Wing's hair fell in a loose black sheet and covered from view the two kissing but Will's heart thundered and he knew what they did. He saw Wing's hand drift down the rounded contours of the painted body, lingering over the mount of the breast, over the inviting softness of the belly. Then her lips followed her hand and slowly in the sunsoaked, shadowsplashed air she kissed the body beneath hers, kissed it with the slow savour of one who does what she does by right, by custom.

The body on the ground moved, lifted itself into the intimacy of the embrace, and the legs came open. Will saw Wing lower her head still further until her hair caressed the thighs and belly of the snake girl, her face bent into the body below her. The palms of his hands were greasy and moist as he saw her buttocks, now facing him, lift as she bent to her self-appointed and so very welcome task.

The snake girl let one hand come up and idly she began to play with the upraised buttocks. She caressed their shape, moulding her palm to each little pointed cheek in turn. Then her fingers slid within the cleft and Will saw Wing push back slightly into the invading hand. Now the fingers ran deep between the cheeks and pushed hard in and Wing's little body jerked. The snake girl had her knees up and Wing was bent right over between her thighs whilst her own more secret place was vulnerable to violation. Will was not close enough to see the moist rosy flesh below where the snake girl penetrated but he knew where her fingers went, what she did.

The snake girl cried out, her body glittering in jagged flames of colour, her hips lifting to the eager sucking mouth. As her passion was fulfilled, so Wing began to cry out, lifting her face and sobbing as her rear clenched the wicked invasive fingers. The snake girl worked them vigorously. Wing sat up, forcing them further in, and plainly came to climax.

She edged forward after a few moments and eased herself off the violating hand. She twisted round and lay on the ground alongside the snake girl. They put their arms round each other and kissed face to face, their bodies pressed together, breasts crushed between them.

Will's skin felt too tight. His chest was constricted and he sweated as if he had a fever. He got quietly to his feet and went into the bathhouse. He slid into the vast cistern where the cold water leaked through and swam briefly in its icy embrace. Beyond him in a square-built pool the hot mineral water steamed faintly, sulphurously.

That night Will lay awake in the dark, his mind helplessly running over what he had witnessed. His body, returning to some approximation of its normal strength, burned. At either side of him the two long warm soft forms pressed close.

He lay still, burning, his chest heaving up and down. His breathing was harsh in the silent warm damp air. It was impenetrably dark, so dark it pressed down on him where he lay.

He felt one of them stir. He kept still. She moved slightly and he felt her listening, felt her thinking. Then a hand was laid hesitantly upon his chest. His breathing shuddered slightly and the hand slipped down his body, warm as silk. In his mind's eye he saw Wing, her

181

hand sliding down the snake girl's body. His body leapt in hot response. The hand on him quested lower, crossed his belly, touched his springing hair and found the thick stem of his urgent sex.

Will didn't know whether his eyes were open or shut. He lay on his back and felt the hand grasp his cock and squeeze gently. His whole soul, his whole body, was all focused on the one part of him and its crying need for release.

The hand caressed him with knowledge and experience. He felt lips at his shoulder, on his chest. The figure reared itself beside him in the dark and bent over him. Hair brushed his face. Warm sweet lips touched his cheek, his nose, then found his lips. Will turned to face her and kissed her fully and firmly, his mouth opening hers and tasting hers and his tongue seeking her tongue. He felt her breasts soft against his muscled chest and moved his body slightly so that his skin could distinguish the feel of her nipples, papery and soft in repose but elastic firm as they became erect.

His cock was a joy. Her thigh was pressed against his and her hand as busy, squeezing, moving up and down. Then she released him. She felt for his hand, found it, and clasping it lightly she led it over her own smooth body, leading it down till it brushed against warm hair. She curled his fingers and he pressed them gently forward, into her, into her sex, warm and open for him. He caught her head with his other hand and pressed her face into his and then he rolled his big body onto hers, pushing away her hands as he opened her thighs and found the way in. His need was urgent but he controlled himself and was gentle. Her legs were parted and his cock found the damp entrance he needed. He lifted his hips and brought his cock up, pushing, urging it in, and she drew up her knees and helped him.

His cock entered glory. She was tight all around him with a lovely firm elastic grip of wet sliding flesh and as he went in and out of her he felt the need to climax rise like a hot flood. He wanted to kiss her breasts but they were below him, under his chest, so he kissed her throat and her ears and her lips.

She was now thrusting up into his body, her own need manifest. He could feel her cunt tremble and he knew that she too was going to come. He lifted himself up on one arm and thrust savagely into her, using all his returning strength to pound his cock into her as they came to orgasm together. She cried out and he let go with a sob and his spunk leapt along his shaft and filled her. He pumped again and again till he was empty. She too came to quietness beneath him and her body drooped back and he bore down softly now, letting her relax with his slack cock still firmly held in her hot wet embrace.

He got his arm under her shoulders and held her to him in the dark. He had forgotten the other girl but now he felt her move as they rearranged themselves. Tiredness washed over him. His body was peaceful. In the watery murmur of the hiding place he fell profoundly asleep. He did not know which of the girls he had fucked.

Will assumed he had been with Wing. Ash, the snake girl, kept away from him apart from in the darkness of the night, and he found himself unsurprised by the knowledge that Wing enjoyed sexual relations with a woman. Some dark part of him liked it. He found the sight of two women in erotic combination enflaming, and that he might use one of their bodies himself was also immensely satisfying to him. Since his sexual rebirth, neither girl had put any clothing on so he followed suit, staying naked himself in their bizarre

183

Eden remote from the rest of mankind. His physical prowess, his muscular strength, returned in a slow wave through the passing hours and days and he experienced a deep mental contentment.

It was to get better.

The next night he slept at first but woke in the murmurous dark to the quiet splendid joy of the two women pressed against him. He moved slightly, savouring the feel of them, the knowledge that they were there and that they waited on him by day and one of them served him by night. It was all the finer because he was strong again. He was a muscled package of energy, of fierce strength, of endurance, of great stamina, with intelligence as well as power, and it pleased him to lie idle in the sun and be fed and washed and be their purpose in life.

A hand was on his body and he sighed deeply and happily. His cock was springy and erect. His balls glowed in anticipation. Hair brushed his shoulder. Lips found his. Her sweet individual woman-smell touched his nostrils. He kissed her, nosing against her face in the dark, tasting the shape of her features. He turned to face her so that he might feel the points of her breasts brush his chest, so that she might rub her body like a cat against his and press her little belly forward into his loins catching his rigid shaft between the two of them, squeezing. Her breathing deepened and he could feel the rise and fall of her breast as she pressed against him. He pushed a leg between her silky thighs and she began to fall back, wanting him on her, wanting him in her. He kissed her throat, her nipples, feeling her arch her back, feeling the heat from between her legs beat up against him.

She drew her legs right up, so far up that for a moment he was confused in the dark. Then he understood. She hooked her legs over his shoulders so that

184

her cunt reared beneath him, gaping, begging for penetration, offering the maximum exposure, the maximum entrance. For a moment he held her legs and dropped his head, feeling his hair brush her inner legs. He took her into his mouth and sucked. She rolled under him and he heard her gasp and moan with delight. Her taste was nectar, sweet, musky, rich and powerful. He sucked and then let his tongue invade her, tasting the inside of her cunt, running his tongue round and feeling its pulpy excitation. He found her clitoris and sucked it till she cried out.

He pulled himself up and lowered his flaming cock into where he had sucked. He was holding her by her calves, her body doubled right over to receive him, and as his cock slid thick and hard into her vibrating inner body, he felt her twist and push to draw him in, further in, till he was buried deep inside her.

He was racked by his lust. He began to thunder into her. His body hit hers with a loud slamming motion and his balls slapped against her. She must have squeezed her cunt because he felt it grip his shaft as he rammed it home again and again, beside himself, caught in his fierce dark joy, wanting her hard and wanting her to want him hard.

He gave a sob and his cock burst as he shot into her. She was throwing her body up to take him, to make his fierce thrusts fiercer, and suddenly her cunt was all different and she was coming around his climaxing cock. Still he thrust into her but now he was letting her down, letting her relax. He let her legs slip down onto the bed and as his belly touched hers, he felt it throb and flex with the potency of her orgasm.

She clung to him, utterly his in the moment of supreme capitulation. He lowered his great head to rub it against her in his wordless joy, and he felt the salt tears on her cheeks. He licked her tears and kissed her face, cuddling her to him. After a moment or two she moved so that she was leaning up over him and now he lay on his back. She stroked his hair back from his brow, kissed his face, and then his mouth. He found her very sweet, very affectionate, and he kissed her back slowly, gently, lovingly.

His body jumped. He felt her kiss his belly, his hips and then slide on down till her face was buried in his hot hairy groin with his cock still slick wet from her cunt. Only, she still was kissing his mouth. Another mouth kissed his cock. He lay warm between the two poles of desire. One girl kissed his mouth, his eyes, his face, his throat. The other kissed his cunt-wet cock. He lay feeling her lip and gently suck what she found there, rubbing her face on him, and almost he began pleasurably to doze, allowing them both the freedom to play with his body and do as they wished.

All about him warm soft flesh pressed. He stirred slightly and moved his hands finding breasts and buttocks. He stroked what he found, fondling a nipple, letting his hands slide within the cleft of buttocks, feeling moist flesh in secret places quiver as his fingers ran lightly over it. The girl at his cock was stroking him, sucking him and caressing his balls. He felt power return to his shaft and it lifted and firmed a little.

They moved and he became aware in the thick darkness that both had their heads bent together over his sex and that two tongues wove about his lifting cock. His exploring hands found a double set of buttocks lifted before him, one to each side, and he stroked them, running his fingers down between them and then seeking lower, further in.

There were two cunts. He had known it, known there were the two girls, but that they should simultaneously give him their bodies, excite and arouse his, argued a generosity of spirit he had no right to expect. For days they had both looked after him. At first they had even half carried him out to perform his necessary bodily functions, he had been so weak. They had tended him, almost worshipped him here in this templelike building with its eternal spring of pure water and the endless sunlight pouring through the tracery of vines that was the roof. They had dealt with his every physical need and they still did. Here in the liberating privacy of the night they caressed his skin with theirs, their skin a soft push on him. They took his intimate body and pleasured it with skill and willingness and emotional abandon. Will slid his fingers into the two uptilted cunts and felt the one soupy wet and the other slightly moist, unused, needing to have its springs released to flood it with the sweetness of its sister.

He pulled himself up and put his face to it. He kissed it, felt it shudder deliciously, and suddenly she rolled and fell across him on her back. He kissed her cunt again and began to suck her in earnest. The other girl was up kissing his shoulders, his neck, his hair. He pushed the girl down and came forward onto his knees to sink his cock into where he had sucked. Behind him he felt hands flutter over his buttocks. He went into the opening that beckoned in the dark and began softly, gently, to bring his cock and it to climax, lifting her with him, fondling her inner places with his veiny member, rubbing on her clitoris with each inward thrust.

Behind him a wicked wet finger found his rear and began to press on it. Will gritted his teeth and contained his growing excitement.

Around his cock he felt the silky smooth cunt begin to grow hot and coarse in its demands. Its heat enveloped him. It seemed to suck his goodness from himself. It throbbed and he felt it vibrate. At his rear a finger slid inside him and his cock exploded.

'Damn!' he shouted. His spunk ran hot into the cunt that held him. He jerked helplessly but though he had come before he meant to, teased by the delicious invader in his rear, he felt the urgent throb around his slackening cock so he pushed in as hard as he could though his cock waned even as he did so. She came, hot and thick, a rumbling juicy flow that was lava-hot. He pushed a few more times feeling her contract about him. He stopped, his head hanging so that his hair brushed her breasts. His arse was being fucked by the finger up it. He got his arms under the girl he had just filled and held her, pushing his face into her soft pillowy breasts. He grunted as his violation continued. His cock slid from its warm bath as his arse stuck backwards towards its invader. Suddenly her other hand came under him, felt his dangling slack damp member and his loose swinging balls. The finger came out of him. Warm lips pressed sweetly to him, kissed his arse, kissed his cock, sucked it a little and then he was allowed to lie down.

They rearranged silently, Will between them, each girl again pressed warmly to his sides. Will held each of them, an arm about her. His cock and balls felt fine and glittery. His arse tingled faintly, deliciously. His belly was soft and empty. Four breasts pressed against his sides. Two cunts dribbled slightly as his spunk slid between thighs from overfull orifices. The two girls were his, his to play with, and he was theirs. He knew now they were both skilled at lovemaking. They could turn him inside out with their sweet demands if they chose and he would die to keep them satisfied and coming back for more. That was all right. That was good. This would be a sweet death, night after night in the watery murmur of darkness. Will felt sleep wash in a velvet flood over his body and he gave way to it, relaxed, a fine animal full-fed.

They were running out of food. Will became aware that the girls fed him as much as he required but ate little themselves. Their bodies were lissom and delightful, barring the extraordinary, brilliant and terrifying snakeskin. He had not been close enough to her in the daytime to find out whether it was decoration or in some ghastly way a natural phenomenon.

He was sitting in the sun when the snake girl suddenly appeared out of the undergrowth quite near him. He gasped in shock. She carried her machete and across the weird mural of her body blood splashed in big red gouts. He sprang to his feet, terrified suddenly for Wing. What if this monster had killed the little Chinese girl? She was a freak and he had all but forgotten it in the hot strong pleasures of the night. Now he could smell the blood on her body rank in the sun and because she was close to him, he saw the streaky little cloud of hair in her groin.

'Where is Wing?' he said roughly. He would kill this thing if she had harmed his little lover.

The snake girl turned and stood to one side. Wing came out of the brush behind her carrying some flayed rabbits. They had been hunting, that was all.

He looked at Wing and the snake girl went by him into the bathhouse.

'What is it?' asked Wing, puzzled. 'We needed meat, Wolf. I think we will have to go soon for we do not have much to eat now.'

'Nothing,' said Will. He was ashamed of himself. Wing went by him and vanished into the bathhouse in her turn.

After a while Will followed them. The snake girl had saved his life and he had not yet thanked her. He felt bad about his suspicions. She had shown no sign of jealousy that he coupled with Wing in the night. Indeed, she had joined in. He had accused her in his mind of murder.

They were in the cold cistern together, gasping and laughing as they washed their bloody dusty bodies. They were fooling like puppies together, pushing each other under, coming up underneath each other, kissing, touching, rolling in the water. He squatted in plain view and they ignored him. Instead they wove their bodies together using the freedom of the water. Now they kissed more often and finally they climbed out of the water, shaking themselves, rapt, it appeared for each other.

Wing kissed the snake girl. It was the closest Will had been to her in the daylight since his recovery. He could see how her hair was oddly streaked and pale at her skull as if it wanted to lift itself away from her. Her patterned skin shone through the water droplets. She was passive as Wing kissed her and when Wing opened her legs, Will's eyes narrowed in shock. Wing held her legs apart and the snake girl lay with her eyes shut, ignoring them both. Will looked where his eyes were led, invited, and he saw that even here the flesh was decorated with patterns woven into the sexual flesh itself. Wing peeped slyly at him, held her hair back with her two hands, and buried her face in the snake girl's body.

Will felt faint shock. The two girls were so close, so deliberate in their actions. Wing had lifted her rear provocatively just in front of him and was wiggling her behind as she sucked down on the other girl. Slowly Will reached forward.

He touched the warm pale saffron buttocks and then he opened them and looked down into the cleft. Wing's little fawn strawberry-shaped bottom puckered and he knew she was deliberately working her muscles. Below he saw the moist webbing of her sex, the skin of her outer labia a darker colour than the rest of her body. He came forward on his knees and began to slide his erect cock into her body, into her, even as she sucked at the snake girl.

His heart pounded as he thrust into the wicked invitation. He began to fuck hard so she juddered against the open sex of the snake girl. Somehow he was angry and he knew his body was dancing to their tune, to Wing's tune. He wanted to come quickly, rudely, but it was too good, a feast too good to gobble. He slowed down and with long firm movements sank his cock deeply into her body and then withdrew it till only the hot swollen tip remained within her. Watery light rippled along his shaft when it was withdrawn. Wing's bent back before him was pale green in the filtered sunlight, the incestuous plants writhing together above them forming a natural trellis with their tendrilled embrace.

Wing trembled and he felt her change and knew she had orgasmed. She held herself for a moment as he still rode into her, and then she lifted her head and broke free from his cock his cock so that it hung before him, erect, a viscous film from her come over it. She rolled from between the thighs of the snake girl leaving them open to Will's eyes, his unsatisfied cock pointing at the magic painted secret flesh of her body. He stared. The snake girl opened her eyes wide in shock. They were vast and blue and brilliant as the sky. Will's hot stone-coloured eyes absorbed her open body, split in welcome to his needy half-used cock. He lurched to his feet and stumbled out of the bathhouse.

He went over through the grove of trees to the cliff. He dealt swiftly and unsatisfying with his need and cursed the worm in paradise that must needs spoil what they had here. He began to run out onto the prairie, forcing his body into a rhythm it could maintain. He needed to find out if his strength was fully returned. Their time was over here.

They ate the rabbits that night and agreed to leave for the Town the following morning. Wing did not know how far away they were. They must go north and make a westing also, but they did not want to come back to the city and must be careful.

Still the snake girl did not speak. Will and Wing went to bed together that night but the snake girl did not join them and Will found he missed her warmth at his side.

He woke very early in the morning hearing the slight shrieks of the creatures of the dawn though it was still dark. He could see very faintly the dark vines above him twisting across a slightly fainter sky. He slipped from the bed and went over to the hot pool where he slid eel-like into the water and allowed its goodness to penetrate his sleepsoaked skin. Then he went over to the cold cistern and washed the faint sour-egg smell from his body. He was cold as he went outside. The air was aching in its purity and the dew was falling. The sky glowed, light over the horizon but still dark above his head. The stars were invisible except far to the west, the shout of the coming dawn washing them from the icy loft of the sky.

The east began to flood softly with light and in its low rays he saw the snake girl sitting on the wet grass, shivering. He stayed still, watching her.

As the sky lightened a mist began to rise from the vast grassland about them so that the light became pearly and dull for a while. Will saw the snake girl move and then take a long iridescent shard of multihued colour and lay it on the ground. After a few minutes, the sky perceptibly brightening, she took another great strip and laid it beside the first.

She was shedding her skin.

When she had peeled her shoulders he went over to her. She jumped slightly when she saw him and he saw how strange she was.

In the night she had cut her hair. Its curious ugly streaky blackness was gone and she had a short pale-wheat fuzz like thick deep-piled velvet over her head. Beads of dew lay on it. As he looked at her she peeled another great strip of snakeskin and he saw cold naked pink raw flesh revealed underneath. She was shivering uncontrollably.

He sat beside her, watching. After a few minutes he began to help her, picking off the frozen shards of colour. All around them mist spiralled silently upwards into the opalescent sky. It was flushed a deep peach in the east.

Will peeled her back and saw ordinary cold human skin revealed more and more. He felt her jump slightly each time his fingers brushed her back. He moved round to her face, his gold-flecked stony eyes softened and greenish-brown. He peeled what remained on her front. She was passive, quite passive, submitting to his hands over her body. He touched her breasts, her inner thighs, her cheeks, her brow, under her arms, and at last she was all naked, freshly skinned and vulnerable.

The mist was nearly gone and the sky was red-streaked. Will ran his hand over the soft warm thatch of her head and his cock leapt. It was the sweetest thing his palm had ever felt, the warm soft velvet of her head. Like moleskin it had no lie of its own. It lay the way he stroked it.

193

She lay back and opened her legs. Will looked at her, considering what she wanted. Then his fingers went in and he found the last of her false skin and gently he peeled the tiny landscape of her sex.

Her body was shivering hard now. He came up over her and slid his cock within her. He let it rest there for a moment. She was dry inside and not ready for him. Holding his cock in her, he began to kiss her face, her breasts, her trembling throat where a pulse beat.

Her eyes were open and they changed first, their blue brilliance becoming hazed. Her skin warmed and flushed partly from the rising sun and partly from the inner heat building in her, the fires he lit with his patient cock waiting for her to respond. Her breasts rose and her nipples hardened. Her arms came round him and she made whimpering noises in her throat and pressed up into his warm strong body. Her cunt softened as it gloved his prick and he felt moisture spring from her inner flesh to bathe and lubricate him. She brought her legs right up and folded them around his body, clinging to him, at last he began to work his cock in her, shafting her new-made body, letting the sun make a warmth on his back as his cock made a blaze in her body.

He began to fuck more strongly and he felt her rise to take him. Her teeth were at his shoulder and her fingers dug into his back. She was hot, very hot about his cock and he got an arm under her arching body and pulled her tight to his chest. Her head dropped back, her lips slightly parted, her eyes closed. Her face was drowned, ecstatic.

His belly was on fire and he burned to climax now. Her body was shuddering against his. Her cunt gripped him with tight spasmodic contractions. He plunged in and let his climax come. He felt his shaft ripple and he did not know whether it was from her or himself. Her submission was gone. Her teeth were bared she fought greedily to drain him, ripping her pleasure from his body and not hiding the extent of it from him.

When he lay beside her she came up and was astride him. Her face was tender and fierce and she kissed his chest and bit his nipples gently. She held his slack cock within her still, her inner cushioning softly holding him.

'Janine,' he said. 'You saved my life. Thank you.'

'I've changed my name.'

'But not your nature.'

'You think not?'

'I think this is how you always were, only you hid it.'

'I hated you going with Wing.'

'I kinda liked it, but I guess I'll stop. I think she prefers you.'

'I liked it. I like her,' admitted Janine. Her voice sank to a low note. 'But women are breast-milk and I guess I'm weaned.' She bent her head and nuzzled him, licking his skin, smiling at him. 'I must look terrible,' she said suddenly. 'I couldn't bear my head black any longer.'

'You are beautiful,' said Will with sincerity. 'Darling, so beautiful.'

She lifted herself slightly and squeezed her muscles. His cock jumped slightly and began to firm again. It was very slidy, bathed in the combined juices of their two bodies. Janine held herself slightly up from him and began to caress his re-awakening cock using only her inner muscles. She squeezed and stroked and rode very slightly up and down and all the time he filled and firmed within her.

'I wanted you,' she whispered as her cunt cradled his cock, rocked it. 'I've wanted you so much.'

After a while he caught her under her buttocks with his two hands and held her just over his belly. He pushed up, fucking her with little gentle slithery movements, his arm muscles trembling with the effort but whole and strong again.

'I thought you hated me,' he said.

She pushed his hands away and now that he was a rigid pole joining their two bodies, she began to fuck just the very tip of his cock in rapid fluttering movements, concentrating on his most sensitive part, squeezing it with the tighter neck of her cunt. His breathing changed and his cock swelled tighter, filling her until she could no longer bear to deny its full presence. She rode down hard on him, feeling the glory of his strong manhood pulsing within her, and suddenly she felt herself flame inside and she lost control so that Will took over and with a rapid series of powerful plunges up into her orgasm, he brought himself to climax once again.

'I was frightened of you.'

'Not any longer,' he murmured. 'Christ, you're so sweet,' Janine climbed stiffly off Will and kissed his body now warm and flooded with sunlight. She knelt over him and he felt her lips roam up and down him as he half slept, his every part comfortable and at ease. She began to lick his groin, lick his curling springing hair, lick his soft wet stick cock, lick his balls.

After a while she made him roll over and she kissed his back, under his hair, down his spine and onto his buttocks. He felt her hold his buttocks open, he felt the sunlight on his arse, he felt her lips silky as they kissed and sucked him there.

She made him roll over again so that he was on his back, and she laid her body on top of his. She lay on her back her head in his groin and her legs one either side of

196

his shoulders. When he lifted his head he looked straight up into her body laced with his own spunk. Her labia, dark-tipped and pansy-soft, wove about the curious little wrinkled lumps and strange bumps and cushionings on her inner sex. He found he felt odd in his throat and there was a tightening in his chest, pleasurable, sore. He brought his arms round under her thighs and felt for her breasts. He caressed them, squeezing the soft flesh up into its points, using his thumbs to nuzzle the sensitive tips. After a while he sat up and holding her legs open he bent his head and kissed at her sex, tasting her, tasting himself in her, mapping her intricate flesh till it was known territory. His territory. His tongue staked a claim on her and when he finally drew her tired body alongside his so that she could sleep, he was smiling.

Last of all she took his hand and turned it palm up. She touched the sapphire stain under the skin where the Amazene had marked him.

'I'm sorry for this,' she said seriously.

'It could have been worse,' he murmured. He grinned at his small joke but Janine shuddered. He had so nearly died.

'That meteor saved you,' she said, 'whatever it really was. I was a little beside myself at the time but the HeliPolice were out in force, you know. I don't think it was a natural phenomenon.'

Will leant on an elbow and looked down into her quiet face. 'You saved me, hero. The special effects were extra.'

'Is this gratitude?'

He kissed her. 'No. Self-indulgence. And long overdue.'

Wing woke them an hour later. It was time to eat what food they had left and to go. Wing saw the peace they had in each other, how their limbs glowed and were relaxed, how their eyes were soft and hazed with carnal release, and knew her time with their bodies was over. She didn't mind. She had not yet found what she wanted, though now after this time in paradise she knew more clearly what it was. She wanted the strength and vigour of man coupled with the softness and intimacy of a woman. She did not really want cock but she wanted to be mastered and to submit as well as being free to steal and invade. No matter. She would make a life for herself in the Town and perhaps there find what she wanted.

LINZI DREW'S
PLEASURE GUIDE

Outrageous Sex and How to Have It

Linzi Drew

There are experts and there are sexperts, and former editor of *Penthouse* magazine, Linzi Drew, is certainly one of the latter. She's a person who knows what it takes to keep the joy of sex alive and encourages her readers to do just that by being honest about their needs and true to their feelings, no matter how 'naughty'.

Her message is 'enjoy, enjoy' and *Linzi Drew's Pleasure Guide* shows us how we can get maximum pleasure out of that most enjoyable of recreational activities. Thanks, Linzi.

Also available from Nexus is *Letters to Linzi*, a compilation of the filthiest fantasies sent to her from men and women across the country.

Sex Toys and Masturbation

What costs nothing, doesn't hurt a soul and feels absolutely fantastic? Playing with yourself, masturbating, wanking, call it what you will! From a very early age, if Mummy doesn't scold us for touching ourselves; we explore that pleasure area between our legs and for the first time experience the warm rush of sexual excitement. Naturally we have no idea why it feels so good, but as we get older we learn the techniques that suit us and give us the most satisfying reward.

Masturbation is the major step for learning about what pleases us sexually. You guys have an organ so designed that I would imagine it's difficult to leave alone in boyhood, but we girls don't have it quite so easy. We don't have this phallic addition dangling between our legs; we have to go much further and explore the treasures hidden within.

The first masturbatory sensation that I can bring to mind is trapping a pillow tightly between my legs and literally riding it to orgasm. Even now it still works for me, but I must confess I prefer to use a man's taut muscled leg whenever one is available! Doctors and

Nurses is a game that I remember playing quite enthusiastically, both with the boy next door and with three or four girlfriends. I don't recall what my views were on this type of activity at the time, but I suspect it was something I thought I shouldn't be doing but which was definitely fun!

One thing that absolutely astounds me about masturbating is that in this day and age it is still a taboo subject. People *still* say it makes you go blind, and the like. Both men and women are actually bashful about admitting they indulge, and we even insult people by labelling them a wanker or a tosser! If you were to walk down the street and call out: 'Hey wanker!', every honest person should turn around and say, 'Who, me?' Mind you, I'm not suggesting for a moment you try this experiment!

Thankfully this isn't the case with everyone. In fact, I know many people with whom I can discuss the delights of self-satisfaction – men and women who feel totally relaxed with the concept of sexually arousing themselves. Bringing myself to orgasm is, for me, a way to relieve stress and relax totally, and it is a pastime that can be enjoyed by each and every one of us without guilt or embarrassment. And girls, we have so many wonderful sex toys to assist us. As a rule men seem to pore over erotica, and need only this and one or both of their hands to bring them instant sunshine. We're very different, and, as luck would have it, there are numerous sex aids on the market to bring us wonderful hedonistic pleasure. I asked a group of my female friends about their masturbating techniques.

Karen, a hairdresser from Berkshire, told me: 'I masturbate a lot. I was at the health club with a mate, and we both had a half-hour session on the sunbeds. When we came out she said to me how boring it was to lie there for thirty minutes. So I told her she should play with herself. I feel you can masturbate anywhere you feel comfortable, whenever you want to, just do it. I couldn't do without it. I remember there have been times when I've been driving home and I'd be that horny that I'd actually plan it out – you know, premeditated masturbation on the way home from work! I'd plan my route so that I'd know exactly where I would stop to finger myself. Sometimes I think I'm sick, but then I think it's fun and I'm not hurting anybody, so why not?'

Carrie, a twenty-four-year-old, happily married mother of two, spoke candidly of her collection of sex aids: 'I've got so many sex toys that if I walk into a sex shop, unless they've had a new delivery in recently, I have every toy in there! Anal beads are my favourite at the moment. I'll put four or five pairs up my arse and two in my pussy. I'll try anything. My favourite vibrator is one that you plug in. It's just the worst thing when you're almost there and your batteries run low. I'll tell you something funny that happened a few months ago. I had this vibrator that you attach different bits on to the end of. The one that I really loved wanking with had this soft cushion-type attachment. So there I was laid back on my bed, my legs spread, rubbing my clit like crazy with this wonderful little vibrating cushion, and I must have got so carried away, it fell off. I just had to have my cushion to finish me off, so I got some Superglue to stick it back on, but the Superglue cap fell off and stuck my vibrator to the bed. I was going crazy!'

Deirdre, a model from Holland, has a very unusual sex toy: 'I use my razor, you know, those wet-and-dry razors. I use that instead of one of those big, ugly dildos, which to me are a total turn-off and make a terrible noise. You just take the wet-and-dry and take the top off. Get rid of the blade of course, and then I just work it up and down against my clitoris. If I want to have an orgasm real quick it's perfect, and you can travel with it too!'

Personally I prefer my fingers with a handy bottle of baby oil, but each to their own! Lisa from the east end of London seemed to me slightly more traditional in her preferences: 'I love playing with myself and do it whenever I've got the time. I suppose I masturbate once or twice a day, in addition to getting fucked regularly, I must add. I own two vibrators and a dildo. One of my vibrators is the silver bullet type and very small, so I can keep it in my handbag and use it whenever I can slip off somewhere private to do so. I've got this big dildo as well that is black and absolutely fucking enormous. Probably about twelve inches. When I wank myself with that I just shove it all the way in and leave it buzzing inside me while I squeeze my clit. I like to wank with that when I'm feeling really dirty, but usually I just use my fingers, cover my cunt in lots of baby oil and then just finger myself. I like to take ages to make myself come. You know, build up to it a few times and just about when I'm on the brink, I stop for a moment and then go for the big build-up again. By the time I finally come, it's so intense it just seems to go on and on!'

Sharon, who works in TV, explained to me in a little more detail the euphoria that can be attained from her favourite sex toys – love balls: 'I've named them anal beads. There's five little balls on a string and I like to stick them up my arse, then finger myself with one hand. Then just as I'm about to have an orgasm, I pull the balls out one at a time, but all the way out. It's incredible, it really prolongs my orgasm.'

I did get around to talking to some male friends about how they like to wank. Micky is single and approaching his fortieth birthday, and has come up with the rather apt title of 'solo flying' for wanking. He told me: 'As well as having sex regularly, I love solo flying. I suppose on average I do it about three times a day. When I sleep alone I always wake up with an erection. A quick wank with one hand, dreaming of the lady in my life or whilst gazing at some sexy girl in a magazine, puts me in the right mood for the day. I don't understand the stigma about it. It feels good, it's free and I for one love it!'

My sentiments entirely! And just a few of these snippets of conversation enlighten us to the liberated attitudes and the various ways that these individuals pleasure themselves. I have a healthy sex life, but I also love to wank whenever time allows and, like Karen, when bronzing my body under a tanning bed, I always let my fingers do the walking. Like Lisa I carry a pocket-size vibrator in my handbag for convenient surreptitious wanks. Sneaking off someplace to play with myself makes it all the more fun. And like Micky I think there's few better ways to start the day than with a wank – except perhaps with a fuck!

Aside from catching a few minutes during a busy day to enjoy an orgasm or two, I like to plan a leisurely few hours alone specifically to play with myself. And there are so many ways to make the whole scenario ecstatic. My favourite music is a must, as is a thoroughly comfortable location – I generally choose my bedroom. I like to dress up in sexy lingerie, so that I can enjoy the pleasure of firstly stroking myself through silky panties, then pulling them off to one side before I really get down to business. I am very aroused by the visual aspect of sex, so I position a mirror at the end of my brass bed. Through the brass rails I like to watch my golden bullet vibrator plunging in and out of my pussy, and I savour that buzzing sound as the whole of my cunt comes alive. Or alternatively I enjoy my fingers, drenched in baby oil, stroking my greasy clit until it swells to twice its normal size and feels like it's on fire!

Talking of using music to add to the stimulating sensation reminds me of an amusing letter I once received. Frank, a widower from Bath, wrote to me to describe his pleasure: 'I love wanking to music. I find nothing more exciting than putting on my favourite classical music and wanking in time to the stroking of violins, booming of the bass drums and clashing of cymbals. I use my dick as a baton, stroking its entire length, building up as the music reaches a crescendo. My favourite tune at the moment is "Rule Britannia"!'

For people like Frank, wanking is probably their entire sex life. There's no shame in enjoying your own body as he obviously does.

Ignorant bigots might have a right good giggle at the thought of some lonely, elderly man stroking his baton to 'Rule Brittania'. But why not? It's his body reaching that mind-numbing crescendo! Dogmatists would exhibit their usual intolerant attitude and cast ridicule on a chap that gets his kicks from plunging his dick into a blow-up rubber doll. But why the hell shouldn't he? It's his dick pumping away inside that plastic paradise. Don't mock what you haven't tried!

Of course, masturbation is often practised by single people who for some reason are without a partner, and by men and women who are separated from their partners for periods of time. For instance, I could say that almost all of the guys in Her Majesty's Armed Forces are wankers, but that doesn't mean they won't fight the good fight! I should know exactly what they get up to; thousands of them write their dirty letters to me describing in explicit detail how pleasurable wanking can be. But believe me, I don't need to be convinced! Here's a few samples of the kind of horny, yet amusing correspondence, starting with a letter from some jolly Jack Tars:

'I expect you get loads of letters from bored, frustrated sailors. Well, we are at present on exercise for four weeks with no contact with the outside world. As most of us are chefs, we just love to eat food of our partners' bodies, but we can't think of anything better than to lick yoghurt off your super-duper nipples and lovehole.

'We wonder what you're up to at this moment in time – 30 May, 9.17 p.m.? We've had a vote and the majority say you're getting it doggy fashion with another cock in your mouth. Were we right? Probably not exactly spot on, but the mere thought of it had us all in a wanking frenzy!'

The next letter from the 'Desert Rats' was short and straight to the point: 'At the moment there are five of us in a tent with a picture of you. About five minutes ago, all of us wanked at the same time and spunked all over your photo. Could you please send us another?'

How could a girl refuse such a plea? Now to conclude these mucky masturbation masterpieces, a squaddie in Turkey wrote: 'Serving in Turkey is hard work and hot work and what makes it bad is that I am bursting for a good fuck. My only contact with sex at the moment is the magazines that my wife has been sending out to keep me on the boil for a bloody good sex session when I get home. I've been ogling some pictures of you. Your ample tits and your sweet cunt always manage to give me a good lob-on. How I would love to slide my cock deep inside your pussy whilst I explore your mouth with my tongue. I long to lick at your pussy. Oh, what a magic taste a good cunt is, and you have one hell of a tasty-looking slit.

'Anyway to the point of my letter. Would you take pity on a sex-starved squaddie and send me a signed photograph to lust over? Perhaps to make it extra special you could see your way to signing it, kissing it and maybe rubbing that sweet pussy of yours all over it? go on, please!'

Somewhat cheeky, maybe, but erotic photographs obviously help these guys keep their spirits and their peckers up!

Naturally I am not advocating that masturbation can replace love, affection and a fulfilling sex life, something I think we all want and need. But it can be an immensely pleasurable pursuit, a welcome addition to a good sex life or, in the absence of any sex life to speak of, a way to keep you going till better times come along!

Aside from giving lonely or disunited people some form of a sex life, masturbation can also provide a valuable way to help keep fraught marriages together. Sadly it's often the case that one half of a partnership is disinterested in sex from time to time, not infrequently when there are other problems and stresses within the marriage. All of us experience peaks and troughs of desire. Everyone has a baseline sexuality which has to do with age, upbringing and their general attitude to sex. And most people are more sexual when they're feeling good about themselves than they are when they're feeling bad. This ego-libido correction is usually stronger in males than in females, so if the problem is only that of a temporary abstinence, masturbation can more often than not see the other half of the partnership through the barren times!

John, an elderly, retired friend of mine from the Midlands, has been married for over forty years, and for the last five years his wife has shown little enthusiasm for sex. John, on the other hand, has an avid interest. He revealed:

* * *

The other night I went to bed dreaming I was rubbing baby oil all over a TV actress. I'll mention no names! The naughty things I think of in the privacy of my own bedroom would astound you. Most of my respectable friends have stopped having sex. One said he'd rather have a corned-beef sandwich and a half of shandy!

Now my wooing days are long since gone, I don't want to get hung up and frustrated. I find the titillation of magazines recharges my batteries. I am Ever Ready! I like to get my rocks off in a passionate way and vary my routine. I admit I enjoy watching porno movies. The women really put the men through their paces. Some people say that too much fucking saps your body and wanking affects your brainpower. What a lot of twaddle! A healthy sex life keeps you young and vital. And every now and then the missus catches me at it and seems vaguely interested!

I know I joke about my pal and his corned-beef sandwich. Of course sex sometimes drops off when you've been married a long time. I now get my rocks off by reading magazines and watching blue movies. My wife understands that, because to us both, friendship counts a lot in our relationship. But it still is wonderful to look back on our early married times.

So far in this chapter we've been discussing masturbation as a solitary pleasure. But mutual masturbation is a wonderful way to learn what excites your partner, and is perfect to indulge in with someone you've just met – both of you can peak sexually, yet still be responsible and practise safe sex. It's also one hell of a way to spend a lazy afternoon! I know from experience that men enjoy watching a woman masturbate, and for me that is a great turn-on. I have one boyfriend who told me the other day that all he needs to do to get me in the mood for a great fuck is for him to ask me to let him watch me play with my pussy. He was right – spot on, in fact – but funnily enough I hadn't even realised how much it excited me! I too love to watch a man wank himself off. Sometimes I can hardly decide where to focus my eyes. Should I stare at his engorged prick or the expression on his face?

Now if you feel exactly as I do that wanking with a partner is perfectly acceptable and immensely pleasing, please keep on at it. On the other hand, if you or your lover can't quite come to terms with it, do relax and give it a try. Put aside a whole evening to explore. Make your bedroom or lounge as comfortable and intimate as possible. Dim the lights just a little, or perhaps buy some candles for that special ambiance. Select some relaxing music and start off by undressing each other. To feel confident, girls, make sure you are dressed in your sexiest undies. You may want to experiment by using just your fingers and hands, but I suggest that, before this delightful planned evening of masturbation, you take a trip to a sex shop and purchase one or two aids to play around with. Perhaps he might start off with a vibrator or a dildo for her; and maybe, girls, you could get him some sexually explicit magazines or some of those exciting anal beads for retrieval just as the precise moment of his ejaculation!

The whole idea is to relax and not be embarrassed about arousing each other manually and allowing the other to watch while we stimulate ourself to orgasm. Let your partner see what excites you, and show them how to stroke you in the most effective, exciting way. That is the key to learning. One of my favourite sex games is to bring myself to orgasm with my lover watching closely; just as I'm about to come, he slips his cock right into my orgasmic pussy. Perhaps I'll try pulling beads out of my arse at the same time. Wow! Am I going to have a prolonged orgasm!

Because this chapter is all about masturbation I have featured lots of letters from my days as editor of *Penthouse*. Whilst editing and appearing nude in a magazine of that genre, I was, as you can imagine, inundated with letters regarding wanking. One that I found particularly sexy focused on solitary masturbation and led on to a couple enjoying mutual masturbation; it was from Dave in Essex. Dave wrote:

I just had to write to you about an incident that was potentially the most embarrassing of my life, but which turned out to be one of the most enjoyable. it was at the start of this recent hot weather. An urge came upon me to go out and buy *Penthouse*. I hadn't bought one for a few months and was looking forward to a leisurely evening alone with my *Penthouse* (while my girlfriend Lisa was out giving private Spanish lessons) and to a good wank. Well, I'd forgotten how good the magazine is. I went to my bedroom, stripped to my boxer shorts and wanked twice over the letters pages alone. Boy, those letters were hot. But that was just the start. Where do you find all those beautiful girls? I went rock hard at the sight of each and every one of them. I shot my load again, imagining that those stunningly sexy women were naked in my bedroom, thickly coating their mouths in bright red lipstick, then slowly sucking me off – one of my favourite fantasies – before putting my throbbing, lipstick-stained knob inside their glistening tight pussies.

By now it was getting dark and I had been lost in my own fantasy world for more than an hour. My penis was purple and sensitive and I was pretty knackered. But I forgot my tiredness when I turned the page and saw the first of a series of shots of you, Linzi – the sexiest selection of erotic photos I've ever had the pleasure of seeing. I came just by looking at your tits. Despite the heat in my bedroom I shivered with pleasure at the thought of what my tongue and tool could do for your exquisite pussy.

Anyway, to get to what could have been the embarrassing bit: I was masturbating over your picture so fiercely that I didn't hear the front door open, my girlfriend come in, climb the stairs and enter the bedroom. I'm sure she could hear the sounds and thought I had a woman in there with me.

At first she was open-mouthed. Then before I could say anything, she pulled up her skirt, pulled down her pants and told me to carry on masturbating, but looking at her pussy and not yours!

Lisa joined me on the bed and at first I carried on wanking, staring at her pussy lips that were getting juicier and juicier as she frigged herself. She told me not to touch her as she spread her legs, faced me and stuck two fingers inside. Her pussy was bright pink and bulging now as I watched her finger-fuck herself until she came. Then she allowed me to suck on her fingers and drink her come. Gripping my swollen dick I told her I wanted to bend her over and fuck her like a dog. I thought I would explode if she wouldn't let me inside her soon. Playing with her boyish tits, she chastised me and informed me that I'd probably been coming all evening and now it was her turn. Relenting slightly, she allowed me to wank her to her second climax, and then she got really generous. She spread open her pussy lips and let me lick her to her third orgasm, before demanding that I fuck her doggy-style to her fourth orgasm of the evening! I think I still came out on top.

Anyway, now Lisa insists on buying me *Penthouse* each month, and every Monday night after her Spanish lesson we play the same kind of game. I wank at home alone in the bedroom, anticipating all that fun to come when she gets home and catches me red-handed!

Lisa and Dave make masturbation a prelude to some sucking and fucking. Sounds like fun to me! I think there's been enough said in this chapter to convince any reluctant wankers that it's fun and free, and that there's no shame in it. I'd conclude by telling you that writing about it has made me feel so randy that I've got to dash off and have a wank, but that kind of frivolous remark gets printed only in men's magazines – besides, typing one-handed is a doddle! But I will nevertheless bring this chapter to a conclusion by recommending some fascinating sex aids.

- A Glow-In-The-Dark Vibrator, available from Knutz, 1 Russell Street, London WC2.
- Anal Love Beads – enormous black rubber ones on a rubber string. Available mail order from the Rob Gallery, Weteringschans 253, 1017 XJ, Amsterdam.
- Strap-On Clitoris Vibrator: 'Judy's Butterfly' is available from Yago Holdings, Unit 18, Roman Way, Coleshill Ind. Estate, Coleshill, Birmingham B46 1RL.

- Vibrator with foreskin which slides back and forth – also from Yago Holdings.
- A copy of the video *Linzi Drew's Striptacular* – one hour dedicated to erotic striptease. And *Members Only*, the adult video magazine presented by and featuring me! Both are as raunchy as the laws of this land will allow and are available mail order from Brittania, and from high street video shops.

LET'S RECAP

- 'The first masturbatory sensation that I can bring to mind is trapping a pillow tightly between my legs and literally riding it to orgasm. Even now it still works for me, but I must confess I prefer to use a man's taut muscled leg whenever one is available.'
- 'Through the brass rails I like to watch my golden bullet vibrator plunging in and out of my pussy and savour that buzzing sound as the whole of my cunt comes alive.'
- 'I use my dick as a baton, stroking its entire length, building up as the music reaches a crescendo. My favourite tune at the moment is "Rule Brittania"!'
- 'Oh, what a magic taste a good cunt is, and you have one hell of a tasty-looking slit!'
- 'Most of my respectable friends have stopped having sex. One said he'd rather have a corned-beef sandwich and a half of shandy!'
- 'One of my favourite sex games is to bring myself to orgasm with my lover viewing at close proximity, and just as I'm about to come, he slips his cock right into my orgasmic pussy.'

Sex in Unusual Places

Making love is a truly sensual experience, and by
varying the locations you select for your lovemaking
sessions, you can enhance and improve your sex life.
Where you make love is as important as when you make
love. If you choose an unusual setting for love, not only
will your vital erogenous zones be stimulated, but your
sense of sight, smell and hearing can be erotically acti-
vated as well.

As I've said before, sex in the bedroom can be wonderful. Sometimes there is nothing better than
thrashing around on a king-size bed or plunging
between the crisp linen sheets with the partner of your
dreams. But every now and again, making love elsewhere can put a new lease of lust into your love life.
Fucking her on the back seat of your car, or shafting her
whilst locked in the stationery cupboard at the office
party might be rushed and uncomfortable, but the
excitement of leaping on the moment and screwing
because you both want it then and there gives the
occasion an added sweetness. One thing I've learnt that
men find incredibly attractive in a woman is her readi-
ness for sex games where and whenever the mood grips

you. The image of taking a willing woman in an unlikely spot plays a part in every male fantasy. I'm not advocating you act like a complete whore, girls, and suggest a fuck whatever the circumstances, but just let him know when and where you want him.

Whilst working as editor of *Penthouse* magazine, my mailbag was often filled with torrid tales of spontaneous and premeditated sexual encounters in various venues. Some of the writers of these explicit letters were so surprised by the excitement and the intensity of their coupling that they seemed compelled to get it down in print and send it off to me. Here's a couple of fine examples:

M.R. of Kent wrote:

For some years now I've had an obsession about screwing girls in cars. It doesn't have to be the exotic model-type creature spreadeagled over the front of my Ferrari – that could never be because I don't own one, and unfortunately don't attract the top-echelon type crumpet portrayed in the likes of girlie magazines – but nevertheless over the last few years I've had some unbelievable sex in my cars. I'm a very safe driver even though I have been known on numerous occasions to savour the sensation of fingering a woman while poodling along the motorway. One such memorable screwing session started exactly like that . . .

Driving along the notorious M25 on the way home from a nightclub, I just knew my date was dying for it. I'd taken her out only twice, and never before had I laid a finger on her, but I knew! We'd only been travelling for a few miles when she eased her bottom back in the seat and propped both legs on the dashboard. I told her to open her legs and she immediately complied. When I slid my fingers beneath her tight, white minidress, she was a little hesitant at first, but when I made contact with her skimpy panties and started to stroke her just where I hoped her clit would be, she moaned and opened her legs even wider. I told her to take off her panties and she couldn't get them off quick enough. I couldn't wait to sink three fingers in that hot twat of hers. What particularly turned me on about this lady, apart from the fact that she had legs that just went on and on for ever, was that she insisted on turning on the interior light of the car, so she could watch my fingers squelch in and out of her cunt. Eyes riveted to her sex, she even used her fingers to pull her pussy lips back, so as to get a good look at my thumb working on her clit. I knew she was going to give me one hell of a time when she took my fingers out and started sucking on them greedily.

My fingers alternating between her pussy and her mouth, I drove off the motorway on to a slip road, and parked up in the first lay-by I came across. If she'd have turned me down at that point, I would have simply wanted to explode. She didn't though; she wanted it just as much as I did. Seconds later I pushed back her seat, wriggled my trousers round my ankles and squeezed into the footwell in front of her. Once in position I slid my hot dick into her with ease. She felt as good as she looked. As I entered her she was still moaning and squirming, still coming from the fingering I'd given her. Her long, slender legs wrapped around me and her tight pussy clenched my dick and squeezed out every last drop of come.

★   ★   ★

The fact that these two rampant lovebirds were sampling each other's delicious wares for the very first time obviously heightened the pleasures of love in an unusual locale. But couples who have been hard at it for years still enjoy a sexual liaison in weird and wonderful places. Ken from Manchester wrote:

My wife and I adore outdoor sex. At every given opportunity we set off for a day in the country with a mind to fuck *au naturel*! My wife Jean is a very game lass. She's just celebrated her fortieth birthday. I reckon life begins at forty, because at present she's randier than ever. She's a very attractive woman, really full bodied and well preserved like a good wine. She has the most adorable tits I've ever laid eyes on, with huge brown nipples that spring to life with only the merest touch.

It was years ago on a camping holiday in the Lake District that we discovered our mutual love for shagging out of doors. One cool but gloriously bright day, we set off all wrapped up to do a little hiking. We'd only managed a mile or two of our fell walk when it started to absolutely pour down with rain. We found this kind of sheltered archway and huddled together to keep dry. I told you about my missus and her wonderful tits – well, being close to these marvellous mammaries for a minute or two, even in the rain, really made me rampant. Pretty soon, in all winds and weathers, I was sucking hungrily on her sweet nipples.

Now Jean is a girl who really loves her tits to be sucked and after five minutes or so, when her beautiful buds were sticking out like chapel hat pegs, she slid one hand inside my trousers. My cock was really stiff and ready, so I bent Jean over and with her arse towards me and her hands clinging on to the wall, I shoved my manhood between her sticky lips.

That was the first of many. Rarely a picnic goes by when we don't find a secluded spot to indulge in a smashing outdoor shag. If there are too many people nearby, we always manage to frig each other to a climax.

If I was to bring to mind all the out-of-the-ordinary settings that I've used for carnal couplings, this chapter might be somewhat long, so I've just selected a choice couple that you might find interesting.

It was a glorious summer's day when my boyfriend and I were out walking my three dogs in a cemetery in West London. The graveyard was split up into two separate areas – one section full of ancient tombs and graves, and the other, grassed over, dotted with benches and magnificent trees. Naturally the latter part was fairly full of people enjoying the sunshine.

My man and I chose a slightly secluded spot at the edge of the dead zone. My dogs were running off, sniffing around and amusing themselves, so we sat down under a tree for a cuddle. The cuddling speedily progressed to necking. Then up popped his erection. He's a very big boy and within a matter of minutes it was peeping out of the waistband of his shorts. Now I too was becoming very aroused, so we snuggled ourselves together, and somehow or other we managed to slip his dick up the leg of my shorts to enjoy a lovely fuck spoon-style. We didn't go unobserved, though. As he slapped it into me time after time, I became vaguely aware that we were being watched by the grounds caretaker who was busily cutting the grass whilst riding on a sit-on, power-driven mower.

When we finally finished our delicious tumble, I noticed he was still circling us, and obviously engrossed in our humping, he had been a little over-zealous in his task – the area of grass that surrounded us was cut down almost to the bare soil!

Another amusing and immensely pleasurable fuck took place while bent over the loo in a film studio. Going back around ten or eleven years now, I had a small role in a main feature film. I only had a couple of lines, and also I was to perform in a simulated lovemaking scene. Anyway, the director took quite a shine to me and we started going out together. He was incredibly randy and had a very big dick, and in addition to that he was a very nice bloke.

When the movie was almost finished, he called me back to do some voiceovers. When I say voiceovers, I mean those ecstatic, euphoric squeals and gasps that a girl makes when she is bubbling up to orgasm. The director took me into a small studio complete with sound facilities and a large screen. My cameo role was then projected on to the screen. Into a microphone I was instructed to breathe and pant all kinds of sexy, dirty phrases to coincide with the lovemaking scene depicted on the screen. All that grunting and groaning made me as randy as a bitch on heat, and luckily it gave my director the horn too. He made our excuses to the sound engineer and dragged me the few feet to the loo next door, bent me over, tore aside my panties and fucked me very hard indeed. My knickers were naturally somewhat juicy from sex, so I slipped them off and popped them in the top pocket of my jacket when I left.

That night I had a date with my regular boyfriend and I was still wearing the same jacket. I can't recall exactly what happened, except that we had a row and I started crying. I fished around in my top pocket for a hanky, and I ended up drying my eyes with panties reeking of sex. That took some explaining!

The 'little boys' room' might be so named because of

the colossal amount of fucking that seems to go on in these unsalubrious places. I recollect one night I was out at a dinner party in a restaurant. There was about a dozen of us there and my mate had the hots for the bloke sitting next to her. He happened to be on a first date with the girl sitting on the other side of him, but that didn't make the slightest bit of difference to my buddy. Between dessert and coffee, the pair of them disappeared to the loo for a knee-trembler, while I had to spend an uncomfortable twenty minutes chatting to this bloke's new bird!

Another of my rampant friends sampled a stiffy at around 35,000 feet when she joined the mile-high club *en route* to Finland on a modelling job. Not only did she get to shag one of the stewards in the confined space of the loo, her arse resting on the stainless steel sink, her buttocks uncomfortable and cold, but so did the other model she was travelling with. Apparently, after guzzling a fair quantity of the buckshee booze, they got a little tiddly, rather randy and egged each other on to proposition the steward. They even tossed a coin to see who got him first!

All the sexy scenarios that I have written about so far fall into the category of unpremeditated sexual encounters. You know what I mean – when you really need some serious shagging so you seize the opportunity and take your pleasures in the most unlikely locations. What I am suggesting is that in addition to these spontaneous frolics you also plan exciting expeditions of sex. Ken and his missus from Manchester seem to have the right idea. Once the happy couple discovered their penchant for outdoor sex, they began to work at it and now contrive their amusement carefully.

There are few sensations as erotic as making mad passionate love on an exotic moonlit beach or wriggling around in a colourful field of golden yellow rape on a warm summer's day. And of course the possibility that you might be overlooked or caught in the act can be an amazing stimulant, although it may have the reverse effect on some couples – the likelihood of getting stumbled upon by a passer-by may give him the dreaded droop! And sometimes the enforced situation of not being able to relax completely whilst frantically fornicating in an unsecluded place causes us ladies to have difficulty reaching a climax. It doesn't with me, I'm happy to say. Being such an exhibitionist, it generally makes me come quicker and more frequently.

So take my word for it, these premeditated fucks are well worth the effort. But I do advise you to do a fair amount of forward planning. For instance, don't decide you're both feeling horny and set off in the car to find this perfect location for some red-hot sex, because you'll probably end up driving around for hours. You'll both get terribly frustrated, end up rowing or shagging in the motor, and if it's in the middle of the afternoon, you might just come up against the problem of Mr Plod tapping on the window when you're straddling your man on the back seat!

Dogging is the quaint British expression used to describe both the voyeurs and the performers who get their kicks from viewing, or participating in, back-seat bonking which occurs in lovers' lanes and car parks around the country. It originated from taking the dog out for a walk – a perfect excuse to slip out of the house, slink off to a well-known spot for courting couples, and watch the lovers perform. However, it is considered extremely bad etiquette to snoop on unsuspecting couples. Somehow or other the voyeur has to be able to decipher which couples actually get off on being watched! Doesn't sound an easy task to me. Consider all those couples who are indulging in a pre-marital affair – I bet it scares the hell out of them. Personally I don't relish the prospect of spectators while I'm snatching a quickie in the car; I may be an exhibitionist, but the idea of all those beady eyes observing me in a dark country lane just doesn't appeal. If it is something you fancy, I would advise you to keep your doors locked to be on the safe side.

A boyfriend of mine, with whom I've spent many a happy hour copulating in cosy car parks, gave me a helpful little hint to keep all nosy parkers from ruining your steamy car sessions. Before you strip off and get down to it in the motor, smear Windowlene all over the insides of your windows. Then you can enjoy yourself completely unobserved, and when you are both sated, a quick rub round with a soft clean cloth and you can drive off home with sparkly clean windows!

To find the ideal private outdoor venue for lovemaking you must keep your eyes open for possible locations whilst on your various travels. Then, when the mood is right and you know exactly where you're heading, you don't waste valuable screwing time. It's advisable to set off for your sexy trip well prepared. Take a couple of soft blankets, perhaps some fruit, bottled water, a bottle of wine or even a flask of coffee. All these preparations might seem like a bit of a palaver, but I assure you the end result is worth it. These days we all seem to lock ourselves away in our own private domain and hardly venture into the great outdoors, but the delight of the wind whistling through your hair and your knickers, and being semi-naked in the great outdoors, can be truly wondrous.

Even when you do chance upon that perfect place for love, things can go wrong. A few years ago I was visiting Italy along with my friend, Marie Harper. We were there on a modelling assignment and Marie got her boyfriend to pop over halfway through the trip to spend a few days with her. We both had the day off and were sunbathing around the pool at a private villa set in some spectacular grounds when George, Marie's man, arrived. The lovers immediately sloped off into the bushes for some sex. A few minutes later I heard an agonising scream which sounded very much like one of pain, not of pleasure. And it was – no sooner had George flipped out his dicky than a wasp had perched on the end of it and stung him. Ouch! Perhaps you should include a tube of insect repellant in your list of requirements for your naughty day out?

When it comes to making love in different and multifarious surroundings, it is often the woman who must take the initiative. If the man in your life is a bit reluctant, do your very best to persuade him. Some guys can get a little set in their ways, so I'm relying on you women to talk him round. Think about it, girls, doesn't he usually make most of the running? When you fuck in bed, in the bath, or on the living-room floor, who is it usually makes the first move? My guess is it's your fella.

Be creative about where and when you have sex. Don't be afraid to take the upper hand. Contrive situations that will give your love life that extra bit of spice. Go out on a date, and halfway through the evening, spread your legs and reveal that you're not wearing any knickers. Pop down to his works and swan into his office in your overcoat. Unfasten a few buttons to show him that you're wearing only stockings and suspenders and your tiniest pair of panties. When you are out visiting friends or your in-laws, insist that he accompanies you to the bathroom so he can bend you over the bath and bang you. It's all the more fun because both of you must stifle your screams of pleasure! Or alternatively, wait until he arrives home and be ready for him. Sit astride the kitchen work surface with your crotch thrust forward and your legs well spread. Play with yourself as he walks through the door and asks you what's for dinner. Fuck your way around your home. If you've a sturdy dining table, that can be great fun. The bath and shower are great favourites of mine, as is doing it doggy-fashion halfway up the stairs.

This letter that I received from Rosemary tells a rather interesting tale of how she took the upper hand and demanded sex when she and her husband went round to his boss's house for dinner:

My husband is always trying to climb the pro-motion ladder. He works in finance and although he had a relatively good job, he still has a fair way to go to reach the top. His boss seems to put him through the paces, and when he invited us over for dinner with him and his wife one evening, my husband Ralph was a little nervous. Gordon, his boss, is a very distinguished gent in his early fifties. I'd a notion that he has an eye for the pretty ladies, and as I'm an attractive, bubbly blonde in my late twenties, I thought I'd dress up in a sexy, low-cut dress to keep the boss sweet. Ralph wasn't sure it was such a good idea, but he didn't push the point.

There were just the four of us at dinner and everything was moving along splendidly. Gordon admired my outfit and gave my slender legs an appreciative glance. He even gave me a big hug when we arrived; his wife Sheila was just checking the dinner at the time. Anyway, the two men sat down on the sofa side by side to talk business, and I sat across from them sipping my sherry. Sheila was still busy in the kitchen and insisted that she should be left alone to get on with it. As the two men chatted, I purposely crossed and uncrossed my legs. My sheer nylons rustled together invitingly. Gordon was not oblivious to my charms and from time to time, in mid-conversation, he'd glance up at me and give me a pleasant smile.

When Gordon popped to the kitchen to see how dinner was coming along, I switched seats and sat next to my husband. It was then that I told him that I didn't have any pants on! Poor Ralph nearly had a funny turn, but he had to cover his embarrassment because it was at this point that Gordon came back in the room to announce that dinner was served.

All through the starter and the main course, I played games with both men. I suppose a couple of sherries and a glass or two of wine put me in that wicked kind of mood. I slipped off my shoes and played footsie with Gordon. At first he was a little timid, but then he responded by moving one leg towards me, enabling my bare, stockinged foot to wriggle right up inside his trouser leg. Still at play with Gordon, I reached out one hand and let it lay dormant on Ralph's fly-button. He gave me a wide-eyed look but didn't remove my hand. I could feel his prick growing hard from my touch.

The meal was first class, but I didn't eat that much. I wasn't particularly hungry, but I was horny. When Gordon and Sheila cleared away the dinner plates and went off to the kitchen to prepare for dessert, I whispered to my husband that I wanted him to fuck me in the bathroom. He shook his head emphatically, so I squeezed his dick a little harder through his trousers and warned him that if he didn't pop upstairs with me to give me a good banging, I'd take his prick out during dessert!

He called out to Gordon that he was just taking me up to the bathroom as I couldn't remember where it was, and we hurried off upstairs. I locked the bathroom door and released his prick, sank down to my knees and gave it a good lapping with my tongue. Now my Ralph usually makes a lot of loud grunts and groans when I suck him, but this time, his lips were sealed!

When his prick was fully hard, he sat down on the edge of the bath and I sat on his lap. He undid the buttons on the front of my dress and massaged my tits as I slowly lowered myself on to his prick. I wriggled around on his prick, desperate to scream out as he grabbed me at the waist and jerked me up and down his length. In more usual circumstances I take a while to climax, but the idea that we had sneaked off from the dinner table to fuck made me very aroused indeed, and I was creaming in only a few minutes, exactly as Ralph shot his hot spunk right up inside me.

When we returned to the dining room the raspberry pavlova was ready and waiting. I'm convinced Sheila had no idea what we had been up to, but I'm sure Gordon knew. It didn't harm Ralph's prospects at all, because two weeks later he advanced one more rung up the ladder.

Some women would probably accuse me of advocating that we become some kind of sex toy, but I dispute that. What I am putting forward is the idea that we as women can decide when and where we make love. If you're not in the mood, he'll have to make do with beans on toast for his tea, not a sumptuous portion of horn on the hob. But when we want it, we should play our erotic games and enjoy our sexual relationships to the full. Sex is only one part of the complicated equation that makes for a stable, happy partnership, but without it many marriages and relationships crumble. If both partners attempt to keep the zing in their love life by regarding lovemaking as a special event that takes time and planning (not forgetting those sudden, uncontrollable lustful urges we all know and love), that will go a long way towards achieving a happy, loving partnership. And we can go on making ecstatic, orgasmic love to the same person for years and years. Or, if you're footloose and fancy free and are well stocked with condoms, you can have a hell of a time as well!

LET'S RECAP

- 'The image of taking a willing woman in an unlikely spot plays a part in every male fantasy.'
- 'I'm a very safe driver even though I have been known on numerous occasions to savour the sensation of fingering a woman while poodling along the motorway.'
- 'She's a very attractive woman, really full bodied and well preserved like a good wine. She has the most adorable tits I've ever laid eyes on, with huge brown nipples that spring to life with only the merest touch.'
- 'I fished around in my top pocket for a hanky, and ended up drying my eyes with panties reeking of sex.'
- 'Sit astride the kitchen work surface with your crotch thrust forward and your legs well spread. Play with yourself as he walks through the door and asks you what's for dinner.'
- 'I squeezed his dick a little harder through his trousers and warned him that if he didn't pop upstairs with me to give me a good banging, I'd take his prick out during dessert!'

CHAMPIONS OF LOVE

Anonymous

When one thinks of modern Japanese culture, one conjures up images of perfection, minimal architecture and polished etiquette. Seventeenth-century Japan was a land of untamed savagery, harsh regimes and ritualistic barbarity. In *Champions of Love*, an exotic band of outcasts feed their sensual appetites against a backdrop of brutality.

Jiro, the statuesque young Samurai warrior, Okiku the nubile dancing girl who inspires his voyeuristic tendencies and Rosamund, a voluptuous Christian woman and survivor of a shipwreck, form an unlikely crew. Their mission is to fulfil a quest for erotic adventure in a time where pleasure is not easily found.

This is the first book in the unique *Champions* series. *Champions of Pleasure* and *Champions of Desire* explore further adventures in the land of the Samurai.

L ooking at his parents as they ate the evening meal, Jiro could hardly believe what had passed in the barn an hour before, while his mother had gone to the temple. His father, a giant of a man, ate with his usual gusto and barbarian manners. After twenty years in the country, his father still acted the barbarian sometimes. His mother, a small, smooth-skinned woman wearing a silk kimono as befitted the wife of a nobleman, seemed a porcelain doll beside him. Jiro's thoughts drifted inevitably to the sight in the barn as he heard the maid move about in the kitchen behind him.

His father grunted and belched slightly.

'Well, Jerry, how are your ship drawings coming?'

Jiro hated being called Jerry, but his father ruled all their lives with his own brand of humour and force. Though his second son had inherited some of his size and colour, he had inherited none of Anjin of Miura's skill at shipbuilding or engineering. The man once known as Will Adams scowled as his half-Japanese, half-English son bowed and muttered that his assigned work would soon be finished. His elder son away at Edo, he wished that the younger lunk he had privately named Gerald, so much like him in size and temperament, would also be a success.

After dinner, the young man stretched, settled his swords into place in his sash, and begged leave to go out. His mother cast him a sharp look. Miru's villagers did not practice nightwalking – visiting girls for sex in the middle of the night – and she could not help wonder what her son was up to.

In truth, all Jiro wanted to do was relieve himself. His prick was heavy, and he knew there was no chance of catching the maid outside at this time. He wandered off into the bamboo grove behind the house, climbing the slope towards the red-painted shrine of Hachiman at the hill's summit. As he walked, seeking concealment, he practised the 'silent tread' taught all the samurai boys by the fencing master. He slipped through the grove silently, and dipped into a small, bush-surrounded hollow. His prick stood out in splendour as he examined it. He rubbed it experimentally, and the reddish staff quivered. As he rubbed again, he thought he heard a movement. Before he could cover himself, he saw the glint of something move in the moonlight. Looking closer, and sliding his feet silently, he saw a bent-over form dressed in a dirty brown shirt. The shirt was hiked up, displaying a round white bottom cleft by darkness. For a moment, Jiro was back in the barn. Without volition he slid forward. The ass before him moved, as its owner, intent on something before her, peered through parted bushes at the small shrine building.

Almost without thought now, Jiro's hands moved. He dropped his trousers, loincloth, and loose shirt. He knelt behind the figure. With deliberation and speed, he seized the figure by neck and hip. Before she could do more than gasp, his prick was probing at her backside. Two incredibly soft and large mounds guided his pole between them. He jerked his loins forward hard and his rigid cock found an opening which yielded only slowly to efforts. He felt through the fingers of his left hand that the woman was about to scream, and he tightened his fingers warningly. Suddenly the ring of muscle gave, as the crest of Jiro's prick completed its penetration and he slid up into paradise. He moaned in delight while she struggled ineffectually beneath him. The weight of his body forced her hand away from the lips of her cunt as she needed to support the sudden weight. Jiro's feeling himself well lodged in her and marvellously supported, began to take stock of his surroundings. His hands snaked around a plump soft belly and explored a full thicket of soft curly hairs. His fingers moved downwards through the mossy growth until he found the beautiful, slick, mysterious folds that were hidden among the hairs. Barely knowing what to do or how to handle it, he let his finger pads explore the sticky folds. He explored some more, and each movement of his hands through the unknown bumps and ridges of flesh brought a trembling response from the girl, squatting on all fours beneath him. He explored further, finding his own large ball-bag swinging beneath, and the root of his manhood disappearing in a ring of muscle. To withdraw now might precipitate another struggle, and in any case, was unthinkable under the circumstances. He ploughed on.

His prick moved up and down in the unfamiliar channel as he got into a rhythm. He explored the folds of her cunt with his right hand, gently probing with the pads of his fingers, sending one digit up the moist channel between the soft plump lips, occasionally exploring the feel of his own prick as it moved in and out of her. Inadvertently, his probing fingers found the protuberance of her clitoris. At the first touch, her body quivered. Jiro, sunk in his own pleasure, his eyes

233

closed, barely noticed. She moved her body unconsciously to encourage contact, and his fingers pinched
the joy button again. This time he noticed as she let out
a breathless moan. It was not long before his inexpert
fumbles became sure strokes as he gently, then more
roughly, stroked the inside of her lips and the slightly
hardening clit.

The girl under him began to writhe slowly to his
rhythm. The two fat mounds of her ass burned his
belly, and in less time than he thought possible, the
pressure on his balls became unbearable. His hips
jerked uncontrollably. His whole body seemed concentrated in one spot. He rammed her again and again in a
frenzy, not forgetting to tease her clitoris as he moved.
His spasms began somewhere down along his spine.
This was nothing like the pale orgasms when he jerked
himself off. This was the real thing, he thought as he
explored within her, inundating her interior with his
thick cream. Unwilling to let go, he was suddenly conscious that the girl, far from fighting him for the last few
moments, was actually gasping in pleasure. His young
prick still erect, he continued probing her. His right
hand continued milking her clitoris, while his left
moved away from her throat and grasped an available
hanging breast. The breast was the largest Jiro could
imagine. He had seen, even managed to feel, female
breasts before in the public bath. But the breast he held
was larger than the palm of his hand, full, and with a
large round erect nipple that he pinched in delight.

Through the thin screen provided by a bush, he
could see the small clearing before the red-painted
shrine of Hachiman. In the clearing danced a nude
female demon. His eyes traced the slim curves of her
ripe female body, the shadow cleft between her legs
with a small heart-shaped patch of hair, smooth-

muscled belly and conical tits. On a long slim neck rested a hideous head: white as chalk, grinning red, long horns projecting from the forehead. Startled for a moment, Jiro recognised a dance mask, as the figure continued its unusual steps.

The dancer, unconscious of the two observers, held a straight sword in one hand which she waved slowly to a beat only she could hear. With her other hand she caressed her body slowly, lingering over her nipples in turn, stroking her buttocks, descending slowly to tickle the spot between her legs. Never losing the rhythm, she was slowly approaching the climax she had not achieved earlier because of a useless male.

Jiro's juices rose once again at the sight of the dancer. He began moving faster and faster into his companion. His hands now probed deep into her cunt, now squeezed her magnificent breasts. He squeezed the two hills together, then pulled them apart, bringing a small moan of distress from the figure beneath him. Soon he approached his climax. He stuck his hand into her cunt, twisting her prominent clit between rigid fingers. She twitched as she felt pain and pleasure mingle familiarly.

This time, as he came, he felt the girl beneath him jerk and force her buttocks back against him, grinding her arse into his belly, forcing the breath from his lungs as he shot his load into her for a second time. Shudder after shudder seized her as she came too. She gave a jerk as the final spasm caught her, and uncontrollably moaned out loud in her pleasure before subsiding beneath him.

The dancing figure in the clearing, hearing the moan, left off in mid-step. In three quick strides she had leapt through the screening bush and stood over the almost comatose couple. The tip of her sword brushed Jiro's neck and the mask, glistening white as death in the moonlight, regarded them dispassionately.

235

Okiku stared at the figures squatting at her feet. For a moment she was furious. Furious at being spied upon, furious at not having noticed the spies, and above all, furious at having been disturbed just before climaxing with her hand. The vision the two presented, however, soon appealed to her sense of humour. The samurai's topknot was askew, he had dropped his swords as well as his clothes in his hurry. He was a fine, large figure of youth, heavily muscled, his skin an interesting pale colour, hint of a beard on his jaws. Her left hand stole to her mound as she thought of the use she could put him to. There was a sucking, popping sound. His prick was ejected from the girl beneath him and he rolled slowly on his side. Okiku gave one look at that fine, glistening instrument and reluctantly came to the conclusion that for the moment, at least, it would do her no good whatever.

Her gaze was shifted to the girl. Rather fat, Okiku decided at first, and her skin glistened unusually in the moonlight. She nudged the girl with her foot, rolling her over. Jiro and Okiku both let out a breath. The 'fat' girl was unusually coloured and shaped, and now that they could see her features, both realised she was not Japanese. Her mouth and eyes, recovering from passion, were both wide with fear. Okiku minutely examined the full body before her and her lust grew. This would be a new experience, and new experiences were something she had craved since her childhood. She kept the sword digging lightly into the young man's neck as she lowered herself next to Rosamund. She explored Rosamund's curves with her free hand, and dipped her hand curiously into the latter's cunt. This last brought a shudder from the blonde girl and a cry, 'No, please, no.'

Jiro jumped, and the sword dipped into his neck, bringing a small flow of blood.

236

'You speak English!!' he called in surprise.

Rosamund turned to him in shock. 'You understand me?! But . . . but who are you?'

He tried to bow but the point of the sword stopped him.

'Miura Jiro at your service,' he said in stilted, hardly used English. 'But my father calls me Jerry Adams when he's drunk. He is from England. Or was, many years ago.'

Rosamund began to cry. 'At last,' she sniffled, 'someone who can help me in this God-forsaken country. Is this truly the Japans?'

Jiro began to answer but was interrupted by Okiku.

'Shut up,' she said. 'Can you understand this woman's tongue? Then tell her that she is going to reciprocate the favour I did her.'

'What?' he asked, confusedly.

'You two spied on me and enjoyed the spectacle and one another. I have a cunt too. This plump foreign devil is going to help me come,' she grinned maliciously, 'since you obviously can't. Explain this to her.'

Jiro started to object, but the sword dug into his neck once again.

'This woman . . . wants to . . . have your body, just as I had a while ago.' He had the grace to blush.

Rosamund stared at him, confused. 'But she's a woman!'

Jiro nodded, and before he could add a word, Okiku's mouth covered Rosamund's and her long and well-trained tongue began exploring the blonde's red-lipped virginal mouth. Rosamund started to object, started to push the slimmer woman away, but was lost in the new sensation. Their tongues explored one another, licked teeth, pushed and heaved one against the other. Okiku eventually stopped to draw breath.

'Tell her I will teach her tongue sumo later, she has such a delicious mouth, but for now, she must satisfy me another way.'

Jiro complied, but before he could explain what sumo was, Okiku had forced the other girl flat on her back. Then she rose and straddled the blonde's face. 'Lick!' she commanded, and Jiro translated the order.

Reluctantly and fearfully Rosamund obeyed the order. Her tongue licked out and barely touched the dark labial pleats. Okiku urged her on by pinching Rosamund's prominent breast and grinding her crotch into Rosamund's face. The slightly acidic taste first revolted Rosamund, but gradually, as she became used to the taste, and more importantly the smell, she began licking in earnest. Though ignorant, her strong tongue and vigorous licking strokes soon had the other woman quivering in delight. Okiku moved her body, indicating which point she wanted attended to, and Rosamund, fearful, almost choking in the close, musky dark, but with a fearful pleasure rising in her, complied.

Jiro's eyes were almost popping out of his head. His swords, toward which he was planning a break, were forgotten. His youthful prick began showing signs of energy again as it raised its head along his thigh. Noticing it, Okiku considered abandoning the delightful tongue beneath her. It would be too dangerous, she decided, and besides, the young man might give up before the right time. Instead, she motioned him forward. She leaned, and with her free hand, separated Rosamund's legs, then motioned the young man between them. He needed no further encouragement. He moved the heavy, long thighs apart and squatting between them, presented his rampant prick at the mark. Okiku's eyes widened in surprise at the sight of the magnificent instrument, and then narrowed in anticipation of the future, as wave after wave of pleasure swept through her.

This time Rosamund reacted to her thighs being parted with less reluctance. She was familiar with the prick that entered her, and raising her hips, she let Jiro's instrument work its way up her sodden canal. Less sore than the first time she was fucked, she reacted naturally, fitting the movements of her hips to those of the man, and transmitting those same motions and pleasures through her tongue and lips to the woman above her.

The three moved as one. Sword forgotten, Okiku rocked herself over Rosamund's demanding mouth, occasionally moulding a perfect breast below her, or pinching her own, sometimes scratching at the muscular shoulders of the youth before her. Jiro drove himself frantically into Rosamund's cunt. He jerked his lips, at first rhythmically, later wildly as his spasms took over his senses. He clutched at available breasts, comparing the full rounded ones and even more enticing small conical ones of the girl who had worn the demon mask. Beneath these two, Rosamund writhed in double pleasure as she gave and received simultaneously from two gloriously demanding bodies and her own.

They came together in a near explosion. All three arched their bodies simultaneously. Rosamund almost fainting from lack of air, bit Okiku's inner thighs, forcing the lighter girl off. Jiro stretched himself full length on the leaf-covered ground, still joined to Rosamund as the dying spurts left his prick and shook his hips. Okiku rolled aside and stretched, her face near his, her thigh cradling Rosamund's blonde head. Minor spasms rocked all three of them. Unable to help himself, Jiro stretched out a gentle hand to cradle Okiku's soft cheek, while the other played alternately with Rosamund's cunt and Okiku's breasts. Rosamund, occasionally exploring Okiku's thighs with her tongue, concentrated on feeling the length of Jiro's body with her hands, finally concerning herself with the point it joined her spread legs.

'Who are you?' he asked. As the question was in Japansese, it was Okiku who answered.

'Okiku, at your service.' She giggled, and Jiro realised she was a girl of about his own age. 'A dancer from Ugo,' she added. That province was far enough to defy immediate corroboration. She pinched the skin of his hard chest. 'You shouldn't have disturbed my dancing, and I would have treated you much better. Much better,' she breathed, as his gentle hand massaged her erect nipple. 'And you? And this beautiful foreign devil beneath me?'

'I am Miura Jiro, and my father is Miura Anjin, lord of the village of Miura and a hatamoto retainer of the Lord Shogun.' He sounded self-important even to himself and hurriedly added with a laugh 'But I am nothing at all. Only the second son . . .'

'And this?' Okiku persisted, her hand caressing the blonde head that lay on her damp brown thigh.

He shook his head in ignorance. 'I'll ask her.'

Okiku laughed. 'And you took her just like that? Without a formal introduction? Quite like a samurai.'

Not knowing what to answer, he turned his attention to Rosamund instead.

'Who are you?' he asked in English.

Rosamund told him her story. Her parents had been English Catholics, forced to leave England during King James' reign. She herself had been brought up by nuns, and upon the death of her parents, had become a novice. Her order had departed for China, to convert the heathen, and a shipwreck had precipitated her on these shores. Hesitantly she concluded, 'Is it true . . . someone told me that they execute Christians here . . .'

Jiro, translating her story to Okiku, paused for a moment, then hesitantly, he nodded. Okiku tensed when she felt his uncertainty.

'What is it?'

'She's a kirisitan,' he said, using the Japanese term.

'A what?'

Jiro explained, and also explained that Rosamund had been a nun. 'The Lord Shogun had decreed that all kirisitan priests be put to death, by crucifixion.'

Okiku shuddered, though her thoughts were not on Rosamund, but on her own troubles. She idly caressed the soft pile of curls on her thigh, and she was rewarded with a warm soft tongue that swept up, then down the length of her wet slit. Her body shuddered, and her passion rose again. Rather than waste time worrying, she curved her body down the length of the blonde girl.

'Tell her I will do it to her this time,' she commanded Jiro.

Spellbound, he obeyed her instruction, and at her urging rolled himself from between Rosamund's pink thighs. Gently Okiku lowered her head and sniffed at the wealth of soft curls between Rosamund's legs. She rubbed her nose gently at the clitoris, and noted its size and prominence with delight. Sticking only the tip of her tongue out, she went exploring, touching the full, rosy surfaces of the outer and longer inner lips, tonguing the sweet channel briefly, lowering her tongue down to the relaxed anus. As Rosamund began to respond, Okiku opened her mouth and with a suck like a noodle-eater, she pulled in the clitoris, passing it through her lips and over her tongue. She expelled it,

241

and repeated the motion again. Rosamund's hands clawed at her back and buttocks. Leaving the clit, Okiku took the left lip of the blonde girl's cunt between her own mouth lips, and ran her mouth, licking all the time, down their length, returning to the quivering clitoris by way of the other lip. Rosamund was now trembling and moaning uncontrollably. Okiku gently bit the fleshy folds, then extruded her tongue as far as it could go into Rosamund's moist channel. She exercised her tongue in ways no prick could move, touching all the points she knew both from her own body and from previous practice, would yield the most pleasure. Rosamund threw all restraint to the winds. Her arse bounced as she shoved her cunt at Okiku's mouth, and she whimpered for more and more lingual attention as a series of orgasms started that she hoped dimly, in the still thinking part of her mind, would never end.

At this sight, Jiro noted some changes in himself. His youthful prick, uninvolved in the action that interested him intellectually to that point, gave a distinct twitch and stretched itself. His hands began wandering over the two sweating female bodies. He compared the two pairs of tits, one soft and full, the other harder and conical. He moved his hands down the crack of Okiku's arse, and his fingers paused at the tight rosebud he discovered. Not wanting to linger, he moved on, gently touching Rosamund's closed eyes, her nose, and then entering her mouth, following her tongue into the hairless cavity it was plumbing. Rosamund spared a few licks for his wandering fingers, even kissing them once, but then returned happily to the familiar muskiness of Okiku's sopping hole.

Fully aroused, Jiro rose to his knees. Commandingly, he pushed at the two bodies. Okiku obligingly rolled on top of Rosamund without losing a stroke. He

242

knelt between her legs, then pushed gently forward. The tip of his prick came into contact with Rosamund's tongue, and his heavy, hairy bag rested on her forehead. He pushed forward, and Rosamund made a channel of her tongue, guiding the thick rigid meat into the waiting hole. On and on he pushed, for what seemed to all participants an eternity. Rosamund felt the whole length of his tremendous machine as it fed slowly into Okiku's gaping channel. Jiro felt as if his prick was entering a smooth, tight glove, just made for it. Though without much other experience, he knew a perfect fit.

When the man was all the way in, Okiku let out a long slow sigh. The cock lodged in her was what she had been waiting for all her life. Since losing her virginity, she had had many pricks up her channel. Fat and thin, long and short. This one, however was just right. She wanted it to rest there forever, as it touched and caressed all her internal membranes with a perfect touch. As if sensing the moment, both her partners remained perfectly still for a while.

At last, lust began to reassert itself. Jiro's prick gave an impatient twitch, and he began to move in the channel. Okiku responded to every move. Her internal muscles contracted rhythmically to meet the demands and comfort the remarkable piece of manhood. She shoved her arse backwards to meet him, bearing the weight of this large young man who now covered her like a huge cloak, hands grasping her breasts. Moving forward, she met with Rosamund's uneducated but willing tongue, that lapped indiscriminately at her pussy and Jiro's long rod. A push of Rosamund's hips reminded her that she had duties in that direction too, and she applied her well-trained tongue and lips to the sweet hair mound that was presented to her. In moments of conscious thought, that grew farther and farther between, she wondered at the way the foreign girl's taste differed from a native one's.

The climax that arrived was long and luxurious for the three. Okiku stretched and arched her back as far as it would go. Jiro's demanding thrusts forced the two joined bodies onto Rosamund's face, and again she suffocated joyously, but this time under the pressure of two climaxing tools rather than one. For the first time in her life she tasted male cream, as the overrun from Jiro's large balls gushed out of Okiku's tight cunt. In her own turn, she wrapped voluptuous legs around Okiku's head as her spasms rocked her and gradually diminished.

ADVENTURES
IN THE
PLEASUREZONE

Delaney Silver

What will sex be like in the future? If it's as exciting as that portrayed in the world of *Pleasurezone Inc.*, then book me a ticket on the next time machine! Of all the characters in Nexus stories, the ones inhabiting Delaney Silver's *Pleasurezone* must be the grooviest. The mysterious Isis majored in psycho-sexual medicine and knows just what's required to take her clients on the erotic trip of a lifetime.

In this extract, the handsome wild child, Josh Mortimer, has his first encounter with *Pleasurezone's* amazing technology. Technology which can make wild fantasies reality, and can cross the boundaries of time to bring the pleasures of the past into the future, with orgasmic consequences.

Two *Pleasurezone* books are available, with a third planned for next year. Delaney Silver is an established author of erotic fiction and may be familiar to readers of *Forum* magazine. While some Nexus authors prefer to find a speciality niche, Delaney adapts confidently to writing about all aspects of sex; and her stories are always fabulously rude.

WWell, could he?

Twenty minutes and another glass of wine later, Josh still wasn't sure. The only thing he did know was that the prospect of even *trying* to 'handle it' was making him randier than ever. That and the fact he'd do just about anything to get closer to Isis. Everything about her was driving him crazy, to the extent he was prepared to trust his living psyche into her slender leather-gloved hands – not to mention his horny male body, if he got half a chance.

And he still didn't understand what she was going to do to him . . .

Without being immodest, Josh was proud of his high IQ. But he also knew that as a mining engineer, his intelligence was of necessity the practical variety. He was a nuts-and-bolts man, an expert with machine tolerances and on-line troubleshooting. So, in spite of his reading, when Isis started throwing 'brain architecture' 'neural resonance' and 'enforced perception shifts' at him, he had to admit she'd lost him. He understood her moist, rosy mouth quite perfectly, but the incomprehensible psychotechnical jargon that came out of it? No way!

'Okay, I'm obviously not as smart as either of us

thinks I am.' He shrugged hopelessly. 'I'll have the idiot's version, please.'

'You're no fool, Josh,' Isis replied, her voice light but serious, 'but the bottom line – '

Suddenly she stopped, pressed her gloved fingers to her lips and smothered an almost schoolgirlish giggle. 'The bottom line is . . . with the sensory re-creator we can make your fantasies real.'

'So it's just a kind of glorified dream machine?'

'Oh no, Josh, it's more than that. As far as you're concerned, it'll all *happen*. Your brain will receive the same messages, both physical and emotional, that it would if the event were actually occurring . . . And you have the choice of three different modes. Either selecting and inducing your own fantasies, living through a pre-programmed, pre-recorded scenario, or what we call an "F & F" . . . which is where we provide the framework but your subconscious directs the action with free choice.' She was warming to her theme now, her voice sparkling, a slight blush rising in the unmarked side of her face. Josh was almost certain she was aroused. 'The last one is the most popular, but whichever you choose, Josh, to you it'll be real.'

'Okay then, let's do it.' Josh sighed. Decision at last. He'd been enjoying Isis's subtle domination of him – *and* the flexing of her obviously prodigious intellect – but it was time for things to get physical. How physical he wasn't sure . . . but his cock hoped very!

'So what happens to my body while my grey cells are getting their rocks off?' he asked casually as they rose, and once again, Isis led the way, 'I suppose I just lie there in a trance.' The prospect offered little comfort to Josh's aching prick, and in spite of his attempt to cool it, the sex-fiend inside the civilised man was still clamouring to get his end away.

'I suppose you could say that,' she said huskily. Her grin was what could only be described as evil, and its effect on her scar was devastating, given what that scar reminded him of. 'You'll certainly have to lie back and think of something.' She laughed that soft foreboding laugh again and Josh felt scareder and stiffer in about equal proportions.

'Let's not hang about then,' he snapped, embarrassed by Isis's slow perusal of his groin.

'Don't worry, Joshua,' she went on, investing his full Christian name with a heavy sensual emphasis, 'you won't be disappointed. In any department. That I can promise you.' Josh felt himself drowning, adrift on the waves of sex pouring out of her. 'Come on. This way,' she commanded, swirling again and leading Josh towards the far end of the room.

To boldly go! he thought half hysterically as Isis pushed open a door concealed in the red baize back wall of the spacious room. Had Captain Kirk ever got this hard being ordered around by women? Josh doubted it. And he doubted too whether the characters in that classic series had ever had an adventure as weird and wonderful as he was about to have . . .

Once through the secret door, they entered an austere white-painted corridor with a second door at its far end – stainless steel this time with only a digital lock to relieve its shiny featurelessness.

Acutely conscious of his aching cock, Josh tried to watch two things at once: Isis's deft manipulation of the control panel, and her sultry swaying bottom in its grey leather casing. She seemed to be one of those people who had a head full of music all the time, and her feet were tapping the floor as her fingers tapped out the entry code.

Josh had a sudden overwhelming urge to see her

body, a stronger need by far than anything he'd felt since coming home. He'd been wracked by lust for women as a sex since the moment he'd touched down, but right now the whole boiling lot of it focused on this slim, grey-clad doctor with her strange scarred face and her sensually delectable shape.

Was she physically involved with the process ahead? Would she touch him? Would he touch her? The steel door sprang open and Isis gestured for him to follow her.

Inside was a vestibule as bland as the corridor, apart from a row of coloured prints on the wall. Josh registered that they were both erotic and oriental; Shunga most likely, the explicitly sexual ancient Japanese art. He would've liked to have lingered and studied them – to check out the back-breakingly gymnastic positions – but Isis was already halfway through another door.

'Wait in here a moment, please,' she said briskly, and ushered him into a luxuriously appointed room that seemed part lounge and part library – all furnished in creams, browns and beiges.

'Make yourself comfortable and I'll bring you something to relax you. Dip into anything that takes your fancy. There's books, magazines, prints, holovids. A lot of clients find that when they actually get here their fantasy inspirations desert them, so we keep a selection of erotica as triggers.'

As she spoke, Isis reached behind her head and pulled out the pins that held her hat. Her thick, vari-coloured waves tumbled forward over her shoulders, and Josh shuddered violently, his prick hardening to iron. His bedmates weren't the only ones turned on by long hair against their skin.

'I won't be a second.' She smiled faintly and left him alone in the strange and sumptuous waiting room. Josh flopped down on to the nearest settee and stared blindly at the heap of leather-covered volumes on the coffee table in front of him.

'She's all different,' he murmured to himself. It'd been like watching a slow, subtle metamorphosis, from the cautious victim who'd been scared to lift her veil to a seasoned sexual professional in total command of her own exotic domain. She's fabulous, he thought, picking up the nearest volume on the table. Who needs mucky books? I've found *my* fantasy.

Nevertheless, the connoisseur inside him was intrigued by what seemed to be a heavy hide-backed photograph album – a ridiculous collector's anachronism in an age of electronic images. The book's cover was unmarked but inside was a series of prints depicting lesbian lovemaking: the first few quite gentle and innocuous, but getting gradually more explicit as the pages passed.

The artwork was superb and detailed, and Josh caught his breath at the sight of a beautiful oriental girl draped over a chaise longue, her slim olive thighs widely apart as a Junoesque blonde licked delicately at her glistening cunt. The genital detail was exquisite, but Josh found himself even more stirred by the ecstatic expressions on the women's faces. They were totally out of it, completely absorbed in the pleasure they were sharing, and not for the first time, Josh wondered what it was like to be a woman who wanted a woman. In his mind he saw Isis's small, elfin tongue probe Tricksie's crimson bush . . .

'Beautiful, aren't they?' said Isis, and Josh nearly jumped through the roof. He'd never heard her return.

'Er . . . yes,' he muttered, snapping the book shut and focusing on Isis and what she was holding out to him: an inch of amber-coloured fluid in a small cut-glass goblet.

'I thought I wasn't supposed to have spirits,' Josh said, more interested in her hand, suddenly, than the glass it held. At first he'd thought she was wearing pink lace gloves, but as he looked more closely he saw that the network of whorls and lines was actually on her skin.

'Another leftover from my accident,' she commented crisply, 'but there's not much more. My hands and face caught the worst of it. Now come on, drink up. You're the one that wants to get on with it.'

'What is it?' he asked, taking the goblet and swirling its contents. The tawny fluid clung ominously to the glass.

'An inhibition-buster,' she answered with a grin. 'And don't worry, it's made from all natural ingredients. It's to help you take the brakes off.'

'Are you licensed to dish out drugs?' Josh was worried now. Nothing was turning out quite as he'd expected.

'Don't worry.' She touched her fingers suddenly to his cheek. The skin of her hands was soft, warm and smooth; there was no tactile evidence of the scarring. 'You can trust me, I'm a doctor.'

'Oh, for crying out loud!'

'No, seriously, I am,' Isis protested. 'I'm an MD. I majored in psychosexual medicine.'

He believed her, although it didn't ease his suspicions about the gungy-looking drink. The first sip was thick and herby tasting, slightly bitter but not unpleasant. It warmed his gullet as he tossed it down, and though he was probably imagining things, he immediately felt less uptight. Handing the glass back, he returned Isis's smile.

'Okay then, I want you to relax and get into the mood,' she said, and Josh could've sworn she was flirting. 'Take off your jacket and tie, choose something to look at or watch, and lie on the settee. Let the ideas come, but don't force anything. Just take it easy, absorb the images, masturbate if you want to. But if you can't fix on a specific act or event, don't worry. That's what usually happens the first time. It's a good thing really. With no particular requirements from you, we can start you with one of our set pieces. Something that'll *really* show you what we can do.'

'What do you mean?' Josh wondered why he'd stopped being worried. He felt no alarm whatsoever now, just a loose, mellow glow.

'You'll see,' she said quietly. 'Now get in the groove while I set things up.'

With that she left him to it. He'd never considered following her but he'd heard the faint click of a lock.

Licking his lips he thought about the potion she'd given him. Was it an aphrodisiac? It'd certainly had some kind of effect on him. He felt curious about what awaited him, but in a gentle, spaced-out sort of way. There was no way to gauge if it'd made him any randier . . . he'd been rock hard since the moment he'd set eyes on Isis.

Masturbate, she'd said. The cheeky cow! At least she could've stayed around and done it for him. He imagined the feel of those lace-patterned hands on his cock. They were slender, elegant hands; they looked as if she could take a man to heaven and back with them. His flesh twitched at the very thought of it. Would she be rough or gentle with him? Would she tease him for hours with featherlight touches? Work the whole surface of his tool into a state of agonising sensitivity? Or would she be swift and clinical, bring him straight to ejaculation with ruthless scientific precision? Assess the number of spurts against a carefully researched norm?

Measure the volume and consistency of his spunk . . .
Oh God, he really didn't care, just as long as she
touched him . . . For the first time in his life, Josh was
ready to beg a woman to make him come.

He thought about orgasm . . .

Christ, he really needed to have one. But if he was
locked in some kind of trance, what the hell would it be
like? A glorious three-dee, electronic wet dream with
spunk all over the ceiling? Or would he wake up at the
point of climax and maybe shoot into Isis's waiting
hand? Whichever it was, the need was getting desperate; his prick was so stiff now it was really hurting. He
looked down and saw the mass of it bulging behind his
zip.

Comfortable as he could be, Josh reached out for one
of the leather-covered books and flipped it open.

Bondage.

It hit him in a series of stark, high-definition images
of bodies in torment. A woman, obscenely spread-
eagled and gagged, was held immobile in an array of
leather and steel. A man was remorsely forcing a giant
prosthetic phallus into her rectum and simultaneously
frigging her clitoris. Juices glinted wetly on every detail
of her shaven cunt: her clit enormous, knoblike and
protruding, her anus stretched open several unbelievable inches. Shocked in spite of himself, Josh wriggled
in his seat. There was something both repellant and
captivating in the image, and he had an urgent need to
understand it, to know the minds of both the man and
woman. Her eyes were wide with humiliation and fear,
yet her quim was dripping; his face was cool, remote,
disinterested. For whose benefit was the scene being
played?

He flipped through a few similar prints and the ache
in his prick got both better and worse. He flung the

book aside in favour of another. His prick was a jumping, steaming rod now, dancing in his pants. Isis's damned jungle juice was driving him crazy. Either that or he was a closet bondage freak . . .

The next selection was more romantic, a selection of classic, stylised themes. A man and woman fucking naked in a forest glade; a samurai warrior parting the robe of an exquisite geisha; a dangerous liaison between a courtier and a half-disrobed queen.

Was this a book for female clients, Josh wondered suddenly. Did Pleasurezone *have* any female clients? Most of the women he'd known were like Julia. They liked the sexual shallows, the here and now of safe, straight positions and manageable thrills. There must be women who went in at the erotic deep end, but surely they were a minority? As a sex they were generally too practical and realistic to need or want a magical mystery tour.

Now here's an oldie but goodie, he thought, turning the page. The picture showed another well-loved fantasy. 'The Seraglio', at a guess. A young woman lay on a brocade-covered divan, almost swooning from the caresses of two other women, who were sliding aside her diaphanous robes and preparing her, it seemed, for the attentions of a prince of some kind. This bearded lord stood to one side, hand on cock, clearly getting off on the sight of the innocent young girl being primed for him. Who wouldn't? thought Josh with feeling. And the girl was in raptures too, her breast being suckled by a giant negress and her cuntlips carefully parted by a slender, naked houri with brightly hennaed hair.

'Layla and the Prince. Do you like it?' said a soft voice beside him, and Josh realised that once again, Isis had snuck in and caught him unawares.

'Yes, I do,' said Josh decisively. He loved it. He'd

always fancied a harem. But when he looked up at Isis, he wondered if another of his long-time fantasies was coming true. It was, after all, every man's perennial yen to have it off with a nurse . . .

Isis had shed her leather suit and now wore a white overall in classic medical white. A doctor's garb, he realised, not a nurse's; and although it was just a simple tunic style, careful darting made the thin white cloth skim faithfully over what Josh suspected was a perfect figure. Slim but curvy; long legs; fine waist; high, rounded, but not too enormous breasts. The plain but prick-teasing garment had a tiny tab collar and ended just above the knee; and on her feet, Isis wore a pair of white canvas flatties. Her thick, brindled hair was tied back in a loose ponytail, and perched right on the end of her nose was a pair of metal-rimmed half spectacles.

Josh blinked, then stared. She was Frankenstein's naughty night nurse, the mad professor, and utterly gorgeous. He'd never wanted a woman more.

'This is an artist's impression of one of our "set pieces",' she said, taking the book from Josh and studying it as if she'd never seen it before. 'Care to try it? It's an excellent example, a *tour de force*, though I say it myself.'

'Why not?' Josh replied, leaping lightly to his feet, revitalised and eager to get stuck in. Isis could be the handmaiden to his prince. 'Any chance of having you in this sex dream of mine?' he said huskily, reaching towards her. Good God, he thought, that stuff was dynamite! He could've thrown her against the wall and shagged her where she stood. Isis evaded him nimbly and said nothing.

Did she have panties on under that cute little smock? Josh did a quick survey. There were no lines showing through, no evidence of lingerie. It'd be a simple matter to slide up the hem, glide his hand up her thigh, slip it into her crotch . . .

'Naughty, naughty!' she admonished, dancing out of his reach as he lunged forward. '*I'm* not what you're here for. I'm just the technician. And to answer your question, Josh – ' She rubbed her hands in a businesslike manner, and Josh suddenly realised she was wearing a pair of fine rubber gloves. Something inside him went 'flip', and if his cock had had a voice it would've whimpered. Oh God, not rubber as well!

Oblivious, Isis went on, 'It's too disruptive for clients to have me in their fantasies. They have to have faith in my expertise, put themselves in my hands, literally. To picture me in some . . . some possibly subjugated situation would undermine my authority and destroy their trust. Surely you see that?

'Not really,' said Josh, advancing again. 'And anyway, how do you stop me dreaming you up in one of these so-called free-choice scenarios?'

'Because, as I've already told you – although you obviously weren't listening – in the Pleasurezone, you're not actually dreaming. You're perceiving an induced reality. The re-creator reads your brain patterns and creates the scenario from the data it receives, and it's programmed to lock out any images of me. So there!'

'You're a mean cow, Isis.' He plunged forward and made a grab at her. Caught unawares, she couldn't stop him. He ran a rapid, exploring hand down her body and gleaned a crumb of sexual comfort. Her breast was firm and proud to the touch, with a nipple, he realised triumphantly, that was hard as a nut. She did fancy him after all!

'Get off, you idiot,' she said sharply, dashing away his fondling hand. 'Look, shall we get on with what you

257

came here for? Or are you only interested in groping? If you don't want the treatment, we'll quit now and I'll have your money transferred back to you.'

Chastened, but still wanting her, Josh stepped back. 'Yes, ma'am,' he said facetiously. 'I'll behave myself.'

'Good. Now, do you see that door over there?' She pointed to one of several doors that opened off the lounge area. 'Behind it you'll find a bathroom. Go in, strip off all your clothes from the waist down and empty your bladder and bowels. When you've done, go through the other door beyond and I'll be waiting for you.'

'I beg your pardon?' Josh was flabbergasted. What the hell was going on? She'd vetoed any kind of sexplay between them, and now she was telling him she wanted to see his dick hanging out! And what the hell was all that about emptying his bladder and bowels?

'You heard what I said,' she replied, her voice like tensile steel.

'Okay. But why do I need to . . . strip and . . . and everything? I thought the action was all up here.' He tapped a finger to his sweating brow.

'Some of it is,' Isis said, coming close again now he'd ceded control to her, 'but for the experience to be complete, there has to be action down here too.' She reached out and closed her slim fingers on his cock, delicately testing its width and solidity through the cloth of his trousers. Josh groaned and she gave him an old-fashioned look over the top of her glasses, mischief bright in both her good eye and bad.

'Don't worry, Josh,' she murmured seductively. 'It'll all be worth it, I promise. Now let's get to it, shall we?'

She gave his shaft one last squeeze – quite lovingly, he thought through his daze – then let him go and left him to it.

The bathroom was also beautifully appointed, but as Josh followed Isis's instructions he was too befuddled to appreciate it. At first his erection made it difficult to piss, but eventually he calmed down enough to get a stream. He'd no problem with his bowels, but wondered, as he sat staring at his own bare feet, why the hell it was all necessary.

She's going to handle me somehow, he decided, loving the idea. He thought of those long fingers touching him – his bare skin this time, not through layers of silk – and smiled. Then, scrupulously, he washed himself both fore and aft, with his penis back at attention almost before he'd begun . . .

'You might change your mind, lady, when you see this,' he observed smugly to himself as he dried his smooth velvety shaft. It looked red and fierce as he held it against the fluffy white towelling: like a weapon, a tool, a rampant pussy-stuffing club. It was no use being modest. He'd a good sound cock on him; every woman he'd ever been with had praised it and he knew they were right. There was no way the good doctor could ignore its charm.

He gave himself an extra little rub, although he knew he was just about as stiff as a man could ever be; then, feeling a burst of ridiculously juvenile braggadocio, he stepped forward and opened the door.

The room beyond was smaller and more intimate than he'd expected, and seemed almost filled by a long white, leather-upholstered couch.

The cradle of fantasy, thought Josh whimsically as he took in its single thick central pedestal and, behind and to the side of where the client – victim? – laid his head, a small bank of electronic gadgetry. He saw monitors, digital readouts, a disk drive of some sort, and – at both the head of the couch and underneath – coils of fine wiring. Isis was sitting on a tall stool, tapping busily at a keyboard, but at the sound of his arrival, she turned around.

She didn't say anything immediately, but took a long look at his swaying erection.

'Good,' she said with a slight smile.

Good? Was that all? Josh's ego deflated, but oddly his prick grew even stiffer. Of course, I forgot, he thought wryly. I get off on humiliation, don't I? He'd learnt more about his sexual psyche in the last hour than in the whole of the rest of his life.

'Okay, hop on the couch,' Isis said briskly. 'Are you feeling comfortable?'

Josh took a moment before replying. The couch had lowered to the perfect height for him to get on it, and as he did so, he noticed that its shape was moulded slightly, and that while the upper part was made in one whole piece, the lower half – from approximately where the base of the spine would rest – was made of two separate but presently flush panels. Unease coiled in Josh's belly as he lay down on the warm leather, and the whole structure rose again, purring almost inaudibly to a height that was ominously convenient for Isis's reach.

'I feel great, thank you,' he murmured airily. 'I've got a stiffy on that's killing me, but apart from that I've never felt better.'

'Fine,' Isis replied, ignoring the sarcasm, 'but what I meant was, have you emptied yourself?'

'Yes, ma'am, I'm a vacuum. What's the problem? Am I going to have so much fun I'll shit myself?'

'I suppose you could,' said Isis consideringly, dropping from her stool to stand beside him, 'but it's simply that we don't want any minor discomforts to spoil things, do we? Shuffle down a bit, please.' Josh complied, and as he did so, Isis took him firmly by the hips, and carefully eased his buttocks into the soft leather indentations. She seemed oblivious to the pulsing erection so close to her rubber-clad hands; but Josh couldn't take his eyes off it. He watched it bobbing obscenely as Isis unbuttoned his shirt and folded it back on either side of his body. Easing the spare material from under his arse, she tucked it neatly beneath the small of his back. The leather couch seemed to kiss the cheeks of his bottom and he could feel the divide beneath his anus. His disquiet grew.

Machinery whirred again, and padded armrests rose up beside the body of the couch. Isis took Josh's wrists – first one, then the other – and placed them on the rests as if he were a rag-doll.

'Now then,' she said in a soft, authoritative voice, 'I'm going to position the sensory transceivers on your body, and as they're very precise and delicate, it's best that I strap you in position too. Whoah! Don't go ballistic.' She pushed down on Josh's chest as he started to rise, 'It's for your own good. You want to get the best out of this, don't you?'

'Yes, yes, I do,' cried Josh, not knowing whether to be angry or excited. He opted for both. 'I've paid good money for this, and I didn't bargain for being strapped in a glorified dentist's chair.'

'Easy, easy,' crooned Isis, coaxing his arms back on to the rests, stroking his wrists and forearms, making soothing little patterns on his hot skin, then suddenly and shockingly clipping on the restraints with a speed that left him breathless. The cuffs were steel, Josh noted in wondering horror, though lined with a feather-soft felt; and as he absorbed the impact of this first set of bonds, Isis ran her latex-clad fingers the entire length of his torso – chest, waist, hips – then on and down his leg to his right ankle. Before he had time to protest again,

261

the foot was locked firmly in place, and, that one dealt with, she walked quickly around the couch and secured the other.

Josh closed his eyes, but behind them, shockingly, was the image he'd seen earlier – the spread-eagled woman in erotic bondage – and several clues slotted neatly and awesomely into place. Empty your bowels, she'd said. No discomfort to spoil the experience. And notice how meticulously she'd folded his shirt out of the way . . . The division in the lower part of the couch assumed a dreadful significance.

'Omigod! What're you going to do to me?' He was appalled by the high whining note in his own voice. Where was the suave sophisticated Josh Mortimer now? The criminally smooth ladykiller who always took control? His eyes flew open, but Isis was busy with her computer array and pretending, he suspected, not to have heard him.

'Are you listening? What're you going to do to me?'

'I think you've probably worked that out by now, Joshua,' she replied, turning away from her mystic calculations. 'Or at least some of it.'

'Maybe I have,' Josh replied, surly with confusion and fear, 'but I think I've paid enough for you to tell me.'

'Quite true,' she remarked amiably. 'So here it is. The next step is to position the transceivers on your body, the sensors that both receive information and transmit stimulation. Pleasurable stimulation, Josh, and for maximum sensation we go right to your pleasure centres to apply it. The brain, of course, is the primary sex organ and the main message goes there. But we'll also be working elsewhere. You being a man, we'll be applying direct stimulation to your prostate gland and the head of your penis.'

262

'Oh God.'

'I shouldn't worry, Josh. You could well end up believing you're God,' she murmured, turning back to her keyboard and punching in a code. The couch's mechanisms whirred again and Josh felt the lower half of his body tilting upwards and curving inwards. His prick seemed to dance before his eyes, stiffer and redder than it'd ever been, a little moisture already oozing from the tip. Isis still seemed unimpressed by its rigid magnificence, though, as she pressed one gloved hand flat on his belly to force his bottom right into the snugly shaped hollows of the leather seat.

'Relax, Josh,' she whispered in his ear, then reached out with her free hand to key in another command.

Josh moaned, then bit his lip as the cradling leather seemed to grip his arse-cheeks, then slowly but firmly eased them apart. The machine's soft purr and his own gasping breath were the loudest sounds in the universe. The couch's inexorable division seemed to go on and on until his legs and his thighs were widely splayed and the twin mounds of his bottom were almost unbelievably stretched apart.

'Relax, Josh,' she repeated, the words whispering in the cool empty air beneath his trembling anus. Josh closed his eyes tightly, trying to deny what was happening and shut out the sensations invading him. He'd never felt more vulnerable, yet the stark exposure was both exhilarating and voluptuous. And even though he knew now what was going to happen, he still jumped with shock as Isis touched a soft cool gel to his arsehole. He twitched, bit even deeper into his lower lip, and tossed his head as she slathered on more of the slippery scented substance, and worked a large dollop of it right inside him.

'Easy now, easy now,' she whispered, her lips close

to his ear and mercifully masking the other small sounds. 'Relax again. More . . . Let yourself go, Josh . . . Open, sweetheart . . . Let yourself open up . . . That's it, my Josh, let it in . . .'

Something firm, smooth and rounded was pressing itself into Josh's rectum. Pressing, pressing, pressing; not cruel yet not kind, it moved remorselessly through the muscle-ring, stretching and opening. It felt huge, gigantic, shockingly good as it pushed in and in, filling him and distending the whole of his consciousness.

'Oh God, oh God, oh God,' he whispered through parched lips. This penetration suddenly seemed as if it were the whole of his life, the only thing that'd ever happened, ever mattered. He wanted to weep, and welcome the intruder in his bottom, while the same muscles that embraced it sought – automatically – to expel it.

'Oh Christ, I'm going to shit . . .'

'No, you're not,' said Isis firmly from somewhere behind his head. She'd done with coaxing him now, it seemed, and Josh felt suddenly and ridiculously frightened. 'It's just your nerve ends telling lies. And I don't know why you're making such a fuss. Surely you've felt anal penetration before?'

'Just what the hell do you think I am?' he demanded, twisting to try and see her, then thinking better of it. Every slight movement reminded him of the phallic object lodged in his bowel, and of the unacceptably delicious sensation of being stretched and invaded in the most intimate and demeaning way.

'What I think you are, Josh,' she said with slight impatience as if talking to a stubborn child, 'is a sexy and imaginative man. A man who's done everything and had everything done to him . . . Why else would you be here?' She moved around into his field of view,

264

adjusting the probe with a gentle impersonal touch that made him feel more exposed than ever and set his prick pulsating unbearably.

He moved uneasily, hating himself for enjoying the sensations it brought. He wanted desperately to touch himself, but his bonds prevented it. He wished that she'd touch him. But she'd turned away to monitor the equipment, as if indifferent to his hugely straining erection. Moving again, and biting down on the resulting moan, Josh wished he could be indifferent to it; but strapped as he was, it reared up at him – in the centre of his field of view – and he couldn't seem to look anywhere else.

'There was once . . .'

Astounded, he heard his own hoarse voice, 'I was just a kid. I didn't want to . . . But I just couldn't seem to help myself . . .'

'What was it?' she asked, coming close again, standing by his head, smoothing back a lock of sweaty hair with infinite gentleness. He was reminded irresistibly of a nurse again, or a priestess, or a mother. To his horror, he felt he might burst into tears. 'What did you have inside you, Josh? A dildo or a man?'

'A man . . .' he whispered brokenly, remembering an experience quite unlike this controlled, clinical penetration. It'd hurt, it'd been a rough buggering and later he'd bled. But . . .

'Did you enjoy him?' she persisted quietly.

'Yes,' he croaked, feeling utterly weak and unmanned in spite of the monumental hard-on swaying before his eyes, 'Yes, goddam you. He tore my arse and fucked me and I loved every minute of it.'

'Well then.' Her voice was no-nonsense; the gentle confessional moment was over. 'If you'll just relax into the feeling, you'll enjoy the probe.'

'How the hell would you know?'

'Tut tut, Josh. What kind of therapist would I be if I hadn't tried the treatment myself?' she asked, slanting a sideways glance at him as she fiddled with a small wire-clad gadget attached to the console at the side of the couch. 'Of course I've had a transceiver in my arse. And one in my vagina at the same time. Now will you stop complaining?'

Josh closed his eyes, his prick leaping again as he saw Isis strapped to this same couch, nude, legs wide open, thighs twitching, dildoes protruding from both orifices . . . Wires trailed obscenely, and he could almost see fluid glistening on her clitoris and labia . . .

'Holy shit,' he shouted, feeling her fingers enclose the tip of his penis. Bare fingers this time. Though he hadn't heard the action, she must've shed her gloves now she'd finished handling his backside. His body rose involuntarily, only to fall back and lodge the probe more deeply in his rectum. The sensations were incredible! The wicked thing seemed to swell inside him, stretching his anus exquisitely. His balls pulsed, rose . . . His prick was on fire, a rod of iron waving and throbbing . . .

'I think I'm going to come,' he moaned, feeling pathetic and completely out of control.

'No problem,' said Isis, easing what seemed to be a small stretchy cuff over the circumcised knob of his penis. He hissed between his teeth, feeling the pleasure roil, then subside as the delicate grip controlled his impending orgasm. 'You'll probably come several times before this is over,' she murmured conversationally, 'and the majority of clients come at least once before they go under.'

Go under? thought Josh dazedly, then remembered that this fabulous trial was simply a means to an end.

Lying semi-naked with wires attached to his prick and a gigantic prod rammed up his backside seemed like hysterically good value already. He turned slowly towards Isis, and his languor dispelled when he saw her priming a small hypodermic.

'What the hell's that?' he demanded, and troubled by the idea of more drugs, he pressed himself down on to the probe in a bizarre yearning for comfort. It jostled gently inside him and he sighed with relief.

'You do like that, don't you?' Isis commented as she applied an antiseptic swab to his forearm, peering at him over the rim of her glasses.

'Of course I do, you sadist,' he snarled. 'But I still want to know what's in that needle. I don't like to think I'm being pumped full of junk I don't know about.'

'Tsk tsk, don't fret. It's just a mild hallucinogen. It helps with the visuals.' The needle went in, hurt minutely, then was gone as she dabbed again with antiseptic. 'You really don't have to worry, Josh. I've told you before. You're perfectly safe with me, I'm a doctor. Would you like to see my diploma?

'I'd rather see your snatch,' Josh said. It'd be nice to just lie here, exposed and stimulated, and see Isis's cunt. She'd be beautiful down there, he decided dreamily. All red and moist and puffy . . . Then, maybe, she could kneel astride his face and let him lick and taste her . . . And as she came all over his mouth, she could throw one of her clever little switches and make him spunk on that sexy white coat of hers.

'Now don't be silly,' she admonished, giving Josh a flash of the stern schoolma'am, something else he found himself liking. 'You've paid for something far more esoteric than little old me.'

'But don't you fancy me?' he persisted. There was nothing to lose anymore: dignity, power, and control of his body were all in the scarred hands of this woman he'd met less than an hour ago. She'd even taken his voice; his words were coming out more and more slurred as the drug took hold. 'Don't lie to me, Isis,' he mumbled, then nodded towards his prick, so stiff and twitchy in the pleasure-giving cuff. 'You fancy some of that, don't you? I'd feel great up your twat. Why don't you climb on board?'

She gave him a long look. A considering look. And to Josh's addled brain it seemed almost as if she might succumb. His hopes – and then his penis – jumped as she slipped off her wire-framed specs, placed them to one side, and reached out to touch his lightly restrained flesh. Her fingers felt cool, and the touch of them was heartbreakingly delicate . . . but sadly, only momentary.

'You have a wonderful body, Josh, and a truly exceptional cock,' she said softly, with a genuine note of admiration. Abandoning his groin, she brought her blighted face close to his. Her voice was level and honest, and her odd eyes seemed to reach right through the narcotic mist and touch Josh's soul. 'If this weren't a professional relationship, I might be tempted. Really. But you must see it's impossible.'

All Josh could see was the most intriguing and desirable woman he'd met in years, but his consciousness was floating now and it was difficult to tell her that. He felt her soft hands slide behind his head, loosen his ponytail and fan his hair out over the shaped leather rest. He didn't protest when she fastened a soft felt-lined strap across his brow, but simply sighed and eased himself deeper on to the probe. You love it, you fairy, he told himself, not quite sure if he'd spoken out loud or not.

Almost on the brink, he felt Isis attach sensors to his

temples and his wrists, then after the sound of tapping keys, the real world began a slow, gentle slide beyond his reach. More tapping, and his body came alive in a strange, almost multi-dimensional way. His prick tingled slightly, seemed to swell . . . and deep in the core of him, a soft warm glow was the most delectable sensation he'd ever felt. Looking around him he saw the whole scene was slightly out of phase, distorted yet strangely unalarming. Isis's scarred face had acquired a bright beatific beauty, and her voice, when she spoke, was alien music.

'I'm going to put a mask over your eyes now, Josh, and I want you to close them as I do,' she whispered. Josh obeyed, lamblike, and felt the soft velvet-lined visor caress his brow and cheek.

'It's time now, Josh. When you open your eyes again you'll be in another world.' He felt the stroking touch of her fingers on his face, so soothing, so much like a lover. 'It's time now, my Josh, time. Time to dream . . .'

WEB
OF
DESIRE

Sophie Danson

Those readers who are familiar with my monthly letter in the back pages of Nexus books will know that a new series of erotic fiction for women, entitled Black Lace, was launched last summer to an enthusiastic response from both a male and female readership.

From January of this year, two Black Lace books will be published each month plus occasional seasonal promotions. The success of the new imprint has proved that women are every bit as willing to buy and read explicit material if it is packaged in the right way. The publishers of Black Lace make no pretensions about the contents of their publications: these are not romantic novels with the occasional sex scene, they are hot throughout. The Black Lace imprint offers a wide range of settings and themes to cater for the demand from women keen to see a steamier alternative to love stories.

I have chosen an extract from one of the first four books released in July 1993. It is by Sophie Danson and is called *Web of Desire*. It's a contemporary story of a woman's discovery of a darker, more challenging sexuality than the one she has been used to. Although she's scared of the feelings she is unlocking within herself, she cannot deny the attraction of this new world. Sophie Danson specialises in writing about more mysterious sexual themes and April 1994 sees the release of *Moon of Desire* – a contemporary tale of a woman's battle with the dark forces that engulf her during the full moon. Compelling stuff!

Sophie Danson

No Lady

Alexis Arven

The Blue Hotel

Cherri Pickford

Cassandra's Conflict

Fredrica Alleyn

Sophie Danson

Avalon Nights

Sophie Danson

Moon of Desire

Sophie Danson

What was Marcie doing? What was she becoming? She looked over the past couple of weeks, and seemed to be recalling a bizarre dream-sequence from a *film noir*. She had walked through the gate into a dark underworld, where inexplicable acts were the only exorcism of unacceptable desires.

As she closed the train door and sat down, she remembered the young man, faceless and helpless, hanging limply from his chained wrists, his flesh seared and reddened from her assaults upon him. Why had she struck him with the whip? What violent impulse had driven her? As the scene filled her mind, the emotions came flooding back, the overwhelming lust for the sweetness of pain and domination. Feelings which Omega had released. Knowledge which she had not known she had.

What was happening to her? What was Omega doing to her mind, to her body? The simplicity of sex was becoming transformed into a dark, seductive world of subtle torment. A delicious addiction, quickly acquired but not so easily broken.

'Good afternoon, Mrs MacLean.'

The Colonel doffed his hat, respectful to a fault as he

275

always was. Was that a knowing gleam in his watery blue eyes? Marcie dismissed the thought as paranoia. Ever since she and Alex had made love, with such naked abandon, in the orchard, she had worried about just who had seen what they had done. Rumours spread like wildfire in a village. There had been one or two comments, one or two obscure, veiled remarks which might or might not mean anything.

'Good morning, Colonel. How are you?'

'Much better for seeing you, Marcie. We haven't been seeing so much of you lately.'

'Oh, I've been away on business,' Marcie replied hastily. 'And Richard is often away. I'll be seeing you later.'

The key turned in the lock, and she stepped into the coolness of the hallway. The only sound was the reassuring tick-tock of the grandfather clock, marking off the seconds until the evening, when Alex would come and ease the tedium of her solitude.

She kicked off her shoes, peeled off her dress and stepped into the shower. The needles of icy water awoke every nerve-ending in her body, driving her into a hyper-consciousness she sought only to shun; and she began to moan, very quietly, very gently, for a comfort she dared not seek.

Marcie enjoyed living in Littleholme, but sometimes it felt as if a thousand eyes were on her. Everyone wanted to know your business, not like in a city where you were just a number, just a cipher. Here, you mattered to a sometimes alarming extent. Marcie thought back to the anonymity of that day in the darkened lift cage, where she had become the ultimate slave to passion. Not just other people's, but most of all her own. No will, no responsibility, no thought.

The ultimate nothing.

And at that moment, nothingness seemed almost welcoming. Even the fear did not seem to matter. To surrender herself, like a helpless child, into the arms of a greater will, a greater passion, seemed the only worthy ambition. Sometimes, thought was nothing more than pain; and pain could be the most exquisite of pleasures.

After dressing, she picked up the post, poured herself a drink and went out into the garden. The heat hit her chilled flesh like a solid wall, and for a moment her head reeled. In the distance, the little brook at the bottom of the orchard was trickling noisily over smooth stones. Beyond the trees, she could just make out the angular figure of Deanna Miles, parish councillor, local author and general busybody, ostensibly watering her hanging baskets, but clearly on the look-out for any scandal or gossip. Well, she would have a long wait today.

Marcie sat down on a sunbed and opened the first of the envelopes. Nothing more exotic or terrifying than a gas bill. Her subscription copies of *Forum* and *Pleasure Principles*; she put them to one side, for bedtime reading. Maybe she and Richard could pick up a few tips.

The last envelope was A4 size, plain and brown. It had no postmark, just a Mailsort code. Junk mail, evidently. She was going to throw it away unopened, but on an impulse she tore it open and pulled out the contents.

It was a fetishwear catalogue, glossy and garish. The cover depicted a vampish woman in a black leather basque, pierced to allow the breasts to poke through, stiff-tipped and threatening. Marcie noted with a shudder that the woman's red-painted nipples had been pierced with little silver rings, linked by a heavy silver chain which distended them.

She turned the page, and entered a whole new under-world she had scarcely imagined existed. A world of master and servant, mistress and slave. On the facing page, a woman in a tight rubber dress and spike-heeled platform boots was dragging along a hapless young man, dressed in nothing but a tiny leather posing pouch, utterly helpless to resist, since she had him fast by the thick brass chain about his slender neck. His mistress's expression was one that Marcie had never seen before: a grotesque mixture of hatred and devotion.

Turning the page, she found pictures of naked men and women, bound with leather thongs; masters and mistresses in leather, rubber and PVC, masked and threatening; boots and masks and harnesses just like the one she had worn on that fateful night at the garden party. As she looked at the pictures, she felt a wave of longing wash over her. A great longing to be part of this world where servitude was safety. To be mistress or servant? Somehow, it did not matter any more. Simply to be redefined and set free.

The sound of the doorbell called her back to reality. She glanced at her watch: three-thirty. She wasn't expecting anyone. After working into the early hours the previous night, and the meeting this morning, she had promised herself a quiet afternoon and then a night of fun with Alex. With a groan, she swung her legs off the sunbed and went to answer the door.

Outside the back door stood the slender, black-leather-clad figure of a despatch rider, his face completely obscured by a black helmet and tinted visor. He was carrying a box and a clipboard. As she signed for the parcel Marcie glanced towards his bike, noticing with surprise that it did not carry the name of any courier service. And he had parked it down the side of the cottage, in the secluded yard, as though he wanted no-one to notice it there.

She handed the clipboard back to the silent courier, accepted the parcel and stepped back to close the door. But the biker stepped forward, taking her by surprise, pushing her further back into the hall.

He clicked the door shut behind him. They were alone in the silent house.

'What do you want?' Marcie wanted to run away, but his leather-gloved hand was on her arm; not holding her fast or restraining her, simply touching her bare flesh. That touch electrified her; and the scent of leather and sweat and two-stroke intoxicated her with sudden desire.

There was a face behind that perspex mask; a face and eyes. Were the eyes cruel, gentle, knowing, stupid? Marcie no longer sought to know. She was speechless with fear, desire, excitement.

When his hands began undressing her, she wanted to cry out with elation, yet she was afraid, too; afraid that this silent man meant her real harm. So she submitted to his urgent desires obediently, almost impassively, as though she felt nothing, when all along her body was a seething mass of unsatisfied desires, bubbling to the surface like marsh gas in some dark, mysterious fen.

Her nakedness evidently did not displease him, for he ran his hands all over her body. The contact of the leather, supple yet harsh, made her moan with pleasure, and her nipples rose up in homage to this strange lovemaking; hard, rose-pink crests of treacherous pleasure.

Naked, she felt doubly vulnerable beside this strange, robotic figure in its prison of leather and perspex. Was there really a man inside the sinister black suit? Did the faceless visor conceal emptiness? Was she being seduced, perhaps, by some beautiful, lascivious android?

The very thought of it dampened her crotch, made her breathing harsher and more shallow. Were there metal claws, instead of fingers, inside those shiny black gauntlets? She shivered as she imagined the metal skeleton beneath the leather skin, like a strange insect or deep sea creature within its carapace. Metal claws, crawling over her naked flesh, exciting her, possessing her.

She reached out and drew down the zipper on the biker's leather trousers. He made no attempt to prevent her; and she slipped her hand inside his flies. Inside, he was naked: nothing between hot flesh and warm leather. Her hand met the upward curving shaft of his penis, and grasped it firmly. It was pulsating with vibrant life. She pulled it out, and saw that it was as beautiful as it felt: smooth and thick and long, with a glistening, rounded head. She wanted so much to lick it, suck it, taste the milk of life as it flooded her greedy tongue.

But as she bent down to suck him, he pushed her away. He had other plans for her.

The biker opened the back door, flooding the cottage kitchen with sunshine. He seemed even more unreal than ever, his leathers gleaming in the sudden light, his cock a sculptured ivory against the black leather. Then he gripped Marcie's wrist and led her outside, into the unforgiving daylight.

'No! I can't! Someone will see.'

She tried to wriggle free, but it was useless. He was inexorable, unstoppable.

Trees and bushes shielded the little yard from the road, and screened it from the rest of the garden. Normally, this was where Richard tinkered with the kit-car he was building, but at the moment it was over at the garage, having some professional work done on the braking system. Marcie darted anxious glances around her. Was she safe from discovery? Could those few trees and shrubs really conceal the indecency of what she was doing from prying village eyes? Strange that a time like this she was thinking of her reputation, rather than her safety. She thought of Mrs Miles, vigilantly watering her hanging baskets, and groaned inwardly. If there was anything to be seen, she would be sure to see it and report on it to the rest of the village.

But her thoughts did not dwell on privacy for very long. The biker had plans for her. His Harley-Davidson gleamed in the afternoon sunlight, superb shiny chrome and well-polished leather, resting on its stand. The scent of engine oil thrilled Marcie as she ran her fingers over the sun-warmed seat.

The biker pushed her gently towards the bike, until her back was up against the back wheel. At first she did not understand what he wanted her to do; then realisation struck. Silently, he lifted her up by the waist and pulled her legs apart, sitting her astride the seat, back to the handlebars. Then he laid her down gently, until her head was on the tank; and with little lengths of cord tied her wrists loosely to the handlebars.

The biker's cock was inside her swiftly and efficiently, and he began to thrust in and out of her like a piston moving up and down inside a well-greased cylinder. His cock was silky-smooth in the soft wetness of her womanhood; and she responded to each thrust with a movement of her hips. They fucked together with rhythmic, well-oiled precision.

Now she was a part of the machine, too. A machine for riding, just like the Harley-Davidson. She gazed up into the sky, and the sunshine blinded her like the reflections from well-burnished chrome.

She came with a cry she could not suppress: a cry of ecstasy unbound, arching her back the better to accept the tribute of his foaming seed.

He came silently, only the faintest shudder betraying his pleasure. Beneath him, Marcie lay moaning, writhing in her ecstasy, the willing victim of her own dark desires.

Later he untied her and rode away, melting like a phantom into the lengthening shadows of evening.

Alex drove her to the airport the next morning. Richard, of course, was far too busy with an 'important client' to see his wife off on her business trip.

'I'll pick you up on Saturday. Have a good trip, sweetheart.'

Marcie returned his chaste kiss and opened the car door. She thought about telling him everything, but something stopped her. She smiled, got out of the car and walked towards the check-in desk.

The trip to Berlin was an unexpected treat, or a damn nuisance, depending on how you looked at it. Marcie could have done without it. She needed to get to the bottom of this Omega thing. She needed to do something about the hostility at Grünwald & Baker. What she didn't need was two days abroad, trying to clinch a deal that wouldn't even have been necessary if Greg Baxter hadn't been so bloody difficult.

When the plane landed at Templehof Airport, Marcie got into a taxi and drove straight to the hotel, a four-star glass and chrome monstrosity off the Kurfürstendamm. She had the rest of the day to kill: the interview with Herr Niedermayer wasn't until the following morning.

She began to wish she had tried harder to persuade Alex to come along. At least she wouldn't have been so lonely. Berlin was supposed to be the fun-palace of Europe, now the wall had come down; but she didn't expect to see much night-life. Maybe she'd go and see a movie, go to the theatre? Whoopee! Welcome to the pleasure-dome.

She ate a solitary dinner, read a magazine, got bored. Maybe it wouldn't be safe for a lone woman to go drinking in a bar? She was just about to give up and have an early night when the phone in her room rang.

'Frau MacLean?'

'Yes.'

'There is a visitor for you. Shall I send him up to your room?'

'I . . . Yes, all right.'

'It'll be the Berlin representative, she thought to herself. Stanhope-Miles mentioned he might be making contact.

She got her papers out, tidied herself up, and a few minutes later there was a knock on the door.

'Komm.'

The door opened, and Marcie drew back in sudden alarm. As she stepped back towards the window she glanced down at the street below, and saw what she had dreaded.

A gleaming black and silver Harley-Davidson.

The biker was as anonymous and robotic as ever, smoked visor firmly down and hiding any trace of a human expression. When he spoke, his voice was flat and emotionless, and Marcie realised with a shock that it was in some way electronically altered.

'Omega summons you.'

A hint of anger flared in Marcie.

'And what if I don't want to be summoned? I can ring reception any time, and six burly security men will come and get rid of you. Why shouldn't I get you thrown out? Just tell me that.'

'Because you would not risk Omega's displeasure. Omega's displeasure is your pain, Marcie. But his pleasure is your delight. And Omega has such pretty gifts for you.'

The biker put down a black briefcase on Marcie's bed, and clicked it open.

'Omega is very generous, Marcie. See what gifts I have brought you.'

She took a few steps closer to the bed and looked down into the case. For a split second her heart stopped and she drew in her breath, remembering the pictures in the catalogue she had received in the post only the day before. A procession of images filled her head: figures in leather and chains and rubber and shiny PVC; figures of her deepest fantasies brought to life.

Marcie stretched out trembling hands and lifted out the garment inside the case. A playsuit of the finest leather, black and fragrant with newness. She pressed it to her face, breathing in its intoxicating scene.

'Put it on, Marcie, Put it on now. Omega wishes it.'

There could be no thought of refusal. Swiftly she unbuttoned her blouse and slipped off her skirt. Stockings, bra and panties followed. Strange how unabashed she felt, taking off her clothes in front of this stranger; this stranger who had, only a day before, ridden her on the seat of his motorbike. It did not feel as though she was taking off her clothes for a man: no, she was standing naked before a gleaming black automaton.

She picked up the catsuit and examined it more closely. A central zip down the back seemed the only way in. She tugged it down, and slid her feet into the slender leather legs, enclosing her ankles with tiny zips and buckles. Pulling up the catsuit, she slipped in her arms and breasts and turned her back on the faceless biker. The sound of the zipper sliding upwards was like the sound of the key turning in a cell door. And it was also the sound of a mother's goodnight kiss. For her imprisonment was also her security.

'This, now.'

The biker handed her a smaller garment of black leather: a mask, designed to cover the whole head. She pulled it over her head, and drew down the zip. At first it felt incredibly constricting, pressing coldly against her face. She would not be able to breathe! Only the holes for eyes, nose and mouth made it bearable. But then the pleasure of it dawned on her. Like the helmeted biker, she was now safe within her own world of anonymous sex.

She stepped in front of the full-length mirror, and was immediately shocked by what she saw. Not Marcia MacLean. No, not any longer. This was no laughing redhead with a friendly bosom. The figure who stared back at her from the mirror was a nightmare creature, both captive and wardress. Black-masked and sinister, two emerald green eyes gazed out upon a figure totally encased in black leather. With a sudden pang of excitement, Marcie noted the little zips strategically placed over her breasts, and the zip running from her navel and down between her legs. There could be little doubt what pleasures they were intended to facilitate. Perhaps she would enjoy the impending games in her hotel room.

'It is time to go now.'

Marcie wheeled round, heart thumping. 'Go?'

'Omega wishes it, Marcie.'

'But I can't go anywhere, dressed like this!'

The biker held out spike-heeled boots and a second helmet.

'Put them on.'

Hands trembling, Marcie pulled the full-face helmet

285

over her head. At least now the bizarre mask was covered. She rammed her feet into the too-tight boots, and fiddled clumsily with the side-straps. She felt a good six inches taller, and scarcely able to walk. Could she really dare walk out into the street dressed like this?

'Come with me.'

Marcia was surprised to hear the electronic voice now coming from within the helmet. An intercom. Omega thought of everything.

To Marcie's anguish, the biker did not lead her down the back stairs, the modest, easy way to the street. He pushed her in front of him, made her walk before him down the broad, sweeping staircase, into the main foyer of the hotel.

Thank God for the helmet, Marcie thought, feeling her face burn under the mask. All eyes were on her, but at least no-one knew who she was. Surely no-one could guess that this leather queen, bedecked in buckles and straps and zips, teetering on spike-heeled boots, was the same woman as the demure red-head in the business suit who had checked in only hours before. And in Berlin, it took a great deal to shock people.

He was behind her, very close behind; not touching, but his presence was all around her, urging her forward. Do not flinch now, it seemed to say. Omega has great hopes for you. Do not let him down. She stumbled on the stairs once, unaccustomed to the ridiculously high heels, and his leather-gloved hand was there instantly, supporting her and fending off disaster. Suddenly she felt safe and proud.

They walked through the swing doors and out onto the pavement. The golden evening light seemed eerie, viewed through the smoky visor; but the heat permeated the leather suit, and little beads of perspiration sprang up on her skin.

The biker lifted the gleaming machine off the stand and straddled it. No kick-start: the merest touch of a button, and the engine roared into life. Electronic ignition: nothing but the best for Omega. The faceless visor turned towards her:

'Get on.'

Marcie had never been on a motor-bike before. She didn't even know how to get on. Cautiously, she swung a leg over the leather seat and her toes found the foot-rest on the other side. Perched up there, she felt extra-ordinarily vulnerable with 1100 cc of hungry horsepower, throbbing through her body, shaking it like a rag doll.

'Hold on to me.'

It was the voice of a sensual automaton, and it seemed to be coming, not from the biker in front of her, but from inside her very head. Tentatively, Marcie placed her hands on either side of the biker's waist.

'Hold on tight. Or you might fall.'

Panic made her tighten her grip. The leather was smooth, hard to get a hold on. Finally she managed to hook her fingers into the biker's belt, but she felt desperately unsafe. She wanted to get off.

But it was too late. With a roar of the throttle, the Harley leapt forward, throwing Marcie against the backrest. She clawed at the biker for safety, pressing herself forward against his unyielding body, a helpless piece of flotsam in the slipstream.

They sped through the streets of Berlin, taking the corners almost without slowing down. The fear was exhilarating, and her pulse began to race. It was a little while before she realised that the laughter she could hear in her head was her own.

The throbbing demon between her thighs used its power over her subtly. With each revolution of the engine, a pulse of energy transmitted itself to the hyper-sensitive flesh between Marcie's thighs, already teased into life by the hard metal line of the zipper, pressing unforgivingly between her sex lips. An involuntary sigh escaped from her lips.

A voice hissed in her ear:

'Dearest little slut. Omega will be pleased with you.'

The biker's voice, little more than a harsh electronic crackle above the roaring of the wind, shook her back to the reality of what she was doing and feeling. A lone woman leather-clad and masked, riding through a city where she knew no-one, with a man whose face she had never seen. And the spice of fear kindled her desire, making her clitoris throb with an insistent pulse, matching the rhythmic hum of the engine, hot and alive between her thighs.

Marcie had never been to Berlin before, but she knew enough to see that they were now entering what had once been the Eastern sector. The buildings were drab and faceless, crowded together in a maze of dingy alley-ways, the tenements so close together that it seemed the sun never quite reached the deepest, darkest corners.

As they bumped over cobbled streets, the metal zipper forced its way more firmly still against her clito-ris, and the zip-fasteners across her breasts began to rub themselves over her nipples, stiffening them in spite of her fears.

'Almost there, Marcie. Great things are expected of you tonight. Do not fail us. Do not fail Omega.'

Suddenly angry and afraid, Marcie cried out above the rising tide of her desire:

'But who . . . Who is Omega?'

The biker's head half-turned towards her. She felt sure that, beneath the darkened visor, a thin, cruel mouth was smiling.

'Omega is desire, Marcie. Omega is *your* desire.'

Suddenly the engine cut, and they coasted to a halt outside the seediest and most garish nightclub Marcie had ever seen. Red and blue neon signs depicted naked women in provocative poses, and yellowing photographs outside the entrance showed men and women dressed in skin-tight leather and rubber. Strong, well-muscled men dressed as executioners, their desire spurting into the mouths of naked 'slave-girls'. Terrifying leather queens: statuesque young women, their heavy breasts encased in skin-tight leather; their whips raised to punish the miserable naked boys kneeling before them. With a shock, Marcie realised how much like these terrifying women she must look.

'We've arrived, Marcie. Do you like it? Get off the bike.'

Marcie dismounted, slowly and unsteadily. She wasn't going inside that club. No way. She looked around her for her best chance of escape. The bike? No, too big for her to handle. She'd never even get it off the stand. She could run, but this tall, muscular biker would be sure to catch up with her. And if she did get away, where would she go? If she went back to the hotel, Omega would be sure to find her.

Omega, it seemed, was everywhere.

'Take off the helmet, and give it to me.'

She pulled the helmet off, and the shame of her leather-masked face emerged into the dingy evening light. To her surprise, not one of the passers-by turned a hair. Of course, they wouldn't. Oddity and weirdness were common currency in this crummy part of town. If she tried to go her own way round here, dressed like this, what would become of her?

She followed the biker across the few feet of pavement, each step leaden and unwilling. She would not go in there; would not cross that grimy, beaded curtain into the seething underworld whose cacophony floated up to her ears from the basement nightclub. She would not.

And yet she wanted to. Wanted to so very much. Her whole body was crying out for her to walk down those steps and enter the world of waking dreams.

'Come with me.'

Silent and trembling, she walked on her spiky heels across the pavement, and through the beaded curtain.

THE GENTLE DEGENERATES

Marco Vassi

The three Marco Vassi books are truly sophisticated adult novels which have received the acclaim of authors such as Norman Mailer – not a man known to mince words. At the end of the 1960s a man is searching for enlightenment through sexual freedom and various partners. The chosen extract from *The Gentle Degenerates* is full of explicit language, but this doesn't detract from the intellectual and philosophical thread which runs throughout the whole book. The first person narrator muses on the human condition and the weakness of human flesh when faced with the object of desire.

The Marco Vassi books stand alone in the Nexus list – they are unlike any others in their frankness of dialogue and intellectual musings. They can be described as 'a good read' however and capture that page turning quality which is so crucial to the success of an erotic novel. The three books in the series are *The Gentle Degenerates*, *The Saline Solution* and *Contours of Darkness*.

Yes, this was the way it should be. The woman's body beneath me, her eyes closed as her face showed a kaleidoscope of emotions, biting her lips, opening her mouth in breathy wonder. Diana opened her legs even further, and her legs and pelvis became a tree trunk and ocean, the thick thighs spread out and leading into her hips, the whole area a wide fleshy pool of sensation. And then her narrow waist rising out of it, curving gracefully up to her boyish torso which then exploded in ripe, sensitive breasts. Her arms lay above her head, as though she were tied to a post, and they too made a long sweeping line from her wrists to her armpits, which now showed in all their hairy vulnerability. I was raised up on my knees and hands, my arms stiffly supporting my body. And my cock lay imbedded in her cunt. From where I looked, I could see the gleaming shaft rising and falling from her pubic hair.

My cock was like a lever and all the buttons were inside her pussy. If I moved up, she would twitch and roll her ass. If I moved to the side she would bring one leg up. If I dropped down and sank deep into her from below, bringing my cock directly between her legs and vertically up into her hole, she shuddered and gasped and brought her hands up to grab my shoulders. She was like a sensual puppet, inert and ready to respond to every manipulation. I admired her great ability to be passive, to trust to her own feelings and the fact that I wouldn't hurt her. So many women kept constantly on guard, waiting for something to go wrong, waiting for the pleasure to depart, that they never were able to just let go and let it happen to them.

I reached down and nipped Diana on the breast. Her eyes opened in surprise and then she smiled. She brought my head down and raised up to place her lips on mine. Her mouth was all giving. It was as though she were speaking a fluid and alien language, very rapidly and in total silence. And although I didn't understand any of the words, the meaning was totally clear. Her tongue became a wonder worker, licking my face, teasing my lips.

I slid my hands along her arms and pinned her wrists to the couch. She let herself fall back again and gave herself to the experience. I leaned down and licked all the skin from between her breasts to her throat, and then around to her jaw and up to her ear. When I plunged my tongue deep inside her ear, she moaned loudly and began grinding her pelvis against me. Her cunt became a hot wet hand squeezing my cock, grabbing it insistently, loving it with a singular intensity. I felt myself sinking into the sloshing tightness of her box when her legs came up and wrapped themselves around my waist. I breathed hotly into her ear and lapped at all the delicate bony ridges inside and around the edge. I felt her nails dig into my forearm. 'Talk to me,' she said, 'tell me what you want.'

I was caught short by the request, and then I let the fantasies go. 'I want your open cunt a million miles wide. You're all pussy, baby, all the way up to your eyes. Nothing but cunt and ass, big ass. I want you to go down and lick my cock, and just keep sucking it and loving it until you can't keep your mouth open anymore.' As I spoke, her breath became heavy and she began to move faster, more rhythmically, now pumping her cunt against me harder. 'I want to spread you over a bed, with your beautiful cunt flying high and your ass inviting, and then have a hundred men come in to see you, to watch you pull your cheeks open, and beg them to fuck you.' She began to moan and writhe. 'You want it too, don't you, you little bitch,' I whispered. 'You want to have all those cocks in your mouth, to have them all come on your tongue so you can swallow them all. You want to go begging on your knees to have them fuck you in the ass. I want to take you in the ass, right now.' She keened and pulled me closer with her legs. 'No,' she said, 'please, not now, just keep fucking me.'

'You want me to fuck you?' I said. 'Yes, please.' I pulled my cock back and kept it at the tip of her cunt. 'Beg,' I said. 'Tell me what you're willing to do.'

'I'll do anything,' she sobbed.

I pulled out of her completely and immediately moved up to her face. She looked at me and a shadow of fear passed through her eyes. I brought my cock up to her mouth, and then leaned down. 'Start licking,' I said. She made a small shrugging motion with her shoulders and her tongue came out to begin its tiny path up the length of my cock. I brought my balls up and dropped them on her mouth. Her tongue kept working, kept moving. Finally I covered her face entirely and felt her mouth go for the sensitive strip between balls and asshole, and she hungrily sucked at it, and ran her tongue up and down in thick, wet strokes. I reached down and pinched both her nipples. Her knees came up

295

and she grabbed my thighs, to force my body to sink more heavily onto her mouth.

I moved back and brought my cock into play, rubbing it all over her face, and on her lips, and then she opened her mouth and with a despairing sigh let the rod sink deep into her. I knelt by her head so that she had to turn her face sideways to suck me off, and then I told her to bring herself off. She stopped sucking and her eyes opened to seek mine. There was a begging request to not do it. 'Do it,' I said.

Then, gently, tentatively, her right hand moved down her body until it rested on her crotch. 'Do it.' I said again. Her legs opened slowly and her hand moved down between her thighs. Her middle finger curved down and slid into her wet cunt all the way up to the knuckle, and then came out again. 'Come on,' I said, 'pretend you're alone. I want to watch.' I pulled my cock out of her mouth and sat back. She closed her eyes and brought the tip of her finger to her clitoris. She started to stroke it lightly, up and down, and suddenly her entire body changed. It became wired, electrified. Her knees came up and her nipples became hard with ridges running through them. She began to roll her head from side to side and her ass started a small pumping motion.

Then the tip of her finger started moving like a vibrator, shaking her clitoris, jiggling it, flicking at it. She started to moan and thrash about. I moved down and lay between her legs. Her cunt was now running juices and very inflamed. I brought my mouth right up to it and drank in the heady aroma. It was too much at once, and with a groan I plunged into her churning pussy. My tongue sank into that steamy box and began lapping at the honey which flowed from it. Her other hand came down and inserted itself into her cunt. I

296

licked and nipped at her cunt lips, and then brought my tongue up to her clitoris, lapping at it and at her finger. Finally, she took her hand away and used both her hands to spread her cunt lips apart, prying them open like a nutshell. The pink slimy inner lips were exposed, and I could feel the tight granular opening, the tiny bud which gave access to the inner heat. She pulled so hard that I thought she would rip her cunt apart.

Now it was pure feasting. I ran my tongue like a scoop from the deep crack of her ass up past her pulsating asshole, between her thighs, and up the length of her dripping pussy, to end right on her clitoris which I took and bit gently with my teeth. Dozens of times I made the same trip, until I had found the rhythm that turned her on. Now I was her sexual object, letting myself have no other function than to give her pleasure, and doing that by finding what gave me the most pleasure. Sensitive to myself, I was best for her. The sweep of my tongue up her privates became richer each time, for now my tongue paused momentarily to dig at her asshole, and changed speed and width between her legs, and plunged deeply into her cunt as I swept between the lips. Her cunt now became a bellows, swelling with air as it bellied in, and then letting the air out with a wet rush.

Finally she began to come. It started in her legs with a deep trembling. Her moans got deeper and rougher. Her fingers twined themselves in my hair and pulled at my scalp, sending tingles up and down my spine. Her ass was like a forest fire, crackling and jumping with awesome speed and strength. My mouth became as excited as my prick, and I lost all sense of what I was doing. I became a slobbering, moaning slave, licking at her cunt, sucking and lapping and moaning into her opening, begging for her to come, begging her to spend

297

all the deepest musky fluids, and discharge them as the waves of energy rolled through her body. And then, with an unearthly cry, she threw her legs high into the air, and her cunt convulsed totally into my mouth, lips quivering, vagina vibrating, the cunt hole itself opening and closing in rapid spasms, and then the juice gushing out, as I drove deep into her and sucked every last drop out, until she was absolutely dry.

Her legs came down slowly and rested on my shoulders. I lay there for a few minutes and then extricated myself. I sat up abruptly and went off into the kitchen. I felt disappointed and a little disgusted with myself. I felt as though I had just seen the same movie for the hundredth time. It was a good movie and I enjoyed it each time, but it seemed fatuous to keep seeing it.

Regina had called me that morning, angry and hurt. She wanted to be in my life, she said, and she was willing to come to New York. She was capitulating rapidly, ready to give up many things just to be with me. And she was still being faithful to me; that's how she wanted it. Once she told me that, when an affair had ended with someone with whom she had been very much in love (although, as she said, 'I didn't know him as well as I know you,') she didn't fuck for months afterwards. It was a clue to her temperament: the romantic bitch. And now it was the same scene, the combination of 'I am strong enough for you,' and 'I can't live without you.' And as usual, I fell for it, letting her do her bitch act, to be followed by her baby voice. And by the time she had hung up I had promised to fly out to the Coast in mid-May, to drive back here with her and her kid for the summer. And then we would make plans for the fall in the fall.

The moment I hung up, I felt as though I had been

had. She wouldn't take 'no' for an answer, and I was her accomplice, or at least some aspect of me was. I spent a good part of the day sulking and running down vicious dialogues in my head, and after dinner, I 'found myself' in Diana's neighbourhood. So I dropped over. She was alone, and after a bit of chitchat we went right to fucking. We have known each other over a year, were once fierce lovers, a Scorpio–Leo confrontation, split up, and have become fucking buddies since. There's a line that describes it: 'ex-lovers like cracked china meet.'

To say that I fucked Diana to spite Regina is perhaps an accurate oversimplification. At the moment I felt shitty because it seemed I had used Diana as a prop in my inner drama. I put on water for coffee and Diana came in, very solicitous. She put her head on my shoulder.

'Something's wrong,' she said.

'Yeah,' I answered.

'I can always tell. Whenever you don't fuck me after eating me, I know it's not all right with you.'

I smiled and kissed her. 'You are a marvellous practical woman,' I said. 'Too bad you're a Leo.'

'Who is she?'

'Her name is Regina. And she lives in California. And she's pretty bad in bed, and a bitch to boot, and dependent at the drop of a hat, and very ballsy, and tricky and unscrupulous. And really a decent chick but not anyone I want to get all excited about. And somehow she's got her hooks into my soul and I can't shake her loose.'

'That doesn't sound right,' she said. 'I've never known a woman to hold you when you didn't want to be held on to. There's something in you that wants her.'

'It may sound stupid,' I said, 'but I think I love her.

And it's all wrong. I mean, it's not what I would have wanted, and I don't even have the feeling that goes with it.'

Diana continued the conversation by bringing her hand down to my cock and fondling it gently. I felt my rod stirring. 'I don't feel right about this, Diana,' I said. But she silenced me in the best way possible, by dripping to her knees and putting her mouth around my dick. Suddenly all thoughts of Regina became two-dimensional. I mean, they still ran through my mind, but they had lost all power to affect me. It was like meditation, where I can sit and watch the thought machine produce its effects and not get involved in any of its products to the exclusion of a total awareness of reality. I wondered what the Theosophical Society would do with the proposition that a good blow job was easily the equal of sitting quietly in the full lotus. I wondered whether Madame Blavatksy was a virgin and whether it was true that Gurdjieff liked little boys.

I looked down at the goddess licking my cock. She was kneeling in the lion pose and tonguing my balls from underneath, moving her lips up the shaft and gobbling the head, then, with a deep breath, bringing her head all the way forward and lodging my cock deep in her throat. Her ass stuck out behind and her breasts jiggled as she worked. I flashed for a moment that it would be a groove to have another man there fucking her in the ass while she ate me, and for perhaps the thousandth time I regretted that I only had one body, and only one cock. I leaned over and ran my hands down her back, letting my nails raise tiny red trails along the spine. She shuddered with delight and grabbed my cock in her hands, pulling it now, jerking off into her own mouth. I felt a kind of disinterested excitement. All the usual sensations coursed through me, but I experienced them as from a distance. I felt extremely cosmic, viewing the known universe from its periphery, watching the galaxies dance, and the many manifestations of energy do their thing. In the incredible faraway was our own scene, a speck of rock chugging around a middle-sized, middle-aged sun in a medium-sized cluster of stars. And among the smallest specks on the speck was poor old Diana kneeling on the kitchen floor sucking my cock for all she was worth, and me digging it, half out of a sense of responsibility and half out of spontaneous enjoyment.

I reached over and grabbed her under the armpits and brought her to her feet. Her eyes were dazed and her mouth a slur of flesh, wet and obscene. She looked like every drugged cocksucker in every piece of pornography that had ever appeared. Of course she was beautiful. It is only our prejudice, our insistence on prim trimness of visage, which makes the dripping cunt-face seem disgusting, when in fact a woman is never more breathtaking than at that moment when every aspect of her essential animal is shown, with heaving breasts, hair stringy around her shoulders, excited ass and hungry twat. This was Diana now, a nameless lusting mouth, wanting cock, wanting the slobbering penetration, wanting gobs of sperm on her tongue, wanting to be pushed down and opened, to be overwhelmed and elevated all at the same time. Mother and child and witch and virgin all at once, the Cocksucker Deity, Queen of All Cunt.

I turned her around and had her bend over the kitchen table. Her knees shook as she bent to let her torso lie flat on the wooden surface. Her cunt gaped at me and the cheeks of her ass spread wide. Between them the tiny hairs were wet and sticky, and formed a web with globules shining, reflecting the overhead light. Still cool, still balanced, I laid my cock into her. She groaned out loud. 'Oh God,' she said. 'Please do it. Fuck me good. Fuck me the way I like it. Fuck me the way you know how.'

'Keep your head, Diana,' I said. 'Stay awake.'

'If I go under,' she said, 'come get me.'

'Right,' I said, as I began to fuck her. And it was just that. It wasn't us fucking, it was me doing it to her, doing it in her, doing it for her. She had to do nothing but lie there, letting her cunt be open. And I began to dance. It was the total dance, the dance of Shiva, the cosmic movement which sustains all movement. I went through all the animal and spirit forms, became everything from a dog to a demon. I growled and hissed, sang and prayed, words poured out like sap from a tree. And everything I was I poured on her, sank into her.

She was silent, but it was a silence that spoke of immense feeling, of deep concentration. Her whole life was in her cunt, while her mind remained alert, aware of the kitchen, of the city, of time, of space, of eternity. She was taking the male role in the Tantric act, while I played the female, and the fact that she had the cunt and I the cock made no difference. Her cunt grew rank with pleasure and meaning. I touched every inch of it, every crevice got penetrated, every wrinkle was straightened. I was every man who had ever fucked any woman, who ever could. Her ass rose higher, the globes gleaming like dew-covered crystal. Her asshole opened and a thin stream of gas escaped. Her cunt bubbled over. I moved inside her for what seemed an endless time. There was nothing to stop me, nothing to make her want me to stop. We were home, where we wanted and needed to be, where each of us in this poor bedraggled species wants to be living, but instead we march around like silly suited zombies and exchange money, and shuffle papers, and make wars.

But fucking is God, fucking is how it begins, fucking is what it is all about while we are here. In fucking everything is contained, all the opposites meet, and there is anger and humour, love and hate, aggression and tenderness. Fucking is where consciousness begins, in that fatal separation of the sexes. In fucking we are whole once more, and out of that wholeness (oh, divine ironic paradox!) another child is born, another fragment, another splinter who will in his or her turn strive to be completed. The history of the world spun from our cock and cunt, and everything that was within the power of the mind to know, we knew then, all mathematics all ethics all poetry all feeling all thought all sensation all the ages of man and all the changes of woman. And then, when we had soared to the outermost reaches of knowledge, we burst through that thin skin and dove into the unknown, the mysterious, the *that* for which there is no concept, no symbol . . . the simple blinding awareness of Being.

Letter from Esme

Dear Readers

It's a bit cold for this, I know, but I couldn't resist taking a last look at the view from my favourite window. Yes: it breaks my heart, but I'm leaving!

It's not that I don't enjoy my job. I mean, apart from the kick I get out of editing all these horny books, it gives me an electric thrill knowing that I'm giving pleasure to thousands of readers too. No, I'm quitting on the advice of my doctor. Who, as it happens, has also invited me to emigrate with her to the balmy shores of the West Indies.

So how will Nexus fare without me? That's for you to judge. Dreadful though it is of me to say this, I don't think they'll miss me too much. I'm leaving you in good hands (and they *are* good hands – I should know, I've been in them myself). There may not be any sexy photos of me in the back any more, but I've managed to persuade some of my friends to model in my place. And it pains me to say it, but they're almost as gorgeous as me!

Before I go, I've got some specially tasty treats in store for my loyal fans. First of all, there's the new cover image. From now on, if you're looking for Nexus books, remember – they'll all be in their smart new uniform!

But while the covers have changed, the stories remain as steamy as ever. If you don't believe me (or, come to that, if you do) read *Stephanie's Trial*. It's the fourth adventure for the dark-haired enchantress, who we find taking a well-deserved break from her exertions at Devlin's castle. Having left as a domineering mistress, Stephanie returns to find that the tables have turned, and she is soon standing in the dock facing the wrath of her former sex slaves.

Stephanie's bedfellow this February is a book I hold very close to my heart – because I put it together myself! *New Erotica 2* is a tightly packed compilation of extracts from 13 of the best recent Nexus and Black Lace titles, including *Adventures in the Pleasurezone*, *Web of Desire*, *Linzi Drew's Pleasure Guide*, *Paradise Bay*, *Wild*, and *The Dungeons of Lidir*. And they all boast a personal introduction from yours truly! I trust you'll have as much fun reading it as I did compiling it. If that's possible!

And for this frosty month of February, Black Lace proudly presents *The Senses Bejewelled*. It's the sequel to *The Captive Flesh*: the next instalment in the licentious life of Marietta. She's now sitting pretty as Kasim's favourite in the harem, but things soon turn ugly. She is kidnapped by her master's greatest rival, and subjected to all manner of humiliations. Not surprisingly, she turns to her fellow slaves for solace.

Well gird my loins, we're off to mediaeval England for *Avalon Nights*, to join King Arthur and his famous Knights in a tale of saucy sorcery. A new arrival causes great upheaval at court, and the noble lords find themselves revealing some very embarrassing secrets. If the plot sounds familiar, you must've read *Knights of Pleasure*, which is very similar. So keep your purse strings pulled 'til next month!

Haring into Mad March, we find *Elaine*. Secretary to a hugely wealthy aristocrat, the young lady of the title is seduced by her boss's wife, recruited into a kinky establishment providing sexual services, and drawn into a sinister plot to blackmail the rich with videos of their filthy antics. Who's a busy girl then?

Now what else have I got up my sleeve . . . *Witch Queen of Vixania*? What is this? I'll tell you. It's a thumping good sword 'n' sorcery tale about the good but naive Brod and the efforts of the wicked Queen Vixia to subjugate him. Unbeknown to the sorceress, though, the young man has a formidable weapon to use against her . . . Sex with Brod is magic, in more ways than one.

Stand by for a Black Lace double whammy in March — and that's just in *Gemini Heat*. Deana and Delia Ferraro are a pair of scrumptious identical twins (yum yum!), yearning for sexual release in the searing heat of an early summer. Unfortunately, they both set their sights on the wealthy Jackson de Guile. It is soon far from clear who's manipulating who, and Jackson is eventually forced to choose between them. A decision that I personally would defer as long as possible.

Have you ever wondered what goes on in the jet-setting world of classical music? Because that's the background to *Virtuoso*. Mika's career as a solo violinist has come to a premature end, but his old friend Serena, another musician, is only too willing to help him get over it. With so many skilled mouths and fingers in one group, nobody's symphony is going to stay unfinished for long!

Ah well, time to fly. Mm, I can feel the cream being rubbed into my skin already . . . but I mustn't get carried away. I've still got to send a big wet kiss to all of you who have been reading Nexus under my editorship. It's been fun, and I'm sure you'll continue to enjoy the books. I shall be keeping an eye on things — I'm getting copies of all new books air-mailed to the West Indies!

Lots of love, and goodbye,

Esme ♡

THE BEST IN EROTIC READING – BY POST

The Nexus Library of Erotica – almost one hundred and fifty volumes – is available from many booksellers and newsagents. If you have any difficulty obtaining the books you require, you can order them by post. Photocopy the list below, or tear the list out of the book; then tick the titles you want and fill in the form at the end of the list. Titles with a month in the box will not be available until that month in 1994.

CONTEMPORARY EROTICA

AMAZONS	Erin Caine	£3.99	
COCKTAILS	Stanley Carten	£3.99	
CITY OF ONE-NIGHT STANDS	Stanley Carten	£4.50	
CONTOURS OF DARKNESS	Marco Vassi	£4.99	
THE GENTLE DEGENERATES	Marco Vassi	£4.99	
MIND BLOWER	Marco Vassi	£4.99	
THE SALINE SOLUTION	Marco Vassi	£4.99	
DARK FANTASIES	Nigel Anthony	£4.99	
THE DAYS AND NIGHTS OF MIGUMI	P.M.	£4.50	
THE LATIN LOVER	P.M.	£3.99	
THE DEVIL'S ADVOCATE	Anonymous	£4.50	
DIPLOMATIC SECRETS	Antoine Lelouche	£3.50	
DIPLOMATIC PLEASURES	Antoine Lelouche	£3.50	
DIPLOMATIC DIVERSIONS	Antoine Lelouche	£4.50	
ELAINE	Stephen Ferris	£4.99	Mar
EMMA ENSLAVED	Hilary James	£4.99	May
EMMA'S SECRET WORLD	Hilary James	£4.99	
ENGINE OF DESIRE	Alexis Arven	£3.99	
DIRTY WORK	Alexis Arven	£3.99	
THE FANTASIES OF JOSEPHINE SCOTT	Josephine Scott	£4.99	

Title	Author	Price	Month
FALLEN ANGELS	Kendall Grahame	£4.99	Jul
THE FANTASY HUNTERS	Celeste Arden	£3.99	
HEART OF DESIRE	Maria del Rey	£4.99	
HELEN – A MODERN ODALISQUE	James Stern	£4.99	
HOT HOLLYWOOD NIGHTS	Nigel Anthony	£4.50	
THE INSTITUTE	Maria del Rey	£4.99	
JENNIFER'S INSTRUCTION	Cyrian Amberlake	£4.99	Apr
LAURE-ANNE TOUJOURS	Laure-Anne	£4.99	
MELINDA AND ESMERALDA	Susanna Hughes	£4.99	Jun
MELINDA AND THE MASTER	Susanna Hughes	£4.99	
Ms DEEDES AT HOME	Carole Andrews	£4.50	
Ms DEEDES ON A MISSION	Carole Andrews	£4.99	
Ms DEEDES ON PARADISE ISLAND	Carole Andrews	£4.99	
OBSESSION	Maria del Rey	£4.99	
THE PALACE OF EROS	Delver Maddingley	£4.99	May
THE PALACE OF FANTASIES	Delver Maddingley	£4.99	
THE PALACE OF SWEETHEARTS	Delver Maddingley	£4.99	
THE PALACE OF HONEYMOONS	Delver Maddingley	£4.99	
THE PASSIVE VOICE	G. C. Scott	£4.99	
QUEENIE AND CO	Francesca Jones	£4.99	
QUEENIE AND CO IN JAPAN	Francesca Jones	£4.99	
QUEENIE AND CO IN ARGENTINA	Francesca Jones	£4.99	
SECRETS LIE ON PILLOWS	James Arbroath	£4.50	
STEPHANIE	Susanna Hughes	£4.50	
STEPHANIE'S CASTLE	Susanna Hughes	£4.50	
STEPHANIE'S DOMAIN	Susanna Hughes	£4.99	
STEPHANIE'S REVENGE	Susanna Hughes	£4.99	
STEPHANIE'S TRIAL	Susanna Hughes	£4.99	Feb
THE TEACHING OF FAITH	Elizabeth Bruce	£4.99	Jul
THE DOMINO TATTOO	Cyrian Amberlake	£4.50	
THE DOMINO QUEEN	Cyrian Amberlake	£4.99	

EROTIC SCIENCE FICTION

Title	Author	Price	Month
ADVENTURES IN THE PLEASUREZONE	Delaney Silver	£4.99	

RETURN TO THE PLEASUREZONE	Delaney Silver	£4.99	
EROGINA	Christopher Denham	£4.50	
HARD DRIVE	Stanley Garten	£4.99	
PLEASUREHOUSE 13	Agnetha Anders	£3.99	
LAST DAYS OF THE PLEASUREHOUSE	Agnetha Anders	£4.50	
TO PARADISE AND BACK	D. H. Master	£4.50	
WANTON	Andrea Arven	£4.99	Apr

ANCIENT & FANTASY SETTINGS

CHAMPIONS OF LOVE	Anonymous	£3.99	
CHAMPIONS OF DESIRE	Anonymous	£3.99	
CHAMPIONS OF PLEASURE	Anonymous	£3.50	
THE SLAVE OF LIDIR	Aran Ashe	£4.50	
DUNGEONS OF LIDIR	Aran Ashe	£4.99	
THE FOREST OF BONDAGE	Aran Ashe	£4.50	
KNIGHTS OF PLEASURE	Erin Caine	£4.50	
PLEASURE ISLAND	Aran Ashe	£4.99	
WITCH QUEEN OF VIXANIA	Morgana Baron	£4.99	Mar

EDWARDIAN, VICTORIAN & OLDER EROTICA

ADVENTURES OF A SCHOOLBOY	Anonymous	£3.99	
ANNIE	Evelyn Culber	£4.99	
THE AUTOBIOGRAPHY OF A FLEA	Anonymous	£2.99	
CASTLE AMOR	Erin Caine	£4.99	
CHOOSING LOVERS FOR JUSTINE	Aran Ashe	£4.99	
EVELINE	Anonymous	£2.99	
MORE EVELINE	Anonymous	£3.99	
FESTIVAL OF VENUS	Anonymous	£4.50	
GARDENS OF DESIRE	Roger Rougiere	£4.50	
OH, WICKED COUNTRY	Anonymous	£2.99	
THE LASCIVIOUS MONK	Anonymous	£4.50	
LURE OF THE MANOR	Barbra Baron	£4.99	Jun
A MAN WITH A MAID 1	Anonymous	£4.99	
A MAN WITH A MAID 2	Anonymous	£4.99	
A MAN WITH A MAID 3	Anonymous	£4.99	

MAUDIE	Anonymous	£2.99
A NIGHT IN A MOORISH HAREM	Anonymous	£3.99
PARISIAN FROLICS	Anonymous	£2.99
PLEASURE BOUND	Anonymous	£3.99
THE PLEASURES OF LOLOTTE	Andrea de Nercist	£3.99
THE PRIMA DONNA	Anonymous	£3.99
RANDIANA	Anonymous	£4.50
REGINE	E.K.	£4.99
THE ROMANCE OF LUST 1	Anonymous	£3.99
THE ROMANCE OF LUST 2	Anonymous	£2.99
ROSA FIELDING	Anonymous	£2.99
SUBURBAN SOULS 1	Anonymous	£2.99
SUBURBAN SOULS 2	Anonymous	£3.99
TIME OF HER LIFE	Josephine Scott	£4.99
THE TWO SISTERS	Anonymous	£3.99
VIOLETTE	Anonymous	£4.99

'THE JAZZ AGE'

ALTAR OF VENUS	Anonymous	£3.99
THE SECRET GARDEN ROOM	Georgette de la Tour	£3.50
BEHIND THE BEADED CURTAIN	Georgette de la Tour	£3.50
BLUE ANGEL NIGHTS	Margaret von Falkensee	£4.99
BLUE ANGEL SECRETS	Margaret von Falkensee	£4.99
CAROUSEL	Anonymous	£4.50
CONFESSIONS OF AN ENGLISH MAID	Anonymous	£3.99
FLOSSIE	Anonymous	£2.50
SABINE	Anonymous	£3.99
PLAISIR D'AMOUR	Anne-Marie Villefranche	£4.50
FOLIES D'AMOUR	Anne-Marie Villefranche	£2.99
JOIE D'AMOUR	Anne-Marie Villefranche	£3.99
MYSTERE D'AMOUR	Anne-Marie Villefranche	£3.99
SECRETS D'AMOUR	Anne-Marie Villefranche	£3.50
SOUVENIR D'AMOUR	Anne-Marie Villefranche	£3.99

WORLD WAR 2

SPIES IN SILK	Piers Falconer	£4.50
WAR IN HIGH HEELS	Piers Falconer	£4.99

CONTEMPORARY FRENCH EROTICA (translated into English)

EXPLOITS OF A YOUNG DON JUAN	Anonymous	£2.99	
INDISCREET MEMOIRS	Alain Dorval	£2.99	
JOY	Joy Laurey	£2.99	
JOY IN LOVE	Joy Laurey	£2.75	
LILIANE	Paul Verguin	£3.50	
LUST IN PARIS	Antoine S.	£4.99	
NYMPHS IN PARIS	Galia S.	£2.99	
SENSUAL LIAISONS	Anonymous	£3.50	
SENSUAL SECRETS	Anonymous	£3.99	
THE NEW STORY OF Q	Anonymous	£4.50	
THE IMAGE	Jean de Berg	£3.99	
VIRGINIE	Nathalie Perreau	£4.50	
THE PAPER WOMAN	Francois Rey	£4.50	

SAMPLERS & COLLECTIONS

EROTICON 1	ed. J-P Spencer	£4.50	
EROTICON 2	ed. J-P Spencer	£4.50	
EROTICON 3	ed. J-P Spencer	£4.50	
EROTICON 4	ed. J-P Spencer	£4.99	
NEW EROTICA 1	ed. Esme Ombreux	£4.99	
NEW EROTICA 2	ed. Esme Ombreux	£4.99	Feb
THE FIESTA LETTERS	ed. Chris Lloyd	£4.50	
THE PLEASURES OF LOVING	ed. Maren Sell	£3.99	

NON-FICTION

HOW TO DRIVE YOUR MAN WILD IN BED	Graham Masterson	£4.50	
HOW TO DRIVE YOUR WOMAN WILD IN BED	Graham Masterson	£3.99	
HOW TO BE THE PERFECT LOVER	Graham Masterson	£2.99	
FEMALE SEXUAL AWARENESS	Barry & Emily McCarthy	£5.99	
LINZI DREW'S PLEASURE GUIDE	Linzi Drew	£4.99	
LETTERS TO LINZI	Linzi Drew	£4.99	

Please send me the books I have ticked above.

Name   . . . .
Address . . . .
         . . . .
         . . . . Post code   . . . .

Send to: **Cash Sales, Nexus Books, 332 Ladbroke Grove, London W10 5AH**

Please enclose a cheque or postal order, made payable to **Nexus Books**, to the value of the books you have ordered plus postage and packing costs as follows:

UK and BFPO – £1.00 for the first book, 50p for the second book, and 30p for each subsequent book to a maximum of £3.00;

Overseas (including Republic of Ireland) – £2.00 for the first book, £1.00 for the second book, and 50p for each subsequent book.

If you would prefer to pay by VISA or ACCESS/MASTERCARD, please write your card number here:

Please allow up to 28 days for delivery

— — — —   — — — —   — — — —   — — — —

Signature: _____